It had to be a dream. Peopl
But if this was a dream, sh

Mica's heart refused to slow down as the stranger moved close to her. Even though she knew he meant to kiss her, she felt more curious than threatened. Tall and dark, he wore a white shirt with billowing sleeves and snug black pants that disappeared into the tops of knee high black boots. She noticed he had his dark hair clubbed back, though bits curled around his angular face. Mica caught a hint of humor in his gaze, along with something far more dangerous.

Instinct shouted this was his domain, and she tried to regain her composure and come up with a reason for being in his room. However, her composure slipped drastically when he took the book from her and replaced it on the shelf.

And touched her in doing so.

Mica gasped when their bodies came into contact. The hard muscle beneath the soft linen of his shirt caused her breasts to ache in reaction to his touch. Heat branded her, and her heart thudded a dangerous beat. She knew she should ask him to back up because he was a virtual stranger. Handsome, but still unknown.

Nothing could have prepared her for the seductive power of his brown eyes—dark, penetrating eyes capable of reading her most intimate thoughts. Tiny worry lines crinkled at their corners, and she felt an unbidden desire to touch him and soothe the frown from his face. His gaze captured hers. Black brows rose in question.

Yes, her mind screamed, regardless of the question. Overwhelmed by the pure sensuality of the man, she didn't move a fraction as he lowered his lips to hers. Just before his eyes closed, she caught a glimpse of passion in their dark depths.

His kiss dissolved any defenses she may have constructed, and she groaned as his arms circled her to pull her closer.

She vaguely recalled a novel where the author wrote, "The heroine felt *devoured.*" She had laughed at the time, but now understood.

For two modern day heroines—
My mom, Mitzi, and my daughter, Cassie.
I'm so proud of both of you!

To my husband, Dave, and my son, Tom,
And to my dad, Rusty—
You are the heroes of my life.

Acknowledgements:

Thanks to my own personal research assistant
Maxine Ganske
Librarian extraordinaire!

To Linda Kichline, editor & publisher—
Thanks for your faithful support of the paranormal genre.
You've given many of us the extraordinary opportunity
to share our hearts with others.

Indigo Bay

***

Barbara Baldwin

ImaJinn Books

INDIGO BAY

Published by ImaJinn Books, a division of ImaJinn

ISBN: 1-893896-43-9

10 9 8 7 6 5 4 3 2 1

PUBLISHER'S NOTE:
This book is a work of fiction. Names, characters, places and incidents are products of the author's imagination or are used fictitiously. Any resemblance to actual events or locales or persons, living or dead, is entirely coincidental.

Books are available at quantity discounts when used to promote products or services. For information please write to: Marketing Division, ImaJinn Books, P.O. Box 162, Hickory Corners, MI 49060-0162, or call toll free 1-877-625-3592.

Cover design byRickey Mallory

ImaJinn Books, a division of ImaJinn
P.O. Box 162, Hickory Corners, MI 49060-0162
Toll Free: 1-877-625-3592
http://www.imajinnbooks.com

One

Cameron, South Carolina –Present Day

"Thomas...Thomas."

The raspy whisper brought Mica Chadwick out of her chair to lean over the bed. Paying little attention to the names and comments mumbled by her aunt, she silently damned modern medicine for not being able to prevent heart attacks and their debilitating effects.

"Michaela, dear, you're here." Her aunt wheezed, then stopped. Mica held her own breath, waiting. She made a grab for the emergency button when her aunt's eyes popped open again and she coughed. A trembling hand blindly groped for Mica's own, and Mica squeezed it to reassure herself as well as her aunt.

"I have to leave soon, Michaela Marie." Her aunt more often used her full name rather than the shortened nickname Mica preferred. Mica smiled now at the sound of it.

"Aunt Theo." A gentle squeeze from her aunt's hand cut off her words.

"It's time...time for me to go."

Mica looked deep into clear blue eyes so like her own. She could see her aunt was lucid, but she didn't like what she heard.

"Auntie, no. You're going to get better, truly." Mica knew what the doctors said, but she told the lie, anyway. At eighty-nine, Aunt Theo's heart had worn out, and Doctor Jacobs didn't know how long she could last. "If you rest and take your medicine—"

"I'm not going lying flat on my back, Michaela Marie.

You know better than that. I signed papers last week at Dr. Jacobs' office. I'll not have tubes and needles and *whatnot* making me look like a porcupine." Her aunt's voice, surprisingly strong, gave Mica new hope.

Just as quickly she began to cough, and Mica supported her so she wouldn't choke. Blue-veined hands clutched Mica's arm until she knew she'd bruise. Still she held her aunt, cooing reassuring words close to her ear and smoothing her white hair with a trembling hand.

"Thomas needs you, Michaela Marie. Go to Sea Crest and be with him." Though her grip had not loosened, her aunt's voice faded to a croak.

"Sh...sh...don't try to talk." Mica didn't know anyone named Thomas, but she refused to agitate her aunt by telling her that. She carefully laid her back upon the bed and pulled the covers over her frail form. Thinking she slept, Mica turned, but Aunt Theo's whispered plea stopped her.

"You're the only one who can save him, dear. And Thomas can make you happy."

"Aunt Theo..." Mica turned back, but noting the closed eyes and shallow breathing, she didn't continue her argument. Her gaze remained on the rise and fall of the coverlet to assure herself Aunt Theo remained with her. She had no idea to whom her aunt referred, not that it mattered. Mica did not need, or want, another man in her life.

She reached out to caress her aunt's gnarled and weather-wrinkled hand, noting a small amount of dirt under her nails. Mica would bet any amount of money her aunt had been working out in the garden again, in the heat of the day, and most probably without a hat.

Her aunt's warm hand tucked into her own formed a bridge to her memories. Mica closed her eyes and thought back to her childhood and the time spent with her aunt at Sea Crest, the old family home on Cameron Island. Even though it had been turned into a bed & breakfast inn years ago, Aunt Theo kept an apartment in one section, and Sea Crest remained a unique place to spend a summer. As an inquisitive and energetic kid, Mica had learned to swim in the ocean, play hide-and-go-seek in the garden maze, and dress up in old, old clothes from the attic.

Aunt Theo's hand stirred beneath her own to scatter the daydreams.

She had recently planned time off to visit Sea Crest. Not only did she dearly love her feisty old aunt, but she needed time to come to grips with her life, her failed marriage, and her career as an attorney. Now her plans would be on hold, for Mica wondered if Aunt Theo would ever live at Sea Crest again. The very thought of her not puttering around the estate and telling stories about the "old days" saddened Mica immensely.

She stepped into the hall and called her mother, who promised she would be up first thing in the morning. When she returned to her aunt's room, panic clutched her chest to find the bed empty, the IV tube dangling uselessly to drip onto the floor. She rushed to the bed to buzz the nurse's station when she saw her aunt's small form in the chair by the window. Relief washed over her even as she started to scold her for leaving the bed.

When her aunt didn't respond, Mica moved closer to shake her awake. The poor dear sat tilted at an uncomfortable angle, but when Mica touched her shoulder to wake her, her hands dropped from her lap and her head lolled to the side. Mica knelt beside the chair.

"Great-great-aunt Theodora Josephine, wake up, do you hear me?" Frightened now, Mica scrambled across the bed and pushed the nurse's button, then slid off to her aunt's side again. She sobbed as she searched for a pulse but couldn't discern a beat.

Nurses pushed her aside. Sharp commands to the orderly had him placing her beloved aunt none too gently back onto the bed. A nurse hovered to check for pulse and respiration, but when she shouted, "Code blue," Mica had seen enough.

"No." The soft-spoken word echoed across the bleak room.

"It's standard procedure, Miss."

Mica knew the nurse only followed hospital rules.

"No. She didn't want the needles." Her gaze caressed her

aunt's beloved face, peaceful now in death. "It's too late, anyway. She's already gone." Tears obscured her vision. Her fingers trembled against her lips as she tried unsuccessfully to muffle a sob.

The hospital staff moved aside to allow Mica her grief. There'd be papers to sign, and reports to file. As an attorney, Mica was familiar with the Advanced Directive Statutes of South Carolina. She also knew there had been no court case to test the limits of living will declarations. The hospital would protect itself from liability. But none of that mattered at the moment.

"Here, Miss, she must have dropped this." She was vaguely aware of the orderly pressing something into her hand before he left the room. Mica bent to place a farewell kiss on her aunt's wrinkled brow. She looked younger now. Perhaps Aunt Theo had been right when she said the time had come to leave.

Mica now realized her aunt would never have been happy in a hospital or nursing home. If Theodora Josephine Ashley couldn't be at Sea Crest, she didn't want to be anywhere. Mica smiled through her tears and said a silent prayer to God to take good care of this very special lady.

She brushed at her eyes, only then realizing she held a paper in her hand, crushed almost beyond repair. Carefully, she smoothed it flat against her chest as she moved towards the light. Her breath caught in surprise as she scanned the legal document.

"Oh, Aunt Theo, what have you done?"

***

Katie French, a lifelong friend, had stopped by Mica's Charleston apartment every day since Aunt Theo's funeral two weeks before. For the first time, Mica felt up to speaking about her aunt's bequest. She still couldn't believe her own father had written the document and never said a word about it.

"It's so exciting, Mica! You own Sea Crest!" Katie, like one of those perpetual motion toys, paced back and forth from the breakfast bar to the couch. She had the energy and personality to run Sea Crest, not Mica. "Well, aren't you excited?" she asked, stopping just long enough to throw Mica a perturbed look, hands on hips, before she started pacing again.

"What do you suggest I do with a bed and breakfast so far up the coast from my law practice?" Mica questioned her. She had come to terms with her favorite aunt's death, but didn't know if she was ready to visit Sea Crest. The inn held too many memories.

"Is it true that Theo's family owned the whole island? How romantic!"

Mica grinned at her friend's enthusiasm. Katie had married her childhood sweetheart and had three adorable kids. She spent her days at the country club, or shopping, or doing volunteer work. She employed a housekeeper and a nanny, and she didn't worry about paying bills or struggling to make sense of her life. Mica sometimes envied her.

Instead, Mica had a routinely predictable and dull life. She had a responsible career. She had made a responsible marriage to a family of strong social standing, even if her husband had proven to be anything but responsible. She always paid her bills on time, visited her parents often—as a good daughter should—and dressed in fashionable, conservative, suits.

As Katie chattered on about Sea Crest, Mica began to think perhaps the time had come for an adventure. She was tired of being reliable. She laughed to herself at the thought, for she and her father had already spent hours shifting cases to ensure she had the time off she requested. Any cases that couldn't be postponed had been given to a junior executive to handle in her absence. She rose from the couch and headed for her bedroom, confident Katie would follow.

Katie plopped on the bed, stomach first, and propped her chin in her hands. She certainly didn't act like a twenty-nine-year-old mother of three. "What are you doing?" she asked.

"You've been badgering me to go to Sea Crest, so I am." Mica watched her friend's mouth drop open. "There. Are you happy, now?"

"Oh, Mica, that's wonderful! I know you'll love it. We had such fun there when we were kids."

"Katie, in case you haven't noticed, we're not kids anymore."

"Michaela Marie Chadwick, listen to me. If you just let your hair down, you *will* relax and have fun. You might even meet someone interesting up there." Katie forever worried about her being alone, though Mica was happier single than married to Richard.

"Yes, ma'am. I promise." She grinned as she gave her friend a hug.

***

A sense of peace stole over Mica the moment she dropped her bags inside Sea Crest's front entrance. She smiled at the smell of lemons, which would forever remind her of Theodora Josephine Ashley, Sea Crest's eccentric matron.

Mica's great-great-aunt had maintained a home here even though she had a manager. She would often help with reservations, set menus with old-time recipes, and greet guests. She had liked people, and wanted anyone who stayed at Sea Crest to feel at home.

A new manager greeted Mica, her nametag identifying her as Mrs. Anna Harris. "Ms. Chadwick, we were all so sorry to hear about Mrs. Ashley. We considered her more a dear friend than an employer."

"Thank you, Mrs. Harris."

"Oh, you just call me Anna. Here, let me take your bags. I expect you'll stay in your aunt's apartment. Well, it's yours now, isn't it?"

Mica nodded as she followed the woman down a short hall to the northern part of the house. She didn't question how the woman knew she had inherited Sea Crest. She was curious, however, about the nervousness in the woman's voice. Perhaps Anna thought Mica intended to take over and oust her from her position. Mica would certainly discredit that notion in a hurry. As much as she loved her aunt, she couldn't fathom giving up a law practice to run a bed and breakfast.

"Oh, my." She had forgotten how Sea Crest resisted change. The manor maintained the grandeur of more than a century ago. A short hall separated her aunt's apartment from the inn, and as they entered the high, oak-trimmed doorway, Mica felt drawn back in time. The sitting room, full of antiques, contained dark, wood furniture with brocade seats, heavy draperies, and even needlepoint pillows on the couch. A small kitchen stood to her left, one of the few concessions to modern times. Directly in front of her, spanning almost the entire north wall, tall windows embraced a set of French doors that overlooked the lovely gardens her aunt had cherished.

"I'll put your bags in here, Ms. Chadwick."

Mica followed the woman into the bedroom. She noticed her aunt had re-papered the room in a yellow rose pattern. It certainly helped brighten the effect of the dark wood highboy, vanity and canopied bed that occupied the spacious room. Again floor to ceiling windows looked out over the garden and fountain.

"Thank you so much for making me feel welcome, Anna."

"Well, you are Mrs. Ashley's niece, after all, Ms. Chadwick." The woman gave her a warm smile.

"Please, call me Mica. We don't stand on formality here, do we?"

"I'll try, Ms...Mica, but you and Mrs. Ashley, well, you're old Southern family, you know, and we do have our traditions to uphold."

"I understand. As long as you're here," Mica saw the smile fade from the woman's face and rushed to reassure her, "I fully intend for you to continue in your current position—you and all the staff. You may tell them as much. I wouldn't dream of changing anything about Sea Crest."

Apparent relief brought the smile back to the woman's face.

"I know you're busy," Mica continued, "but would you have time to show me around? I haven't visited in a while, and then I spent most of my time here with Aunt Theo. I want to familiarize myself with the rest of the inn."

"It would be my pleasure to show off Sea Crest to its new owner, but would the morning be soon enough? We have guests arriving and leaving today."

"Of course. Tomorrow will be fine." Mica nodded

agreement, and Anna left to prepare for the new arrivals.

Mica unpacked her things and stored the bags under the bed before opening the doors to the patio and gardens. She bent to pinch dead leaves from a rosebush and realized the plants and flowers weren't in the best of health. Weeds choked out some of the verbena, and unwanted ivy tangled among the azaleas.

Her aunt had refused to hire a gardener, insisting she could take better care of her *babies* than anyone else. Because the gardens remained private and not readily accessible to the inn, it appeared no one had thought to do anything with them since her aunt's death. Mica made a mental note to remedy that situation.

She sank down on one of the stone benches which surrounded the fountain and stared at the granite Cupid standing in the center of a small pool. She cocked her head to the side and smiled. This Cupid had no little bow and arrows, as the original concept of Cupid should have.

She recalled a story her aunt used to tell. At the time, Mica had thought it so romantic. Generations ago, the owner of Sea Crest had fallen in love with a mysterious lady and had commissioned a statue of Cupid in Charleston. When delivered, the workmen accidentally tipped it over on the stones, snapping off the hand that held the bow and arrows. The man had been very angry, but the lady had told him she loved him truly and would not let him have the statue replaced with a new one. Mica could still hear her aunt's voice at the end of the story.

"The man then told his beloved it made no difference that Cupid had no bow and arrows, for his heart had already been captured by the most wonderful woman in the world, and his love would be hers throughout all time." Her aunt would sigh, then add, "Michaela Marie, someday you'll find just such a man, and Sea Crest will be safe in your hands."

Mica now frowned at Cupid. "You and my aunt must have crossed signals when it came to me. I sure haven't met any man as handsome, endearing, and romantic as Aunt Theo always said were in her time."

Feeling foolish talking to a stone statue, Mica left the garden to wander through the rest of the inn. As a child visiting her aunt, she had loved to hear stories about Sea Crest. In the early 1800's, a plantation with acres of crops and flowering gardens covered the entire island. During the War Between the States, the manor housed soldiers, then the family turned it into a boarding house to make ends meet. Eventually, the land around the manor house was sold to pay taxes.

Over the years other beach houses were built, but the island still retained much of its primitive atmosphere. She couldn't recall when the house had been converted to a bed & breakfast, but it still stood above the rest of the homes in elegance.

She strolled down a short hallway that opened into the community living room where guests could enjoy television, a game of chess, or just relax. She smiled, for this room also reflected Aunt Theo's personality. Yellow washed the walls in cheery brightness. Floral pictures hung on any available wall space, and fragile porcelain bouquets sat atop the mantle. Like the rest of the inn, however, the room contained furnishings from the 1800's. Even the television and lights were somewhat disguised in period decoration.

Mica ran her hand over the banister's natural wood as she passed the stairs. A small reception table sat in the shadow of the curved stairway. Although the regulations governing bed & breakfast inns stipulated a maximum of five guest bedrooms, the dining room she entered could easily seat fifty. The smooth, polished sideboard offered guests a buffet-style breakfast. A huge chandelier had been converted to electricity, but lent the room a nostalgic air. After the turn of the twentieth century, the kitchen had been built onto the back of the house, whereas before it had been a separate structure.

Mica glanced out the back door to find a light rain falling that would prevent her from walking on the beach. She shrugged. Long days and nights loomed before her to indulge in that delight, so she returned to her apartment to relax for the evening.

***

Mica jerked awake, her neck kinked from where her head

had been cranked lopsided on the couch. The noisy static from the television indicated it was well past midnight. She rubbed her neck as she stood and picked up her plate and cup from the coffee table. What had awakened her? Usually if she fell asleep in front of the TV, she slept like the dead until morning.

Halfway to the kitchen, she froze. Loud male voices floated in through the open French doors. While Mica couldn't discern what they said, she could hear the anger. She grabbed a flashlight from the kitchen drawer and cautiously slid the screen door open and stepped onto the patio flanking the garden.

She frowned as she held her breath to listen. The yellow circle of light waved back and forth as she searched the garden for intruders. The voices, though not as loud, were still disturbing in their intensity. Where on earth did they come from?

She tilted her head. Now, it sounded as though the voices came from the inn's second floor. Mica's exasperation rose as she stomped back into her apartment. She would *not* allow anyone to disturb the other guests, and if they couldn't keep the noise down, she would escort them out the door immediately. The flashlight fell to the couch as she grabbed the wrapper that matched her silk pajamas, tying the belt as she walked briskly down the hall and up the stairs. She had no trouble finding her way since lights were kept on all night.

She softened her steps as she moved down the hall, listening all the while to the voices. The yelling became loudest when she reached a door at the opposite end of the hall from the stairway. She pushed aside any guilt for eavesdropping as she put her ear to the heavy wood. Strange, though the voices appeared to come from here, the key remained on her side of the door, which indicated no guests occupied the room.

Determined to stop the argument as the volume grew, Mica reached down to turn the key and open the door. A tingle shot up her arm, crossed her shoulders and settled in her chest to constrict her breathing. Sounds much like the surf at high tide pounded in her ears and her vision blurred for an instant. She jerked her hand from the doorknob as the door swung open to reveal not a room but a long corridor.

Nervous at the thought of invading another person's privacy, but eager to end the commotion, Mica stepped through the door. Humid air surrounded her as a warm breeze swept down the hall. She thought perhaps this section had been shut off for repairs, since apparently the air conditioner didn't work. The hallway appeared to have a design similar to the rest of the inn. Plush carpet tickled her bare feet, and the hall contained dim lights of the same style. Most of the doors along the corridor were closed, and no light filtered beneath them.

She stepped through the first door she found ajar, expecting to confront the unruly people and ask them to keep it down, but she found the room empty. She forgot her reason for coming upstairs as the glamour of a bygone era wrapped her in warmth and welcome. Burnished oak furniture and book-lined shelves filled the room.

The only illumination came from an antique oil lamp on the desk, and she reached behind her for a light switch. Not immediately finding one, she moved across the room and turned up the lamp's wick, frowning. Anna should not use such a dangerous source of light in this corridor. Although lending an historical air to the room, if a lamp should tip over—Mica shuddered at the thought.

The books on the far wall captured her attention. When she moved to examine them, she released a soft, slow whistle. One of Aunt Theo's ancestors had spared no expense in recreating the past, she thought as she pulled a heavy volume from the shelf. She caressed the leather-bound tome as she read the title, embossed on the rib in gold leaf.

In her surprise, she nearly dropped the book as she quickly glanced up at the other volumes. Law books—all of them — in mint condition even though the ribs stated they were South Carolina Law Statutes for 1840! She would definitely have to ask Anna Harris about this section of the inn.

***

The downstairs clock struck twelve as T. Logan Rutledge stood silent and undetected at the doorway to his study. It would appear his housekeeper's new-fangled idea of carpet in the hallway served more purpose than ordinary comfort for his plantation home. The plush covering must have muffled his footsteps as he returned to his study.

Arguing with his stepbrother, Neil, all the way out the front door, he had not been quiet as he stormed back upstairs. Now, he must deal with another intruder in his home. His anger still simmered, and he opened his mouth to castigate her, but for some reason the raven-haired beauty's womanly curves softened his anger and turned his blood warm.

For just an instant, he wondered if this could be another of Neil's tricks. No, his stepbrother had the habit of foreshadowing his hand, and Logan never had trouble reading his mind.

He heard a soft whistle then a gasp as the woman pulled a book from the shelf. Thinking she was another of his housekeeper's myriad assortment of cousins and nieces, he felt sure she gasped from the weight of the book, since most of the lower class could not read. Before he could reprimand her for wandering above stairs, she moved towards the desk light and he caught a glimpse of long, trim legs through the silk of her wrapper. Was he mistaken, or were those trousers she wore beneath the calf-length jacket?

Captivated, he watched as she tucked a strand of hair behind one ear. Odd, but he could never recall seeing such a statement in contradictions. Here stood a beautiful woman, but with hair as short as a man's and wearing trousers. Still, she was a fetching piece, and he thought perhaps he'd take advantage of her presence.

"Excuse me?" He said, coughing discreetly.

The woman screeched at his simple words and whirled to face him, the book clasped against her bosom. Logan's breath caught when she came full into his view, her blue eyes wide and her dark brows lifted in an expression of surprise.

She stood before him wrapped in peach silk, her black hair swirling about her face, and her eyes huge. With the light now behind her, he could see most of the rest of her slim figure beneath the thin covering she wore. What he saw enticed him to gamble that she had not been sent by his conniving stepbrother, but had ventured from below stairs to visit the master of Indigo Bay.

He stepped further into the room and poured himself a brandy from the glass decanter behind his desk. She didn't say a word. When he gestured to her with the glass, she shook her head and clutched his law book closer to her breasts. He gave a hearty sigh.

"Are you another of Mattie's cousins, or a niece, perhaps?"

"Mattie?" She managed to squeak out the one word.

"Ah-ha, so you are. I thought as much. Most times, though, her relatives are too timid to show themselves above stairs. You are different." He downed the last of the brandy, set his glass back on the cart, and walked over to stand in front of her.

She was tall for a female, for she tilted her head only slightly to look him in the eye. She smelled of fresh air and sunshine, and his fingers itched to touch her sun-kissed skin. Never had a woman so quickly captivated him. Under normal circumstances, he kept a very tight rein on his emotions, but she drew him closer with her sky-blue eyes and pouting lips.

Were her lips as soft and hot as they appeared? His mind rushed headlong over a waterfall of emotions, and he had yet to know her name, much less kiss her.

And he did want to kiss her. More than once. Why shouldn't he? After all, why else had she come to his study dressed so seductively if she were not some promiscuous miss out for an adventure?

"I will relieve you of your burden." He gently removed the book from her clasp. "In the future, please do not take the liberty of removing these books unless you're dusting the room. They're far too precious to me, and besides, they have no pictures to glance upon."

"Law books?"

Ah, they were making progress, for she uttered two words that time, and apparently was smarter than most, for she could read. He reached past her to put the book back on the shelf, and his chest came into contact with hers. Instant fire scorched him even as he heard her suck in her breath.

She stared at him. Sooty lashes blinked rapidly as though she was trying to clear her vision. The heat of her already burned into him, and he felt the urgent need to kiss her pink lips that even now trembled so close to his. He lowered his head toward hers.

Mica's heart refused to slow down as the stranger moved close to her. Even though she knew he meant to kiss her, she felt more curious than threatened. Tall and dark, he wore a white shirt with billowing sleeves and snug black pants that disappeared into the tops of knee high black boots. She noticed he had his dark hair clubbed back, though bits curled around his angular face. Mica caught a hint of humor in his gaze, along with something far more dangerous.

Instinct shouted this was his domain, and she tried to regain her composure and come up with a reason for being in his room. However, her composure slipped drastically when he took the book from her and replaced it on the shelf.

And touched her in doing so.

Mica gasped when their bodies came into contact. The hard muscle beneath the soft linen of his shirt caused her breasts to ache in reaction to his touch. Heat branded her, and her heart thudded a dangerous beat. She knew she should ask him to back up because he was a virtual stranger. Handsome, but still unknown.

Nothing could have prepared her for the seductive power of his brown eyes—dark, penetrating eyes capable of reading her most intimate thoughts. Tiny worry lines crinkled at their corners, and she felt an unbidden desire to touch him and soothe the frown from his face. His gaze captured hers. Black brows rose in question.

Yes, her mind screamed, regardless of the question. Overwhelmed by the pure sensuality of the man, she didn't move a fraction as he lowered his lips to hers. Just before his eyes closed, she caught a glimpse of passion in their dark depths.

His kiss dissolved any defenses she may have constructed, and she groaned as his arms circled her to pull her closer. She couldn't remember ever being kissed this way. His lips, firm and warm, touched her with gentle persuasion, yet she could sense the underlying passion. His mouth traveled from her lips to her ear, where he nibbled on her lobe before sucking gently.

She vaguely recalled a novel where the author wrote, "The heroine felt *devoured*." She had laughed at the time, but now understood, as his lips scorched a path back to her mouth to communicate his desire once more.

Her body melted into a puddle of heat. She ached with pleasure so intense it hurt. Her fingers curled into his shirtfront as her legs threatened to turn to jelly. She could feel his heart beat against her breasts, pounding in answer to her own erratic beat.

"What is your name, midnight minx?" His husky whisper reached her through a haze.

"Mica." She moaned as he rained kisses against her closed eyes.

"Mica? That's too masculine a name for one so delicate. Is there more?" Each word was punctuated with butterfly kisses along her brow and nose.

"Michaela Marie." His kisses were driving her crazy; otherwise, she would never have told him her middle name.

"Ah, a beautiful name for a beautiful woman." His kiss stopped any reply she would have made, the heat from his lips traveling through her to turn her blood to fire. She stood on tiptoe to get closer.

"Come to bed with me," he whispered, pulling her tighter against him.

His suggestion brought Mica to her senses, astounded that the man's sensuality had carried her away.

"No!"

She pushed away from him, and his arms dropped to his sides, but he remained close enough to block her escape. He no longer touched her, but Mica could feel his heat and passion as though he did.

"I don't think...I really shouldn't be here." It was all she could think of in way of explanation.

"I know that, sweet thing, for this is Indigo Bay, and I

know all who belong here." His full lips lifted in a sensuous smile. "But that is of no consequence, for tonight, if you will allow it, you will be my guest."

He executed a bow, and Mica felt the urge to curtsy as a lady would when a gentleman asked for a dance. It only deepened her chagrin to glance down and realize she was not wearing a dress, but silk pajamas. She needed to get out of here before she lost the rest of her dignity and begged him for something she had thought she no longer needed. She glanced around for an excuse, her gaze settling on the drink decanters he had reached for earlier.

"May I have a glass of...water, please?" She gave him what she hoped was an enticing smile.

"Water? I have sherry and brandy, but no water." He now seemed in no hurry to continue his seduction, and that made Mica more nervous. When he moved towards the table, all fluid grace like a wild animal on the prowl, she *knew* she was in trouble.

Except for his kisses, which she couldn't blame entirely on him, he appeared to have the integrity of a gentleman. She used that to her advantage and allowed her Southern drawl to slip into her words, aware of its effect on men. "I really would like water, please. Sherry and brandy will make me wilt right on the spot, I assure you."

He gave her a sideways glance, and she fluttered her lashes. "Well, if you insist on water, I'll have to fetch it, for all the help are beyond hearing in their beds at this hour." He stopped to whisper close to her ear. "As we shall be, just as soon as I return."

Mica sagged against the desk and gave him a weak smile before he turned and walked out of the room. In the next instant, she sprinted to the library door. When a quick glance assured her he was nowhere in sight, she raced down the hall to the door through which she had come.

In her haste, it slammed behind her, but she didn't care as she twisted the key in the lock. Heart pounding and knees weak, she rested her head against the wood's cool surface. What in the world had come over her to make her act the way she had? And with a perfect stranger no less! She could only blame it on his overwhelming sensuality. She'd never met a man with such seductive power.

As she made her way down the stairs to her rooms, she recalled just how perfect he had been. He had a lean, muscular body, silky hair and laughing eyes. The best part had been his searing kisses—hot, sweet and more than adequate to send even the most sensible woman into ecstasy.

She fell into bed exhausted, but determined to find out the next day exactly what kind of rooms Sea Crest's second floor contained. More importantly, she wanted the name of the stranger who not only inhabited those rooms but also had managed to breach all the defenses she had so carefully constructed since her divorce.

Two

Mica woke the next morning tangled up in the sheets and feeling disoriented. It took a few minutes to remember she was in Aunt Theo's bed at Sea Crest. As she lay staring at the ceiling, she recalled her strange dream. At least she thought it was a dream. Her body immediately tingled, and her lips throbbed as though the kisses had been real.

"Hogwash!" she muttered, sliding from bed. As she walked to the kitchen, she recalled Katie's wish that Mica would meet a man while on vacation. That must have been the impetus for her dream. A tour of the inn would dispel any imaginings of handsome men who lived upstairs.

As she fixed her coffee, she noticed that two buttons on her pajamas had fallen off.

"That's weird." She plucked at the fabric. She knew she had tossed and turned most of the night because of the condition of the sheets, but to have torn off the buttons on her favorite pj's?

More disturbed by her dream than by two missing plastic buttons, Mica showered and dressed. She wanted Anna to give her a tour before breakfast, where she hoped for the opportunity to meet the guests.

Anna sat at the reception desk just inside the main door. "We've only got one guest this morning, but we're expecting another couple tomorrow," she replied cheerfully when Mica asked about the guests. She provided a running dialogue as they climbed the steps to the second floor, the polished wood railing gleaming in the early morning light.

"It appears you keep a tight rein on the housecleaning

staff," Mica commented.

"Yes, I try. Since we only have five guest rooms, it's not hard to keep things clean with two regular maids. I help when I can get away from the desk. Ah, here we are."

Mica experienced a sense of déjà vu when they reached the top of the stairs. It appeared exactly as it had in her dream. Even the silk flower arrangements on the wall tables were the same colors. She hadn't been upstairs since she was a little girl. Could a person remember such small details from that long ago?

The stairway divided the hall in half, and a person could go left or right along the corridors that flanked the stairwell. A beautiful, scrolled-wood railing enclosed the stairwell to prevent accidents.

Each of the doorways had ornately carved doorframes, all alike. "These lead to guest rooms," Anna stated, pointing to the doors directly in front of them at the top of the stairs. She moved along the east corridor, where there were two doors similar to the west side. "Not all of these are guest rooms. As you know, South Carolina law limits the number of guest rooms a small inn such as this can maintain. One room at the end of the corridor is a reading room available to the guests."

Mica noted the small lights on the walls that cast the hallway in a warm, mellow light. Their design replicated the earlier gaslights that had been popular before the advent of electricity and gave the hallway a turn-of-the-twentieth-century air. Odd, but she recalled the lights in part of the inn flickering like real candles, not burning with the steady glow of electricity. Why would she dream about a time before electricity?

"What about these two?" Mica asked about the doors at the end of the hall.

Pointing to the right, Anna stated, "This opens to a large linen closet. I can show you how we keep it if you'd like."

"That won't be necessary. From what I've seen, you keep everything spotless." Mica was curious what the housekeeper had to say about the rest of the inn. "What about this door?"

"Oh, that doesn't go anywhere."

Mica cocked her head to the side and glanced at Anna to see if she were teasing. It would appear the answer to her dream lay in this woman's knowledge. "Why on earth would there be a door that goes nowhere?"

Anna laughed lightly. "I asked your aunt the very same question when I began working here. She simply stated, 'Because it's the Georgian style, that's why.'"

Mica arched her brow, but before she could respond, Anna said, "That's all your aunt would tell me, but Cook gave me the whole story. Seems there was a fire generations ago, and the manor house, which was connected to this section by a hallway past that door, burned beyond repair. It was never rebuilt."

"But the door wasn't taken out?"

Anna nodded in confirmation. "The way I understand my history, the Georgian style meant everything had to be balanced. Notice the rest of the upstairs—the stairs are right in the middle. There are two doors on each side, each doorway is exactly the same in height and style, and there's a table right in the middle of each wall. Your aunt was a stickler for tradition and preserving the past."

Mica could surely attest to that. However, it seemed odd to have a door that led nowhere. Glancing down, she saw an old-fashioned skeleton key inserted in the lock. "Why is the key still there?"

Anna shrugged. "The key turns, but the door won't open. I assume it's been welded shut somehow."

Mica reached down to turn the knob, just to see for herself. The same tingle she remembered from last night immediately shot up her arm, this time even stronger. She jerked her hand away from the knob and stepped back, colliding with the railing that circled the stairwell.

Obviously, Mrs. Harris didn't notice Mica's astonishment because when a chime sounded from below, she turned and walked to the top of the stairs. "Coming?"

"Where?" Mica asked as she rubbed her hand up and down her jeans leg, still feeling the strange tingles from her contact with the doorknob. She swore she heard the rasp of a voice beyond the solid wood barrier.

"Why, to breakfast, of course. We have a fascinating guest you'll enjoy meeting."

Mica turned and followed the housekeeper. Maybe it wasn't a dream at all. Regardless of what Anna thought about the door, last night's incident was too vivid for Mica to put the door, and whatever might lie beyond it, from her mind. As a good homeowner, she felt it her duty to investigate any strange and odd occurrences.

Mica revised her definition of *strange and odd* upon meeting Dr. Joseph Bigley, a professor from Columbia University. His bright blue eyes, set in a deeply tanned face, twinkled when he introduced himself. An abundance of fuzzy gray hair and bushy gray eyebrows contradicted his youthful face. Gray sweats completed the picture. However, his strong grip when she shook his hand conveyed the impression that all the gray didn't mean the man was old.

"I hope you'll excuse my casual attire," the professor said. "I thought I would forego breakfast and jog my daily five miles up and down the beach, but when I heard you'd arrived I wanted to introduce myself."

"I *am* impressed, Professor Bigley. On a good day, I can only jog three." Mica allowed him to seat her, and since they were the only residents at the moment, she nodded for Mrs. Harris to commence serving.

"Please call me Joseph. I've been vacationing at Sea Crest for many years and was a great fan of your late aunt's. I offer my condolences." Before Mica could answer, his next words sent her head spinning. "I hope to speak with your Aunt Theo again quite soon."

"I beg your pardon?" Mica's eyebrows arched. Her coffee cup clattered back onto the saucer.

"Oh, dear, I'm sorry. You have no idea on Earth who I am or why I'm here, or do you?" The last words were stated in a hopeful voice, as though the explanation would be difficult and he hoped to avoid it.

"Professor Bigley, I only arrived yesterday, and I'm afraid I don't know anything about you. But I do know my aunt died over two weeks ago, so I'm afraid it would be impossible for you to speak with her."

"Tsk, tsk, another skeptic," he said. "Here, have some eggs, my dear, and try this delicious sausage. You're entirely too skinny. It's no wonder you can only jog three miles."

The professor continued eating his hearty breakfast in silence as Mica stared at him, her curiosity aroused by his abrupt change of subject. After several sighs and two cups of coffee, he finally acknowledged her presence again.

"Ms Chadwick, do you believe in the paranormal?" His blue eyes glowed with a serious light, and Mica dared not laugh.

"Do you mean ghosts?"

"Yes, among other beings trapped in the netherworld between life and death—or between lives."

"Professor, I'm an attorney. I deal in fact—evidence and provable, material objects. I'm afraid I wouldn't have gotten where I am by believing in ghosts."

His eyes twinkled as he laughed. "And I, Ms Chadwick, am a professor of psychology who has spent his life studying people. I'd say from the slight quiver in your voice, and your nervous plucking of the tablecloth, that you might not *want* to believe in them, but perhaps you're not quite sure."

The image of a dark-haired, handsome man flashed across Mica's mind. His warm, firm lips touching hers across the distance of her dream sent shivers down her spine. She reminded herself she was twenty-nine years old. Far too old to believe in dreams, much less ghosts.

"Professor Bigley, I'm well aware of the legacy in the South to believe in legendary heroic ghosts from the past, but that doesn't mean *I* believe in them," she said, but to convince the professor or herself? "Please feel free to conduct your research at Sea Crest, but I'd prefer you do it in such a manner that you don't disturb the house or grounds, or any other guests who might arrive."

His mysterious smile was back, as though he alone knew a secret. "I don't intend to dig up old bones, if that's what you're thinking. The object of my research doesn't lie buried beneath the earth we live on."

Mica eyed him, unsure how to respond. With his fuzzy hair and spectacles that kept slipping down his nose, he seemed to be an ordinary, harmless old man, but Mica shivered as though someone had just walked across her grave. Why did she have the distinct impression life would never be quite the same around Sea Crest?

***

Early that evening Mica strolled the beach fronting Sea Crest. She stretched as she walked, rolling her shoulders to relieve the tension. The day had been spent with Anna going over the inn's books and reassuring the woman that she had a permanent job for as long as she so desired. While Mica enjoyed the ocean and the restful atmosphere surrounding the resort, a lucrative law practice awaited her in Charleston. The time would come when she would have to resume her life.

"What life?" She scoffed as she plopped down on the sand and stared out over the blue expanse of water. Part of a top-notch law firm, she had great job security, considering her father and uncle had promised her a full partnership when she turned thirty. But was that what she really wanted—a nice, secure, responsible job? Finding loopholes for large corporations to take advantage of the law could not compare to the excitement she had always felt as a law student working for the public defender's office.

Even in the elite social circles that now drew her into their inner sanctum, the excitement had disappeared. The glamour and glitz of rubbing shoulders with Charleston's upper crust and being recognized at high society parties held little appeal. Mica realized she didn't need the glamour, but she did yearn for the excitement. She wanted to feel she made a difference.

She turned her back to the ocean, content for the moment to watch the sun set behind the houses lining the shore. Sea Crest stood majestic among the smaller private dwellings and single story resorts. She was glad the island council had set down strict rules as to what could and could not be built here. She would have hated to see the trees and gardens dug up for some high-rise. That had been Richard's plan when she had brought him here for a visit several years ago.

The sun dropped behind the island, allowing the night to slowly claim the shore, just as dark thoughts of Richard Norden, her ex-husband, claimed Mica's thoughts. She had thought their marriage would last a lifetime, even if her father had been the one to arrange their meeting and push her into marriage. Richard had been funny and bright, and most important by her father's standards, he came from an upstanding Charleston family.

In the three short years of their life together, however, Richard had drained his trust fund, invested in and bankrupted three businesses, and had started in on Mica's savings. When she made it impossible for him to access her accounts, he had become abusive, something her parents did not know to this day. Her father had never understood why she divorced him, and her mother? Well, Mica's mother came from a long line of happy marriages and couldn't see beyond that.

Mica rested her chin on jeans-clad knees, glad she had grabbed a flannel shirt to throw over her sleeveless shell because the breeze off the ocean became cooler as the night closed in around her. She closed her eyes, allowing her other senses to absorb the sea breeze, the tang of salt in the air, and the cry of a lone gull down by the water's edge. But her mind refused to rest as the lulling of the waves suggested she should.

The very characteristics her father so admired in her as a lawyer had been the downfall of her marriage—her outspokenness, her tenacity and her honesty. Richard had not liked her questions about his expenditures. He applauded her career since it put money in the bank, but at home and social functions, he still expected her to be a quiet, Southern lady with feathers for brains and no opinion of her own.

While Mica didn't mind being pampered once in a while, she didn't want someone who bought her expensive presents and flowers instead of showing her love and understanding. And she definitely didn't need a man who told her what her opinion should be. She wanted honesty, and a relationship with someone who could love as strongly as she could, but who would not try to change who she was.

She sighed and glanced around her, realizing the lateness of the hour by the rise of the tide and the coolness of the night air. Oh, well, the tide wouldn't come as far as where she sat, and no one was waiting for her and dinner at the apartment. For once and all, she wanted to exorcise Richard from her mind, just as the divorce had rid her of his presence in her life.

As she watched residential lights wink on one by one, Richard's fair face didn't come to mind. Instead, a faint melody drifted across the beach, carrying the image of dark brown eyes, glistening black hair, and a body that was pure sensation. How could a dream be so real—the man, the words he spoke, his hard body pressed against hers in the study?

Mica closed her eyes, her senses sharpened in the night. Once again she could smell the freshness of the leather-bound law books, feel the linen softness of his shirt, and see the twinkle in his eyes as the oil lamp reflected his awareness of her.

Oil lamp? How strange that she would dream of oil lamps instead of electric lights. She supposed her profession would fill her dreams with law books, but there had been something peculiar about the books. What was it that now stirred restlessness inside her?

She focused on a shadow shuffling along the back side of the inn toward her aunt's private gardens. Shaking off thoughts of dream men, she rose and brushed the sand from her jeans, walking up the path towards the inn's lights.

"Professor Bigley?" Her question brought a squawk from the little man, who spun around to face her, clutching a metal box against his heaving chest.

"Ms Chadwick, you scared the dickens out of me!" He gasped the words even as he shuffled the box into one arm and shoved his glasses back up his nose with the other shaking hand.

Mica tried not to laugh, because she realized the man was intent on his investigations. He just didn't look like a ghost buster. "I'm sorry, but what if I had been a ghost? You wouldn't have heard me coming then, would you?"

"As a matter of fact I would have, young lady. Besides, ghosts are not nearly as mean as people have been led to believe. I wouldn't have been frightened by a ghost."

Mica's arched her brows. The man really believed what he was doing. As though he read her mind, he held out the metal box in his arms. "I know you're skeptical, so let me show you. This is my own design, guaranteed to pick up the beta impulses known to be associated with ghosts. The spirit, you might call it, is made up of energy, instead of basic matter like you and me. This energy pulsates at a phenomenal rate—too fast and too high-pitched for human eyes and ears to pick up." He turned one of the knobs on the machine, and Mica could hear a faint click, click, click, like a Geiger Counter. The needles of the dials, however, stayed flat against one side.

"It doesn't appear to be working." She tentatively reached a hand out and tapped a fingernail on the glass cover of one dial.

"Of course not, because there are no ghosts in the vicinity. If there were, an alarm would go off to alert me. Then I could activate the camera, here, which would automatically take a photograph every five seconds."

Although Mica watched as he pointed to the devices on his ghost detector, she remained skeptical that it would do anything at all, much less photograph a ghost. "I thought you said the energy impulses were too fast for us to see. How can you photograph them?"

"This is a special film, developed for NASA's use. It is much, much more sensitive than what you or I would normally use."

"I see." Mica didn't, but she wouldn't destroy the professor's illusions. She cocked her head to the side. The music she had heard earlier drifted towards them again. It sounded close by, but Mica couldn't recall a piano anywhere on the premises. "Do you hear that, Professor?"

She watched him quickly adjust the knobs of his machine, his eyes flickering from the dials to the area around them. "I don't hear anything. What do you think you hear?"

"I hear a piano, but then, it couldn't be played by one of

your ghosts, could it, for your machine isn't telling you anything." She couldn't help the laughter that crept into her voice.

The professor took her joking with good humor. "Perhaps they aren't out and about just yet, Ms Chadwick. Would you like me to come get you should I find one? After all, this is your residence."

"Thanks, but no. I don't need part-interest in any ghosts. My portfolio is quite full at the moment."

He laughed with her. "But think of the publicity—the notoriety—the adventure!"

"Good night, Professor Bigley," Mica said as she turned toward the private gardens.

"Aren't you ready for a little adventure in your life, Ms Chadwick? A little excitement?"

She didn't answer, but kept walking, her heart pounding in cadence with her rapid footsteps. She stepped through the French doors, locking them behind her, but she could not lock out the echo of his question. Regardless of what she had told the man, she did long for an adventure. She had grown tired of her responsible, sensible life. But where, on sleepy little Cameron Island, could she possibly hope to find any excitement?

As if in answer to her question, the music she had heard earlier rose to a crescendo before returning to a soft, haunting melody. She knew without doubt the source of the music lay directly above her, and yet hadn't last night been a dream? Didn't Mrs. Harris confirm that this afternoon when she told Mica the door led nowhere?

Then why did her heart pound with anticipation? Why did her palms itch to touch the doorknob again, to see if the same electric tingle gave way to sensations she could not describe now that she was awake? And why, if it had all been a dream, did her feet lead her through the darkened corridor to the stairs?

Her breath came in short gasps. Her hand trembled on the banister as she ascended the steps and turned to face the door. She had to know. She had to find out for herself. Was the man she envisioned last night a dream? Or someone real?

The key turned in the lock, sending a frisson of excitement racing through Mica. The door swung open to a corridor exactly as she remembered from last night. Her hand trembled so badly, she dropped the key. As she stepped through the doorway and bent to retrieve it, she felt the zipper in her jeans pop.

"Damn!" She put a hand to her stomach and turned. She would have to return to her room and change. But then she heard it—the beautiful strains of a waltz played with such emotion she felt wrapped in warmth and caressed by invisible, soothing fingers.

Though her heart beat quicker, it wasn't from fear, but from the same sense of anticipation she had felt downstairs. She wouldn't go back, not now. Some inner sense told her the stranger waited just ahead, past the flickering wall candles to where the light spilled from an open doorway.

She placed the key in her pocket and pulled the door shut behind her. Pulling her flannel shirt closed to cover her broken zipper, she stepped down the hall and into the room. Her gaze focused on the man, elegantly attired in a black tuxedo, though his tie hung askew and his jacket had been left abandoned in the center of the floor.

He sat at a grand piano, his head thrown back, eyes closed, oblivious to everything around him. His body swayed with the rhythm. Mica found her gaze mesmerized by the stroke of his long, tan fingers across the keys. He didn't play the piano. He seduced it, coaxing sounds from the instrument and becoming part of the music he created.

Wild thoughts took flight with the music. Her skin tingled at the thought of his hands caressing her skin, bringing her to a fevered pitch. Together reaching the ultimate pinnacle. She was so wrapped up in passionate thought, she didn't realize the music had stopped until he spoke.

"I wondered if you would appear for me again tonight."

He swung around to straddle the bench, and Mica noted that his black vest and the starched white shirt beneath it were opened to his waist. She had an unobstructed view of his muscular chest, lightly sprinkled with dark hair. She leaned against the doorjamb, not sure her legs would support her. His gaze was more intense than she remembered, his shoulders broader, and his smile just as inviting.

"Who are you, lovely lady?" His voice seduced her as surely as though he touched her.

"Michaela." She, Michaela Marie Chadwick, renowned attorney who could convince a jury her client was innocent by her adept use of the English language, couldn't think of anything more to say than her name.

"I know your name, Michaela Marie." Her name flowed from his lips like the music he played. "But who *are* you? And why are you dressed as a farm hand? You could not possibly hide your femininity beneath trousers and a man's shirt." As he spoke, he reached high, arching his back and flexing his arms to stretch his muscles. It was enough to make Mica's heart stop.

"Who are *you?"* She might have convinced herself she wanted an adventure, but this man, so blatantly sexual and seemingly unaware of it, could end up being more than she bargained for. It would be best to find out more about him, and how he came to be at Sea Crest.

He grinned at her as he unwound his long legs from the bench and walked towards her, all fluid grace and elegance. "I do apologize, my dear lady." He gently took her hand and lifted it to his lips, giving her a bow that came so naturally, Mica would have thought him a member of the cast of *Gone With the Wind*. "T. Logan Rutledge, your dutiful servant."

The elegance of his words, the gentleness of his gestures, touched a chord deep within Mica, and she almost curtsied in return. Her face flushed when she glanced down at her attire. While she had never been concerned with fashion, she suddenly felt terribly out of place. He laughed at her frown, touching her shirt collar's soft flannel.

"At least you are comfortable." He spread his arms and gestured at the layers of clothes he wore. "I have had to torture myself with a tight tie and too many layers of hot cloth. All this for the unenviable delight of having Miss Sophie

Wainwright, trussed up like a peacock in monstrous feathers and ruffles of satin, try to break my eardrums."

She laughed with him. She couldn't help herself. He painted a picture as vivid as his music. He captured her hand, and when he tugged, she followed him to an old-fashioned settee against one wall of the enormous room.

"You have a delightful laugh, Michaela Marie. Your eyes sparkle, and your whole face glows."

She sat facing him, close enough so he didn't have to release her hand. Close enough she could feel his heat and the raw male magnetism surrounding him like some mystical aura. She tried to concentrate on what he was saying.

"T. Logan Rutledge." She repeated his name. "That doesn't tell me much about you."

"One night I find you in my study, wearing little more than silk unmentionables and a very seductive smile. Now, here you are again, this time with more cloth covering your curves, but with eyes holding a secret and lips begging to be kissed. Why must you waste time talking?" As he spoke, he traced her lips with his thumb, his other arm sliding across the back of the couch to rest on her shoulders. Just when Mica thought he would kiss her, he turned, stretching his legs out in front of him and clasping his hands behind his head.

"What would you like to know?" His eyes and voice were full of laughter, and again Mica found herself smiling.

Even in the tension of just moments before, she felt comfortable with this man she barely knew. But now he had given her the opportunity to remedy that. Trying not to sound like a lawyer in cross-examination, she said simply, "Tell me everything."

"Do you have a lifetime or two to spend on a very boring recitation? I dare say after five minutes, you'll wish to be at Miss Sophie's instead."

Mica turned and sat cross-legged on the couch, propping her elbows on her knees and chin in her hands. The action brought his black brows together in a frown.

"You are not exactly the conventional lady, are you?"

It was her turn to smile, turning his earlier comments back

on him. "After I have listened to your story, perhaps I will tell you mine. However, it will require the same diligent attention and length of time, I assure you."

Mica suddenly felt lighthearted and free, as though the restrictions placed on her by family and society all her life were no longer there. The invisible bonds, which had dictated how she spoke, dressed and behaved, suddenly didn't matter at all.

Logan sat there, staring at her as though he wanted to devour her. *There was that word again.* Mica's stomach flip-flopped.

She swallowed to ease her throat's dryness, then spoke. "Mrs. Harris said the door wouldn't—"

"And who is Mrs. Harris?"

"The housekeeper at Sea Crest, of course."

"So, you live at Sea Crest. You're not visiting Mattie?"

"Who's Mattie?"

He mimicked her. "The housekeeper at Indigo Bay, of course." He laughed with her, his rich chuckle reaching across the short distance to caress Mica's senses. "I am certainly glad we have established the servant's hierarchy."

"But no one knows you're here. It was only by accident that I followed the voices last night."

"Ah, last night. You must have heard me arguing with my stepbrother, Neil. If word of my arrival had to be slow, I wish it had not reached him quite yet. I would have liked to re-establish my father's accounts and reacquaint myself with the workers, firmly establishing myself in control of Indigo Bay before I had to deal with him."

That explained a lot, Mica thought. While she couldn't recall her aunt ever referring to any part of Sea Crest as Indigo Bay, she supposed if Logan leased this part as his private residence, he could call it what he wanted. That also meant there would be no need for the other employees of the inn to be concerned about it. Apparently Mrs. Harris, who was fairly new herself, didn't know about Logan because he had only recently arrived. But it was odd that her aunt wouldn't have told her about the man.

Logan reached over to tuck a strand of her hair behind her ear. The intimate gesture was so natural, Mica tilted her head towards his fingers without conscious thought. She forgot for a moment how strange their circumstances were. She felt comfortable and secure here. Peace stole over her as effectively as Logan's husky voice soothed her.

"I do not want to discuss my hot-tempered step-brother, or either of our gossipy housekeepers. I want to know about you—what do you do when you're not spying on me at night or wearing outlandish clothes?"

Mica couldn't take offense at his mention of her trespassing, because she had come into his quarters unannounced. "At the moment, I'm on vacation. My aunt, well actually, my great-great aunt, bequeathed Sea Crest to me when she died. While I don't know the first thing about managing it, I decided to spend some time here."

"I'm not familiar with Sea Crest, nor your aunt...?"

"Theodora Josephine Ashley." Mica had to smile when she said the name, knowing her aunt wouldn't like to be introduced, even in a conversation, as Aunt Theo. "Sea Crest has been in the family since before the Civil War."

"Civil War? I am definitely familiar with that term, especially with a stepbrother such as Neil," Logan snorted.

Mica thought his comment odd, but his fingers, which had lazily circled her ear, now slid to the back of her neck. It took little effort on his part to pull her towards him. During the entire time he had talked, she had wondered why he didn't put those lips to better use!

His breath, warm and tinged with the scent of mint, caressed her cheek as his lips touched her skin. "I don't want to discuss families or plantations or housekeeping staff anymore. I want to know about you."

"But I was telling you about me."

"There are other ways of learning about a person besides talking." He pulled her closer. And Mica didn't resist. His voice had spun a silken web about her, and she found herself willingly trapped in his embrace. His lips touched her brow, and she sighed, realizing she had been holding her breath in anticipation of his kiss. But even as he kissed along her eyebrows, down the bridge of her nose and across her jaw, she craved more.

Logan felt her moan vibrate through his body. Her heat combined with his own to fan the flames of the fire she had started last night. He had been delighted when she appeared, as though by magic, at the door to the conservatory, for he had spent the entire day trying to find her. Mattie had no visiting relatives, and though he had only been back at Indigo Bay for two weeks, he thought he knew most of the people in the immediate area.

For now, it didn't matter where she had come from. She was here in his arms. He couldn't explain the attraction he had felt last night, nor the intense sense of loss when he had returned to the study to find she had disappeared. Her seductive green eyes held secrets he longed to discover, and in her kisses he detected an untapped wealth of passion.

Michaela Marie consisted of more than physical desire, he knew, but for now, he would content himself with the exploration of her lush curves and smooth, silky skin. He quit teasing her with butterfly kisses and finally captured her mouth with his. The intensity of her response caught him unaware and totally unprepared for the heat racing like wildfire through his blood.

As if he had waited a lifetime for her to come to him, unspent passion now simmered just below the surface. His hand moved inside her shirt to cup her breast, the weight and fullness of it just right in his hand. His thumb flicked across her nipple, which stood rigid against the cotton of her chemise. He groaned as his lips left hers, not wanting their kiss to end, but knowing he had to taste her.

He heard her faint whimpers of desire as his lips wove an erotic path down her neck to the curve of material covering the treasure he sought. His hand pushed the material up over her flat stomach. Her skin was hot to the touch, on fire as surely as his own. He groaned as he cupped her breast, his hand large and brown against her delicate beauty.

"God, you're beautiful. I've waited my whole life for you

to come along." He kissed her breast before he flicked his tongue to tease her nipple erect.

Awash with emotions foreign to her systematic, orderly existence, Mica couldn't reply. Never in her wildest imaginings would she have thought kissing could be so erotic. Logan kissed her as though he had spent a lifetime perfecting the art, and Mica found herself more than willing to let him practice on her. That is, until he once again asked her to stay.

"Stay here tonight, with me," he whispered against her throat.

She pushed against his chest, struggling to pull her tank top back into place. While he allowed her to regain her modesty, he didn't move far from her side.

"No, I can't stay here. It's just not possible."

"But why not? You said you own Sea Crest, so I assume you've reached your majority. Is there someone waiting to take you home? I'll have Simon..."

"No!" Since he had just recently moved to the area, he must not realize how close she lived, and she wasn't going to tell him. The less he knew about her the better. If she didn't want to pursue a relationship, she would prefer he not know how to find her. She cleared her throat. "May I have a glass of water, please?"

The scowl that had brought his dark brows together instantly cleared. His eyes twinkled, and straight white teeth flashed in a grin. He stood and walked to a wall table that Mica had failed to notice earlier. "Would you prefer brandy or sherry?"

"No, water, please." She stood and moved to the end of the couch, ready to make a run for it when he left the room to fetch the water.

"Well, you are indeed fortunate. Just today, I had Simon put water decanters in all the rooms." He handed her a crystal glass, the smile never leaving his face. He sat lightly on the arm of the couch, one leg braced on the floor, the other bent with his foot on the cushion. Mica idly thought he should have more respect for the antique settee.

"Simon?" She clutched the glass, because her hand shook

and her voice cracked. She hated the squeak in her voice, and the fact she had reverted back to one-word sentences. No man had ever put her on the defensive so quickly.

"Are we back to that, again? Simon is my butler, who is married to Mattie, my housekeeper, remember? Tomorrow morning, I will introduce you to the entire staff, from the gardener and stable boy on up." He rose and moved towards her. "But tonight, you are mine alone. I do not wish to share you with anyone."

He reached to take her glass, and Mica panicked. She could think of only one thing to do—an old trick, but usually effective.

"Damn!" Logan jumped back as she knocked his glass of brandy and it spilled onto his shirtfront.

"Oh, dear, I'm so sorry. Let me get a towel." She stepped towards the door, but he grabbed her wrist. His eyes twinkled with amusement, as though he guessed her game.

"It won't hurt a thing. Leave it." He pulled her closer, his words soft and not the least angry over her clumsiness.

Mica's gaze fell to his chest, where golden droplets of brandy glistened among the dark hair. She pinched her lips tightly together to repress the sudden desire to lick the drops away with her tongue.

Logan's warm hand gently cupped her chin and tilted her face until she met his gaze. His brandy-tinged kiss, this time seductive and leisurely, still held a promise of passion.

She pulled away from him with reluctance. "I'll get a towel so it doesn't stain." She stepped back so they no longer touched, but she still felt as though they did. A reproachful look entered his eyes, and she added a promise she didn't know if she could keep. "I'll be back."

This time when she closed the door behind her, she pulled the key from the lock. She couldn't have said whether it was to keep Logan from following her, or to keep anyone at the inn from finding out about him. Her hand trembled as it closed around the cold metal. Her fist continued to shake when she pushed it against her pounding heart.

Three

Several things about T. Logan Rutledge didn't add up, and Mica swore she would get to the bottom of the mystery. At least that's what she told herself as she jogged down the deserted beach early that morning.

Last night as he kissed her and touched her, she could have cared less about any mystery. She couldn't seem to think straight when in the same vicinity as he. She recalled the soft glow of candlelight on the black sheen of his hair, and the heat of his body, which rivaled the moist warmth of the night air coming through the open balcony doors.

Candlelight? No air conditioning? And what about all those antiques?

She tried to rationalize the unusual circumstances. Candlelight was romantic, though he couldn't have known she would come to see him again. The night was cool enough to forego air conditioning, and many houses in the area were full of antiques. Sea Crest had its share of them, though some were reproductions. She suspected that some of Logan's could be, too. Much of the original furniture had been sold off sometime in the past to pay for upkeep. She knew that much from stories her aunt had told.

Mica came to a stop at the back gate, bending slowly at the waist several times as she brought her breathing back to normal. As she headed back to her apartment, she admitted that she could play the devil's advocate all day and still have no answers. She draped a towel around her neck and grabbed a mug of coffee from her small kitchen before she skirted the breakfast room and slipped unnoticed out the inn's front door.

She walked several yards past the circle drive to where

the lane just began its curve. She turned around to face the house. Sipping her coffee, she squinted against the morning sun that had risen above the roof. She stepped several yards to the left, then slowly walked back to the right, never taking her gaze off the building.

At one time, she had thought about being a mechanical engineer. Now she realized why her grades in high school drafting had indicated she find another career. She couldn't for the life of her picture the layout of the Sea Crest's upstairs from looking at the outside structure. The inn appeared much larger from the outside than when she had toured it. However, she had no way of knowing the size of individual guest rooms. That could explain the difference in size.

"There you are, Ms. Chadwick." Mrs. Harris said, interrupting Mica's thoughts. "I was just telling the Barkers you may have already left for the day."

"I will be gone soon. Are they the Barkers?" Mica added in a whisper, nodding toward the odd-looking couple who followed some distance behind her manager.

Mrs. Harris glanced over her shoulder before whispering back, "They're our newest guests, and they have a rather strange request. I told them they would have to speak with you."

"You're the manager and would normally handle this if I weren't here, wouldn't you?" Mica was reluctant to get involved with any of the inn's lodgers. Besides, there were things she wanted to do—the most important to investigate the mysterious Mr. Rutledge. "Speaking of guests, what can you tell me about—"?

"Hello, hello, I'm Harold Barker, and this is my wife, Nadine." The short, rotund man grabbed Mica's hand and vigorously pumped it up and down while waving the other in the general direction of his wife. Mica had no time to introduce herself before the woman stepped forward.

"Harold, please dear," she said, patting her husband on the arm. Mica couldn't see that the man had done anything wrong, so she supposed the wife just liked to be in charge.

When Mrs. Barker turned her attention to Mrs. Harris and

Mica, Mica picked up on the condescension in her voice. "I don't see why it's necessary to tell everyone in creation what we are about. However, since your manager felt we should speak directly with you, well, here we are. Now, do you have a problem with that?"

Mica switched her gaze from the wife to the husband and back. Nadine Barker was as tall and thin as her husband was short and fat, and her dyed red hair was in sharp contrast with his bald pate. While Mr. Barker shifted from foot to foot and worried his shirt collar with a pudgy finger, his wife glared down her nose at Mica with arrogant self-assurance.

Mrs. Harris shrugged her shoulders when Mica glanced her way, as though to say she had no idea what the woman was talking about. Mica decided to play the diplomat and try to get rid of the couple as quickly as possible.

"Welcome to Sea Crest, Mr. and Mrs. Barker. I hope you enjoy your stay." That was innocent enough.

"See, Harold, I told you there wouldn't be a problem, but no, you had to try to tell all." The woman blustered openly to her mate, whose suddenly flushed face matched the dark red of his shirt.

"But, dear, you didn't tell her anything yet." Obviously henpecked, Mr. Barker ducked his head after he spoke, as though a blow would follow his words.

"Of course I did, and she said we were welcome." The woman turned on a sandal-clad heel towards the inn.

Mica tried to be polite as she said, "Excuse me. I did welcome you to Sea Crest, but can I ask about the nature—"

"Of course, I suppose you must know something of our business," Mrs. Barker interrupted. "I assure you it's legal, and when we find the treasure, it will legally be ours, even if it is somewhere on the island."

"Treasure?" Oh, great, just what Mica needed in her life right now! Not only did she have Professor Bigley looking for ghosts, now she had a couple of fortune hunters invading her aunt's sanctum.

"See, she didn't know anything about it," the husband stated.

"Of course she knows. You told her first thing, but the fact remains it will be ours."

Mica found it curious that the woman talked to her husband as though he were a child. She used her no-nonsense attorney voice to quell their bickering. "I think I can clear this up quickly and you can go about your business. As long as you are guests at Sea Crest, you will be treated hospitably and left to your privacy. However, I shall expect you to follow the same rules as the other guests."

"And those are?"

The haughty angle of the woman's nose and her demeanor grated on Mica's nerves, and she had to remind herself they were guests. "Simply that you respect other guests' property and privacy concerning your activities. This is a small, quiet community, and the neighbors won't tolerate mischief. Although the beach is public, the property around Sea Crest is private, and you won't be able to dig for treasure. Even on the beach, you'll have to observe the posted rules."

"But the treasure isn't on the beach. The journal clearly states—"

"Harold!" It was obvious Mrs. Barker didn't want Mr. Barker divulging any more of their secret, and that was just fine with Mica. She had other things on her mind at the moment.

"Mrs. Harris, if you would be so kind as to show this charming couple to their room?" Mica applied all the Southern charm she had learned, then forgotten, in modeling class. She had effectively dismissed the annoying couple, but she'd managed to do it with such grace they smiled at her as they turned to leave.

She watched as poor Harold took two steps for every one of his wife's, his head down in abject apology as she ranted and raved at him for heaven only knew what.

She shook her head. A ghost-hunting professor and a treasure-hunting odd couple. She couldn't wait to tell Logan about the strange people populating her side of the inn.

Now why had she thought of that? Wanting to share part of her life with him indicated she had some feelings for him.

Mica didn't know enough about Logan to justify what she felt when around him.

She mentally put herself back on track as she retraced her steps, slipping through the private gate to the gardens, and then through the sliding doors. She definitely didn't want to run into the Barkers.

In less than an hour, she had showered and changed into a colorful broomstick skirt and blouse, brushed her hair and pulled it up with a clip in the back.

As she dropped into the front seat of her car, she decided the local historical society might have some information about the island community, since all the homes dated back to before the turn of the twentieth century. While she knew they wouldn't have architectural drawings and floor plans, perhaps she could dig up an old photograph or two, or some kind of document referring to Sea Crest as Indigo Bay. The strange name by which Logan referred to her home stuck in her mind. It was almost as though she had heard it referred to as such before.

She drove across the causeway, the only road linking the island with the mainland. The recently repaired black asphalt sent the August heat waves up in front of her, and Mica reached into her purse for her sunglasses. She laid on the horn when an erratic driver braked in front of her then turned left from the right lane. It appeared the small town of Cameron had become overpopulated, for the roads were already congested with traffic.

When she finally arrived at the museum, she idly thought about turning around and going back, suddenly in no mood to talk to curators about architecture. But since she was already there, she fervently hoped she could find the information she needed. Otherwise, she would have to make a trip that she knew would end badly.

***

Why wasn't anything easy? Mica slowly rotated her head, trying to relieve the tension that had built at the back of her neck during her four-hour search at the museum. She hadn't found what she needed, so her only other source of information was her parents.

She drove south on Highway 17 without paying any attention to the scenery. While she knew she shouldn't dread seeing her parents, they would make her visit difficult. Her father would ask her to return to work, and her mother would mention Richard. She could have put off this trip to another day, but she had a fascination for history and mysteries.

And, of course, she couldn't forget her simmering attraction for Logan. She didn't want to be away from Sea Crest for even one evening and miss the chance to see him. He was the mystery she would like to solve. This morning, she had started to ask Mrs. Harris about him when the Barkers had interrupted. In a way, Mica was glad, because at this point, she wasn't sure she wanted to share her thoughts of Logan with anyone else.

Finding out about Logan wasn't easy. If the lady at the Historical Society had been more helpful, Mica wouldn't have to make this trip. However, very few records prior to the Civil War remained intact. They had located only one reference, in an old ship's log, to an off-coast island named Indigo Bay.

Other than that, the historical documents referred to Sea Crest and the homes on the island simply as retreats. Apparently, families used the island to get away from bouts of malaria that periodically spread through the plantations. Mica hoped her mother still had Grandmother's old letters and family Bible. That might be her only hope for information at this point.

She stopped by her apartment for her mail and did a little shopping, purposely dragging out the rest of the afternoon. She didn't arrive at her parents until well after four in the afternoon. Though she had packed a bag, if she could help it she didn't intend to stay the night.

"Michaela, dear, what a pleasant surprise!" Her mother's lilting voice reached her as she slid the verandah doors open. "Come give your mother a kiss."

Mica dutifully bent and pecked her mother's cheek before slipping into a chair on the other side of the glass-topped patio table. As her mother finished addressing an envelope—probably an invitation to another of her famous cocktail parties—Mica took time to observe her. The sun picked up the silver highlights in her black hair, but somehow it didn't detract from her youthful appearance. At fifty-four years old, Karen Chadwick was still a very pretty woman.

The pink dress she wore accented her creamy complexion, and Mica suddenly could not recall ever seeing her mother in jeans and a sweatshirt. A descendant of an old Charleston family, she still clung to the Southern ideals of ladies, and prestige, and the social stratum. It wasn't that her mother flaunted their wealth or snubbed those without membership to the Country Club. It was just her way to be the genteel "lady of the manor."

Mica poured herself a glass of iced tea and tried to decide how best to broach Sea Crest with her mother. If she asked too many questions, Karen would become suspicious and want to know exactly why Mica wanted the information. She needn't have worried, for her mother gave her the perfect opening.

"How are things up at Sea Crest, dear? Are you enjoying your little sojourn?" She couldn't use a simple word like *vacation*.

"Sea Crest is as beautiful as ever, Mother. Visiting has made me interested in some of the history of the place. I was hoping you still had some of Grandmother's or Great-grandmother's correspondence or journals. I'd like to see if they wrote about it and the previous owners."

"Sea Crest has always belonged in the family. On the maternal side, of course. Why would you think there had ever been any other owner?" Just the tone of her mother's question put Mica on guard.

"No reason, really. I was just curious as to when some of the other homes were built, and when the island started being sold off. Surely we have some old letters or something?"

Her mother tapped a manicured finger against her cheek. "Well, Grandmother, Aunt Theo and I sorted through so much stuff about twenty years ago and donated it to the Charleston Historical Society. After all, we can trace our roots back to one of the first families to settle in Charleston, you know."

Mica groaned. "Of course." She had been brought up on

her mother's stories of ancestry and knew them all by heart.

"There may still be some old letters up in the attic in a trunk. I'll try to remember to have your father bring it down one of these days, if you promise to visit again. You know, you don't spend very much time here, even when you're in the city. I still think it entirely too frivolous for you to have an apartment when we have so much room. Of course, it was different when you and Richard were married."

Mica could feel a headache coming on.

"How is Richard?" Her mother asked. "Have you spoken to him?"

"No." *Why should I?* Mica kept that thought to herself.

"Well, he did call, and said he would go up to Sea Crest this week."

"You *told* him where I was?" Something close to panic closed around Mica's throat, and she swallowed hard to relieve the tightness.

"Don't yell, dear. Of course I told him. You can't reconcile your differences if you don't talk to him."

"We're divorced, Mother. I don't *want* to reconcile any differences!"

Her mother huffed, sitting up very straight and giving Mica that I-know-what's-good-for-you look. "It's not like he found someone...had an..."

"An affair, Mother?" Mica had learned at an early age that one didn't speak about sex with her mother or politics with her father. Just to agitate her, Mica stated, "There are reasons other than adultery for getting a divorce. I think I would have preferred it if he had screwed someone else rather than doing it to me financially."

As predicted, her mother gasped. "Michaela Marie! Don't speak that way in this house."

Mica was saved from a response when Lucy, the Chadwick's housekeeper, came out on the verandah. She had Mica's bundle of mending in her arms.

"Whatever did you do to your clothes, Miss Michaela? These things are chewed up!" Lucy held up Mica's jeans and silk pajamas.

"I didn't exactly break my zipper or pop my buttons on purpose, Lucy." Lucy had been in the Chadwick household since Mica was born, and had patched up not only her clothes but also her scraped knees and bruised pride more than once.

"Break? Pop? There ain't no zipper anymore—the teeth are done gone! And how'd you lose buttons when the thread's all nice and tight in these little loops? Both buttons broke in the middle?"

Mica would have examined her garments, but her father joined them at that moment. Lucy just clucked her tongue and turned back to the house.

"Ah, the wanderer has returned," her father greeted her. "I knew it wouldn't take a month for you to get yourself straightened around. Good thing, too, for the Sanderson's case is on the docket for next week."

"I only came for a visit, Father." Mica couldn't let him jump to conclusions. "I'm not ready for work yet."

"What?" His gray eyebrows came together in the middle as he scowled first at Mica then her mother, who gave a slight shake of her head as she patted his hand. It had been her mother's silent *I'll tell you later* signal for years. Mica still reddened with embarrassment, just as she had when her father hadn't understood about cramps, bras, and boyfriends.

He cleared his throat. "Well, get it fixed, whatever it is, and come back to work."

Mica wondered how easy it would be to *fix* having the unbidden image of Logan in her mind, or to erase the urgency she felt to return to Sea Crest and see him again.

"And how is Richard?" Her father's question brought another rapid shake of the head and hand patting from her mother. He jerked his hand free and said with a frown, "Be damned if I'll be quiet, Karen."

To Mica, he added, "He deserves more time, Michaela. He'll change if he has you backing him. But then, you'd better get yourself straightened out, too. We have too many big cases for you to be gone too long. We need your smile and soft voice to sway the jury and—"

"Father, I'm twenty-nine years old and can manage my

own life!" She hadn't meant to yell, because she knew her father didn't understand how talking about Richard upset her. He and her mother had married when vows meant forever, and they were still very much in love. She softened her voice with a smile. "Besides, as an esteemed attorney, you should be ashamed trying to use my looks and sweet, honey drawl on unsuspecting jurors." She rose as she spoke and bent to give him a kiss. As gruff and unbending as her father had always been, she still loved him dearly. "Have to go. I promised Katie I'd be there for dinner."

"What? You can't mean to leave before dinner?" Her mother sighed.

"You weren't expecting me, and I know how Lucy cooks. Next time, I promise I'll call first and stay longer." Mica hugged her mother, reminding her to check on the old letters.

She breathed a huge sigh of relief as she slipped into her car. Her parents were dear, sweet people, but when would they let her run her own life? Pointing her car north once again, she made a mental note to call Katie that evening so she could vouch for her lie.

***

Mica maneuvered her way into the apartment at Sea Crest with her bag and purse over a shoulder, a pizza in one hand and keys in the other. She grinned at the note Mrs. Harris had left stuck to her door. It seemed Sea Crest's guests had a minor confrontation on the beach that day. Professor Bigley's ghost monitoring machine and the Barker's metal detector set each other off.

Mrs. Harris' scribbled message indicated she would give Mica the details tomorrow, if she wanted them. However, the Island Beach Patrol had put an end to their argument before it escalated to a fistfight between the Professor and Mrs. Barker.

Oh, boy! Although she wasn't personally responsible for her guests, Mica felt she should probably say something to them. She chuckled at the thought of Mrs. Barker beating up the poor Professor.

Mica flipped the remote control as she ate pizza, disgusted with the lack of good programming. She grumbled to herself as she cleared away her supper plate and tidied the apartment. Her stomach churned, and her palms became sweaty as she rearranged some books on a shelf, just about knocking over a fragile figurine.

"What in blue blazes is wrong with you?" She spoke the question out loud, but already knew the answer.

She wanted a sign—something to tell her Logan was upstairs—just as his voice and music had the previous two nights. Tonight, however, no sound drifted in through the open windows. No haunting melody beckoned her forth. Did she again dare invade his residence without an invitation?

He had been on her mind the entire trip back from Charleston, and she realized she wanted to see him. No, she *had* to see him again, just as she had to breathe and eat to survive. It wasn't just to erase the thoughts of Richard that her parents had forced to the surface.

Logan had accepted her in his life with few questions asked. Her clothes hadn't mattered, and he hadn't even cared what she did or where she came from. His gentle words and interest in her were so different from the attention she had received from the other men in her life.

Mica looked down at her skirt and blouse. At least she would look more like a respectable woman, instead of having Logan see her as he had before—first in pajamas then in jeans.

"You said it didn't matter to him," she taunted her reflection in the mirror.

"It doesn't," she answered, but nevertheless she ran a brush through her hair before grabbing the key and hurrying from her apartment.

Moving soundlessly through the upper hallway, Mica cringed as the key grated in the lock. She glanced over her shoulder at the other doors, but since it was early the other guests must still be out for dinner. It simply would not do for anyone to see her sneaking around like a thief in the night.

The now familiar tingle shot up her arm as she turned the knob to let herself into Logan's residence. A quiver of anticipation pumped adrenaline through her system, and her heart pounded in her chest. She knew it was more than the excitement of doing something no one else knew about. This nervousness could be directly attributed to the prospect of seeing Logan. While he seemed to want to advance their relationship faster than Mica could handle, it hadn't precluded her from wanting to see him again.

Discouragement slowed her footsteps as she checked the library, and then the music room. There were low burning lamps in each, but no sign of Logan. Well, what did she expect, coming in unannounced at such an early hour? A man as handsome as Logan surely had dates. It might be hours before he came home. And he might not be alone. Disappointment clouded her vision as she turned to retrace her steps to the door.

Suddenly, her gaze landed on a closed door. It was a room she had not been in before, and it seemed to beckon to her. She turned the knob to find it unlocked. Every law she had ever studied flashed through her head, but none of the statutes she was about to break could have made her release the door and leave without investigating.

The instant she stepped over the threshold she knew Logan slept here. She could feel his very essence surrounding her—his aftershave, the strictly male feel of the place. Heavy draperies were open to allow the evening breezes through, along with a sliver of moonlight. A chair sat by the fireplace and a desk was positioned near the windows.

Mica trailed a hand across the counterpane, which was light colored but not frilly. She thought the furnishings looked old, but then they fit in with the rest of the decor. Dreamily she leaned against one of the posters, trying to imagine Logan asleep on that bed, his beautiful hair mussed, his lips parted as he dreamed.

Did he dream of her? If so, were his dreams as erotic as hers had been the past two nights? She straightened and shook herself, knowing beyond doubt she should leave. Not only wasn't Logan here, but her thoughts were definitely getting away from her better judgment.

"I'll be down for something to eat as soon as I bathe. We kept the fire contained to the ..." Logan's voice carried down the hall, but Mica couldn't move fast enough to hide.

Suddenly, he stood in the doorway, and Mica couldn't be certain who was more surprised. His hands clutched his open shirt, pulled halfway out of his pants and covered with black soot. His arms and face were completely black. Had it not been for his voice, Mica would never have recognized him. She swallowed. He didn't look pleased to see her this time.

"Well, Michaela Marie, so you do keep your promises." He walked right past her to another door, and Mica could hear water splashing. Before she could slip out of the room, he returned, this time bare-chested and with some of the soot wiped from his face. "When you said you would be back, I didn't realize you meant not until the next day."

His sarcasm stung her like a blow, but she couldn't find it in herself to walk away. In fact, she couldn't look away from his gloriously muscled chest that heaved with righteous indignation. Her palms itched with the need to calm his agitation with a caress. No, she wanted to touch him to try and calm her own feverish state.

She took a deep breath and said, "I'm sorry. It's just that things were moving so fast. You were...I haven't been divo..." She groaned. Once again he turned her mind to mush. He stood not three feet from her, clad only in his trousers and smelling strongly of smoke, and all Mica wanted was to wrap her arms around him and kiss him and beg his forgiveness. All her recently found self-assurance flew right out the window. She took a step forward, but his next words halted her.

"If you're a married lady, I suggest you leave right now. I prefer not to have my life ended by some cuckolded husband."

"I'm not married." She spoke the words softly.

"You say you are from Sea Crest, but all the other plantations are across the bay. I doubt you could walk there at night, so where the hell have you been, and why do you keep disappearing?" The last words reached Mica's ears as an exasperated shout.

Remnants of arguments with Richard flashed through her mind, finally lifting her mental fog and spurring her into action. Why had she thought this man different from any other man?

They all wanted to dominate, and she refused to give them total control.

Without a word she turned on her heel and stormed towards the door. This time she would make sure the key she felt in her pocket became permanently welded in the lock.

"Wait." His touch on her arm was electrifying—the heat from his hand instantly melting her anger. When she did not turn around, he stepped closer, running both hands up and down her arms. The heat turned to goose bumps then back to fire, burning through her back as he pulled her against his chest.

"I'm sorry." The two words, whispered against her hair, completely unraveled her. They weren't what she was used to from the men in her life.

Logan circled her with his arms, knowing he would probably ruin her clothes but wanting to feel her against him—to know she was real and had returned yet again to see him. He could no longer smell the smoke from the fire. Instead he breathed in the clean, lemony scent of her hair, felt the soft curves of her body as she relaxed against him.

God, she made him crazy! Here one minute, gone the next without a trace. He hadn't meant to shout at her. His anger reflected his frustration at being unable to locate her though he had searched throughout the day. He knew so little about her, and yet when she softened in his arms like this, there was nothing else he wanted to know.

He turned her around, enchanted by her dainty gesture as she tucked her hair behind her ear. Her eyelashes fluttered over bright blue eyes as she glanced up at him, then away.

"I missed you," he said. "I searched and searched, but couldn't find you." Each word brought him closer to her lips, which she opened as though to deny what he told her. He didn't give her a chance, instead kissing away her protests.

He had dreamed of her last night—dark erotic dreams in which they had traveled the road of passion time and time again. She had been hot and willing, and he had felt complete for the first time in a very long while. Now, as she returned his kiss, opening her mouth to his questing tongue, that feeling of completeness stole over him again. The warmth of her hands as she cupped his face erased all doubts as to the rightness of her belonging with him. If only he could convince her of that so she wouldn't keep running away. If only...

He flinched as she unwittingly brushed against the burns on his neck. She immediately stilled, tilting her head back to break the kiss.

"You're hurt." Her tender words tore at his heart. How long had it been since anyone had cared?

"It's nothing serious. Just some cinder burns. We had a fire in the north field, and it took everyone to put it out. I'll have to wait until morning to assess the damage. It's too dark to tell how many acres burned." He started to release her, but then caught her hand and lifted it to his lips. "If I leave you to bathe away the stench of smoke, will you promise to be here when I finish?"

Her blue eyes glittered mischievously, and he traced the upward slant of her lips as she smiled. He didn't want to let her out of his sight. He loved the silky feel of her skin and the warmth of her body, and yet he knew she would probably not consent to take a bath with him so he wouldn't have to stop touching her.

"I promise I'll be here."

"And do you mean *here* in this room, or *here* on the island somewhere, or perhaps just *here* in the state of South Carolina?" He realized that her escapes had been made because of his amorous advances. Though he couldn't seem to help himself where she was concerned, he knew he would have to proceed slowly.

"I'll stay in this room. I swear." He watched her glance nervously around his bedroom. Wanting to make her feel comfortable but not wanting her far from his sight, he refused to consider putting her in the library. Instead, he pulled her towards the fireplace chair, releasing her hand only after she had settled herself on the soft cushions.

He moved towards the bathing room that he had just installed upon his return to Indigo Bay. He left the door open a little as he stripped off his soiled breeches. He spoke, wanting to hear the sound of her voice to reassure himself she had, indeed, stayed.

"I lay awake last night rehearsing what I would say to you when I saw you again. Shouting at you in anger wasn't what I'd planned. I apologize. Will you tell me where you went?"

Mica closed her eyes as his voice caressed her with its deep Southern drawl. The rest of her senses alerted her to the sound of his pants being removed and the splash of water. Her own skin tingled as she pictured him lowering his muscular body into the water, his hands slowly soaping a washrag, then rubbing it over every inch of himself to...

"Michaela Marie?" His voice became urgent, and she realized he thought she had broken her promise.

"Yes, I'm still here." Her voice squeaked, and she cleared it as she fought to suppress her wayward thoughts.

"Well?" More water splashed, and Mica squeezed her legs together against the achiness building deep inside her. Dear God, why hadn't she suggested she wait in the library?

She tried to keep her voice steady as she spoke. "I spent the day trying to find out about you, if you must know the truth. There is no record of Indigo Bay, except for one reference back in the 1800's." She raised her voice to be heard over the splashing. "Most records were destroyed during the Civil War."

"That's the second time you've mentioned a civil war. Exactly what do you mean?" Logan's voice came out of the bathroom muffled, and Mica clutched the arms of the chair as she envisioned him rubbing himself dry with a fluffy towel.

"You know, the War Between the States." Many Southerners still refused to use the term Civil War.

"What?" Logan stuck his head through the doorway, gifting Mica with a glimpse of bronze torso, lightly sprinkled with dark hair, contrasting sharply with the white of a towel slung around his neck. She swallowed. Every muscle in her coiled tighter than a spring. Every nerve ending sang along her skin from the explosive current in the air.

When she didn't say anything, he disappeared around the door again.

"Leave it to a woman to get war and politics confused," he said with a chuckle. "The war of 1812, to which you must be referring, was between the United States and Britain. Although it was before my time, my father fought, using Indigo Bay as a refuge for American privateers." He came into the room buttoning a shirt over clean brown trousers, but this time Mica didn't notice his devastating appearance. What he'd just said didn't make sense.

She didn't have time to sort it out before he said, "Of course, with President Fillmore in office now, we don't have to worry about any more fights with the British. He's made it clear he won't tolerate—"

"What did you say?" Mica tore her gaze to his. "President *who?"*

He gave her a quizzical look. "Even if you can't vote, you've surely listened to dinner discussions and know Millard Fillmore has been our President since Taylor died in July."

He bent to kiss her lips, unaware of the shock his words had caused. "Stay right here. I'm going to get a tray from Mattie, and we can eat up here tonight. Tomorrow will be soon enough to see the rest of the manor."

Mica didn't even realize he had left. Very slowly, as though she had never seen it before, her gaze shifted around the room, pausing here and there to study the furnishings. Her heart beat painfully against her ribs, and yet it beat so loudly she could hear its slow thump, thump inside her head. Other impressions bombarded her—oil lamps, mint condition 1840 law books, and Logan's clothes, which, now that she thought about it, had never seemed quite in fashion.

She forced herself to relax the stranglehold she had on the chair and rise, moving to the doorway. Though the light was dim, she could detect the pattern of the wallpaper. She searched in vain along the entire length of the wall—from doorway to corner—and could not find a single light switch or wall socket.

Her hands shook as she brought them to her mouth to stifle the scream bubbling up inside. *No way could this be happening.* Either this was some great practical joke, or she had slipped over the brink of sanity and entered a dream world of her own design. Either way, Mica wanted no part of it—Logan or no Logan. She might have dreamed him up, but she could not imagine how the rest of this came about.

Tears blurred her vision as she raced from the room and descended the stairs. She had to get out of here—back to her safe life and her nice, responsible job. She reached for the doorknob, shaking so hard she had to clasp it with both hands.

"Michaela Marie? Where...oh no, not again!"

She heard Logan's shout and the crash of dishes and jerked harder on the door, intent on getting back to Sea Crest before he could stop her.

She bolted through the door only to realize it led outside. In her panic she had taken the wrong turn. A wide verandah stepped down to a circular drive before a lush lawn took over the rest of her view. Where was she? How had she gotten away from Sea Crest?

Before she could find any answers, she heard footsteps behind her. Instinctively, she raced down the steps and turned to her right. At the first opening in shrubbery, she turned again. The small amount of light from the moon showed her the way across more lawn.

Her ears roared as she raced through the night. She gasped for breath but refused to slow down even though her heart pounded and her side ached. Did she hear waves crashing in front of her, or was it only her frantic heartbeat? If she got to the beach, she would be able to orient herself and locate Sea Crest.

She didn't stop until she felt the water lap at her ankles. She held her side against the pain as she turned towards land to locate Sea Crest's lights.

She screamed when Logan grabbed her arm and spun her around. She pounded on his chest with her fists. "Go away—leave me alone! I don't know who put you up to this, but it was a cruel joke!" Tears streamed down her face, but she didn't care. She had trusted him, kissed him, and look what it had gotten her.

"Michaela! What's wrong with you? Why do you keep

running away from me?"

She could see the confusion sketched in his scowling features, feel his concern when his whiskey-colored gaze met hers. His voice bordered on panic. Perhaps he hadn't wanted to hurt her, but he had still been party to the joke.

"You blew it, Logan!" She shouted her outrage at his betrayal. "I may have let you sucker me into a few kisses, but you went too far tonight." At his look of further confusion, she continued to yell. "George Bush is President, and there is no way your dad could have fought in a war that took place over a..."

His look of astonishment made her stop. She gazed beyond him to the sandy stretch of beach. There were no clusters of bright-colored beach umbrellas stuck in the sand, ready to be rented the following morning. For as far as she could see, there was not one piece of litter scattered anywhere on the pristine sand.

She turned tear-filled eyes back to Logan, who had remained at her side even as she ranted and pounded on him with her fists. His eyes were full of sympathy, as though he understood her loss, even if he didn't realize what caused it.

"I don't understand," she whispered. "Where am I?"

With hands once again gentle, Logan turned her away from the ocean. He wrapped one strong arm around her, pulling her back against his chest. He fanned the other one out in front of them to encompass the entire island.

"Look before you. All that you see is Indigo Bay—my plantation—my island. It has been worked by my father, and his father before him." With a work-callused hand, he brushed her hair back from her face. She blinked several times before her eyes cleared enough to see what Logan saw.

She gasped. There were no lights up and down the length of shoreline, no privacy fences stretching to the edge of the sand to ensure each owner's territorial rights. Only the soft glow from several illuminated windows in one enormous house broke the darkness. She listened intently. Where was the traffic noise, so constant even from across the bay? Where was the odd odor so often prevalent because of the clogged bay and stagnant waters?

She shivered, and Logan's arms came around her to ward off the chill. But he couldn't remove the deep-down cold that had nothing to do with the breeze blowing into shore. This time, she didn't fight his hold, because he seemed the only solid thing in a world suddenly gone topsy-turvy.

She tipped her head back until it rested on his shoulder. She recalled other things that hadn't made sense from the beginning—things her mind had blanked out because of her fascination with Logan. Antiques that looked new. Mint condition law books that were, in fact, new. A house that had no air-conditioning and no electricity. And most important of all, a man who had the manners and gallantry of a gentleman from the antebellum South.

How could this have happened to her? She turned her head to rub her cheek against the soft linen of Logan's shirt, convinced that if she was having some crazy dream, at least he had been a nice part of that craziness.

Still, before she woke herself up, she had to ask, "Logan, when did Millard Fillmore become President?" His arms tightened around her shoulders as though he were afraid his answer would send her away from him again. "Please. It's important." She felt his sigh against her neck, his breath warm and real.

"Zachary Taylor was elected two years ago. When he died this past July, Vice-president Fillmore became the new President."

"What year, Logan?" Mica tightened her grip on his arms to anchor herself for the rest of his response. Even so, nothing could prepare her for the instant vertigo she experienced, nor the sudden black void that opened up and swallowed her at his answer.

"1850."

Four

Soft voices woke Mica. She felt a gentle hand brush hair off her forehead. The touch stirred such pleasant feelings inside her, she refrained from opening her eyes for fear it would stop.

When she could delay the inevitable no longer, she opened her eyes and focused her gaze on Logan, his face etched with concern. He noticed her open eyes, but he didn't stop the wonderful caresses along her forehead and down the side of her neck. If anything, he increased the pressure of his hand as it stoked the front of her shoulders and down one arm. She sighed in contentment and allowed her eyes to drift closed again.

"Michaela? Don't try to sleep again, at least not yet. The doctor said when you woke, we were to keep you awake for awhile." As his warm breath grazed her cheek, she felt his hand tremble and heard the worry in his voice.

"You were worried about me?" She shifted her gaze to his glittering brown eyes. She had been self-sufficient for too long. She had always done the worrying, and she doubted anyone except her mother ever worried about her.

"Of course I am. Did you think I wouldn't be? You fainted on the beach. After I brought you back to the house, I immediately sent for the doctor. He, by the way, wondered if I had fetched a mermaid from the sea."

His smile, tender yet teasing, caused Mica to flush with heat. A heat that spread like warm sunshine down her neck, across her breasts and belly to pool very low in her anatomy.

To cover the blush she knew stained her cheeks, she glanced around the room. "This is your room."

He shrugged his shoulders. "It was the first bed I came

to." His smile grew wider. "I've wanted you in my bed from the first, though I would have preferred it under different circumstances."

His head lowered towards her, and though Mica realized he meant to kiss her, she felt no panic. She knew he was a gentleman—a gentleman from 1850! That thought came crashing in on her, squeezing her chest and creating a pain at the base of her skull.

"Ahem. Here is the tea you requested." A woman's voice from the doorway interrupted her panicked thoughts, but increased Mica's headache. Logan placed another pillow behind her, then took the tea tray from a petite gray-haired woman with a cheery smile.

"Thank you, Mattie. Oh, Michaela Marie, this is Matilda Brown, my housekeeper, but we call her Mattie. I feel I should introduce you—since you're not her cousin." A tease had entered his voice, but Mica felt only a cold, black helplessness swirl around her.

"I know that."

He frowned at her tone, and Mica regretted her surly answer. The blackness closed in on her, and Mica welcomed it to avoid making up lies. Or worse yet, trying to make Logan understand the truth. Just when the blackness would have swallowed her completely, Logan's soft voice beckoned her back.

"Michaela Marie, don't run away from me again. Nothing can be so bad that you must hide away."

"You don't know any such thing." She refused to leave the soothing blackness behind her closed eyes, but she couldn't deny him some kind of an answer.

"You are right. I don't." He chuckled, but his next words were quite serious. "I will not ask you for answers, Michaela. I can only hope that, in time, you'll become comfortable enough to share yourself with me without my asking."

"Time?" Mica's eyes popped open. Her gaze flickered to the lamp on the bedside table that cast wavering shadows against the pale walls. "What time is it?" She tried to rise from the bed, but Logan pushed her back down.

"It is still the middle of the night, and you are not going anywhere." At her look of panic, he softened his tone. "If I have to stay here all night, you'll lie there and rest."

"But you don't understand. I *can't* stay," she whimpered. She had no idea what would happen if she remained on his side of Sea Crest. Would the key work the next time she tried to return home?

Logan studied her for a long moment, and Mica felt uncomfortable beneath his stare. At last he let out a sigh as he took one of her hands between his two warm ones.

He spoke softly, his voice comforting even as he said, "I said I wouldn't question you, but I fear I must ask one after all."

Mica held her breath. She knew she couldn't lie, and the chances of again evading the truth were slim.

"Do you trust me?"

"What?" she asked, blinking in surprise.

"Do you trust me?"

She lifted her gaze to his. His dark brown eyes drew her. In their depths she saw warmth and caring. She didn't know enough about this man to fill a thimble, but her heart gave her the answer to his question.

"Yes, I believe I do."

His audible sigh made her realize he hadn't been as sure of himself as she had thought, and that endeared him to her all the more.

"Then trust me to know what's good for you, and that includes staying here with me." At her immediate sound of protest, he gently put a finger to her lips. "Wait. I will make no demands on you. Let me show you my island. Let me share its beauty and its secrets with you. Learn who I am. I promise you'll not regret it."

Mica could never recall an offer quite like his. She gazed at him. He wore an earnest, little-boy expression, and she felt honored that her answer could mean so much to anyone.

She briefly thought of her parents and the argument they had before she left—the control they wished to exert over her life. Her mother had also mentioned Richard would be paying her a visit and she really didn't want to see him.

Then Professor Bigley's words echoed in her mind, asking if she feared a little adventure. She allowed herself a smile at that, for she doubted the Professor quite had this in mind. Logan returned her smile, and she thought, *Why not?*

If she were very careful, he would never know where she came from, and when the time came, she could leave and have no regrets. She fumbled along the side of her skirt until she felt the hard metal key in her pocket. The solid weight of it gave her the confidence to stay, because she knew she could not deny him, or herself, the chance he offered.

"I have no clothes." Her protest lacked conviction.

"I'll send someone over to Sea Crest to fetch what you need."

"No!" She realized her error when surprise etched his features, then a brow arched in question. She faltered as she tried to think of a plausible excuse.

"It wouldn't be...my staying here wouldn't be proper, would it?" She could only hope he accepted that.

"Ah, you're right about that. Hmm..."

"I'll write a note, asking for some things to be delivered to…" she paused, not knowing if the same towns existed in this time as in her own.

"Cameron. To the Belleview Hotel," Logan said, completing her sentence.

Oh gracious! Aunt Theo's hospital used to be that hotel. Well, at least the town existed, which would make it less likely she would make grievous mistakes in geography.

Of course, her note could never be sent, so she'd have to come up with some other way to obtain clothes. She sank back on the pillow, the headache she had tried to ignore blocking her ability to think anymore.

Logan lightly touched her forehead with warm fingers, brushing the hair from her eyes as he graced her with a smile. "Rest now, and we'll talk more later."

He rose from the edge of the bed, and panic assailed Mica. "Don't leave me!"

No matter what her decision to stay in this unknown world,

she felt safe only because of Logan's real and solid presence. He was a force she hadn't reckoned with, but now depended on.

He bent close to place a light kiss on her brow. "I won't leave you, Michaela Marie, but you have to rest." At the look of panic she knew remained in place, he sighed and resumed his seat on the side of the bed. "All right, I'll stay until you sleep."

She reached out and linked her fingers with his. As she drifted off to sleep, wrapped in a feeling of security and warmth, she had the impression her very own guardian angel kept watch over her.

***

Logan had never felt this way before. As he sat beside her, their fingers entwined, all his gentlemanly instincts rushed forward and squeezed around his heart. He wanted to protect her from whatever fears she had and solve all her problems. He longed to be her escort around town and show her off, and yet a selfish inner voice told him to keep her entirely to himself.

She had the look of a sophisticate, and he calculated she had to be past the age of twenty to have inherited her aunt's estate. Besides, most young women weren't allowed to travel unattended. Even so, she appeared very young and vulnerable lying there in his large bed.

He pondered the mystery surrounding her sudden appearance. Even if he overlooked that, it fell beyond his realm of experience to understand why a look from her could cause his heart to pound and his blood to rush. And her kisses—never had such quicksilver heat consumed him.

He glanced out into the dark night, but within seconds his gaze again rested on the sleeping beauty. She had been frightened that he would leave her and confused about her surroundings. Those feelings made him want to keep her safe and protected. Every man wanted to feel like a knight in shining armor, he thought, grinning to himself.

He gently brushed a thumb across her lips, parted slightly in sleep, and felt her warm breath against his skin. Heat coiled deep inside, and his hand trembled as he stroked her smooth cheek.

He thanked the good Lord who saw fit to send him his own damsel in distress. He only hoped he had the patience not to push her too fast, for he didn't want her to run away again.

He thought to move her to a separate room, for his physical arousal created an ache he knew could be appeased if he crawled into bed with her. Damn, it would be hard not to seduce this luscious, dark-haired beauty who had trusted him enough to fall peacefully asleep in his bed.

Trust. Because of that honorable word, Logan spent a restless night in the chair beside Michaela.

He jerked awkwardly when Simon shook his shoulder early the next morning. Stretching the kinks from his lower back, he only half listened as the butler informed him Neil waited in the downstairs study. While he cursed the untimely interruption, the situation between him and his wayward stepbrother needed to be settled. Logan did not want to it put off.

He gently tucked the covers over Michaela Marie, chuckling to himself, for he could not remember a time where he had offered a woman his bed without him being in it. He would ask Mattie to ready another room for Michaela to use during her visit. If the time became right to make love to her, the distance between bedroom doors would be of little consequence.

Having cheered himself with those thoughts and a splash of cold water to his face, he walked out the door to take care of the business at hand.

"Have Lana bring some coffee as soon as possible," he instructed Simon as the butler opened the door of the study for him. The click of the closing door resounded in the silence as Logan faced Neil.

"Good morning." His brother did not acknowledge the greeting, but kept his head bent over some papers on Logan's desk. Logan shook his head in despair. Neil just would not let go and kept trying to find some piece—

"I didn't burn your goddamned field, Logan, yet you've

already spread the vicious rumor all over the island." He stormed around the desk to stand toe-to-toe with Logan. "If I wanted to take over, I'd just kill you and be done with it!" He swung away from Logan and moved to the liquor cabinet, pouring himself a rather large glass of whiskey for so early in the morning.

"I'd go easy on that if I were you." Though they were close to the same age, Logan always felt himself older and in charge of a temperamental younger brother.

"Don't tell me what to do! You're always trying to tell me what to do. Remember, I lived here with Father, working from sunup to sundown, making this damnable island produce indigo—the prize of the South," he added with sarcasm. "You were off with your studies, taking all that your dear mother would send you, when it should have been mine."

Logan studied his stepbrother as he guzzled the whiskey and poured more. They had the same build and were within months of being the same age, but there the similarities ended. Neil was as fair and blonde as Logan was dark. While Logan supposed Neil could be considered handsome, he had a mean streak that radiated around him and emanated from his cold, green eyes.

There had never been any love lost between them. Somehow, though, Logan always felt he should try to make Neil his brother, if not in blood, then at least in word and deed. Unfortunately, Neil would have none of it.

Logan knew Neil had always been jealous of his relationship with his mother, who had married Neil's father. While Neil's father had been consumed with making money and seeing the island produce more and more, Elizabeth Rutledge Seaton had bestowed her time, energy and love on Logan. Though she had tried to share that love with Neil, the boy would have none of it and had been moody from the day their parents had married.

"This land should have been mine! I worked it with my own two hands—these hands." He thrust his arms straight at Logan, the whiskey in his glass sloshing over the side onto the carpet.

Though Logan knew it would be useless, he tried to reason with him. "Neil, I've told you before, the Will—"

"Goddamn you! You could have forged the Will. You're the goddamn lawyer. You could have written anything you wanted." He guzzled the rest of his drink then slammed the glass down on the desk. He turned towards Logan, his eyes glazed with drink, and his step faltering as he rushed him, arms upraised as though he would strangle him.

Logan neatly sidestepped his brother, grabbing an arm and twisting it behind his back, locking his own arm around Neil's neck. He exerted pressure until Neil quit struggling, but he held on until he felt the tension leave Neil's body. Even drunk, Neil could be a formidable opponent. Logan just wished he would use all that energy in helping at Indigo Bay, instead of wasting it on hate.

Neil hung his head in defeat, his voice a whisper in the silence. "Jacobs told me you thought I started the fire."

Logan let Neil go, stepped back, and said softly, "Jacobs doesn't know when to keep his mouth shut. I'll have to speak to him about that."

One look at Neil's slumped shoulders and haggard face, and Logan said without thinking, "Neil, stay here at Indigo Bay. Together we can make it great again—the way it was."

The instant the words were out, Logan realized his mistake. Neil's shoulders squared, and his head snapped up, eyes again glittering with hatred. Although Indigo Bay had always belonged to Logan's family, Neil felt when his father married Logan's mother, the plantation should have been his.

"I don't need your pity, *Brother.*" He sneered the word. "But I give you fair warning. Indigo Bay should have become mine, and I won't rest until I have set the record straight." Without a word of farewell, he turned and jerked open the door, storming out of sight before Logan could stop him.

"Get the hell out of my way!" A crash of dishes in the hallway followed Neil's rude command. A muffled shriek accompanied by a thud brought Logan to the doorway to assess the damage.

"Good God in Heaven, what—"

"It weren't my fault, Mister Logan, sir." Lana, one of the maids, crawled on her hands and knees, scooping dishes and silver back onto the tray. "Why, he just came out of there like all the demons of hell was right on his heels, that's a fact."

Nodding her head vigorously, Lana dropped the last of the morning cakes back onto a plate and then plopped right down in the middle of the hallway as though cleaning up the mess had tuckered her out for the day.

Logan laughed outright at her antics and received a toothy grin in return. A groan swung both their attentions to where Mica sat propped against the wall.

"Oh, mercy heavens," Lana exclaimed, scrambling across the hall on hands and knees.

"Christ!" Two strides brought Logan to her side, squatting down so his eyes were level with her own.

Mica's heart beat in funny little thumps as Logan's wide eyes searched her face, and concern etched his brow. She managed a weak smile as she glanced between Logan and the maid, the last few minutes a blur of frenzied movement. When she awoke alone in Logan's huge bed, voices raised in argument had led her downstairs.

"You weren't there, when I woke up." She thought how handsome he looked, even with stubble on his chin and rather wrinkled clothes. Had he stayed by her side all night and never gone to bed?

"I know. I had to speak with Neil." His voice remained soft, but Mica could see a visible change in his features as he took in her bare legs sticking out from the short hem of one of his shirts. She had changed when she got up because her own clothes had been wrinkled and spotted with soot.

Her skin grew warm beneath his perusal. Her heart pounded faster as his voice lowered to a deep, seductive whisper. "Had I known an angel slept in my bed, you can rest assured I would never have left her side."

As always, his glittering gaze and powerful presence reduced her to fidgeting. She nervously tucked her hair behind her ear. "Angels always have blonde hair."

"Not mine." He tucked her hair behind her other ear, placed

his hand on the wall beside her head, and leaned forward. Mica closed her eyes in anticipation of his kiss.

"Ahhhhh." The heartfelt sigh jerked them both upright. They had forgotten the maid sprawled at Mica's feet, a moonstruck expression on her young face.

Mica's face flamed hot with embarrassment. Logan just laughed as he stood, then gracefully lifted the maid to her feet. Before she could utter a word, he scooped the tray from the floor, placed it in her hands, and turned her toward the kitchen.

"Off you go, Lana."

"Oh, but sir, the lady. Perhaps I should—"

"I will see to the lady. You just see to not spreading any gossip, do you hear?" While his voice remained gentle, Mica could hear the underlying thread of steel. From the expression on Lana's face, she knew the girl would obey the master of the house.

Mica struggled to get to her feet and at the same time not reveal more leg than she already had. When she saw Logan staring, she had the distinct impression she shouldn't have come downstairs without her own clothes on. With sudden clarity, she recalled the difference in centuries and could have kicked herself for not realizing it before. Propriety would be her downfall, she feared, for her more liberated self might not allow her to bow to nineteenth century conventions.

She had barely regained her balance when Logan swept her off her feet and into his arms, striding towards the stairs.

"Put me down. I can walk." Even as she protested, she curled her arms around his neck.

"Uh-huh. That's why I found you sprawled all over my hallway carpet just moments ago?" He chuckled as she hid her face against his shoulder in embarrassment.

"I heard voices—angry voices like the other night—and I came in search of you. I didn't intend to arrive at the door just in time to get hit by a human tornado."

Logan sighed as he stood her on her feet, this time in a different room from where she had slept. She glanced around at the feminine furnishings before allowing her gaze to question him.

"This was my mother's room. I thought you might be more comfortable here." His gaze slid down to her bare legs, and Mica had the delicious feeling that she made him uncomfortable.

A devilish desire to tease him came over her. She stood on one foot, sliding the other slowly up her bare leg, reaching down as though to scratch her instep. All the while, she watched Logan, who swallowed convulsively as his gaze followed her movements.

Lowering her foot to the ground, she widened her stance a little and slowly stretched. Her hands reached for the sky, which in turn hiked his shirt up to mid-thigh.

The groan could have come from Logan or her, she really didn't know. Instantly, he crushed her against him, his lips covering hers and his tongue begging entrance.

Between hot, moist kisses, she felt rather than heard him grumble, "You don't play fair, lady."

"I couldn't come downstairs in my wrinkled clothes, could I?" She rubbed against his chest with her own, the whisper of cloth mingling with the sharp intake of his breath.

Mica would in no way consider herself naive, but the instant rush of passion she experienced in Logan's kiss unnerved her. Her entire body tingled as though struck by lightning, and she felt the distinct, heavy achiness between her legs that, before Logan, had always come much later in foreplay.

Logan continued to kiss her, his lips finding the incredibly sensitive places behind her ears, the hollow of her neck, even her eyelids. She gave her body over to the sensuous pleasure of his attention. His tongue teased at the corners of her mouth, and she opened for him.

She had always thought this type of kissing vastly overrated, but Logan surprised her again. As his tongue swept the edge of her teeth and teased her own tongue to respond, her knees buckled.

"Oh, dear God." She grabbed his shoulders and tipped her head back, unable to draw a decent breath. "Oh, wow."

She dropped her head to his chest, sucking in air like a drowning person.

Still he held her in his seductive grasp. His hands massaged her back, rubbing up and down her spine, then he cupped her fanny and pulled her harder against him. No amount of clothes could have kept her from feeling his arousal, which in turn heightened her own inflamed state. It took every bit of willpower she could muster not to curl her legs around his waist and allow him to make love to her as they stood. At that insane moment, she wanted him that badly.

She tried to slow her breathing and get herself under control. She could feel the rapid beat of Logan's heart—could almost hear it thunder in the room's silence. Well, at least the attraction couldn't be termed one-sided.

Though she ached to continue, she felt sure women of his century didn't seduce the men. The last thing she wanted was for him to think her a strumpet. She pushed against his shoulders to gain some distance. While at first reluctant, Logan did relinquish his embrace, but kept his hands on her hips as she tried to step away from him.

"If you're going to tease me, you must be willing to accept the consequences." The rebuke, though voiced gently, brought her head up. She scanned his face and realized he suffered as much discomfort as she did.

"I'm sorry...I had no intention...I..." Geez, would he always reduce her to incoherent thoughts? Before she could formulate a better answer, he released her with a sigh and walked to a large cabinet set against one wall.

"Do you know, when you get excited you speak in monosyllables?" The teasing quality had returned to his voice, and Mica was glad. The sexual tension had been thick, and she knew if he had kissed her again, she would not have let him go. At the same moment, the thought crossed her mind that she wanted more than sex from this man.

His comment helped take her mind off his magnificent body, at least for the moment. "It's entirely your fault if I can't speak. I don't know why, but somehow you reduce me to a blundering idiot. I'm usually quite capable of holding my own in any conversation. What's that?"

She had come to stand beside him and peered into what appeared to be a very large closet. Clothes hung in a neat row across it, and several pairs of shoes and boots were lined up along the bottom.

"My mother's wardrobe. I think it would be best if you found something to wear until we can retrieve your clothes." He turned his sexy grin on her again. "If you stay in my shirt much longer, I'm dreadfully afraid you won't be in anything at all."

"These are your mother's clothes? Won't she mind?"

"Mother died...some time ago."

Mica's heart went out to him. Seeing the sadness in his expression, she guiltily thought she should be nicer to her own mother the next time she saw her.

"I fear you are somewhat taller than she, but perhaps something will suffice for the time being." He turned and walked away from her before she could say thank you.

At the door to the bedroom, he paused. "I'm sorry Neil ran you down. It was extremely rude of him. Hopefully, you will have the opportunity to meet him in a better light in the future."

"It's not your fault your brother acts like a jackass." She gritted her teeth and grimaced at her slip. She had no right calling anyone names, much less someone she didn't know. However, from what she could gather, this stepbrother of Logan's couldn't be counted on to act in a very civilized manner.

Logan chuckled, turning part way around to glance in her direction. "You really are quite unconventional, aren't you?" At her indifferent shrug of a shoulder, he added, "You're really quite adorable, too."

She could only stand with mouth agape as he closed the door behind him. Adorable? No one had called her that since she was five years old. Even then, it had only been her Uncle Gene, who was family, so that really didn't count.

She donned a simple skirt and blouse, along with some strange underwear cut much like a split skirt slip. The shoes in the closet were much smaller than the size nine she wore. Realizing her shoes were probably still in Logan's room, she decided she'd just have to go barefoot.

She glanced around the room but couldn't locate her clothes either. Rocking back on her heels, she gasped. If her clothes and shoes were nowhere in sight, then she no longer possessed the key!

She stumbled on the long skirt as she scrambled out the door and down the stairs, calling for Logan. In her fear over the disposal of her clothes, along with the key, she tripped over the last step and would have fallen if not for a pair of strong arms catching her awkward descent.

"What on earth? If the servants had not already been up, you surely would have awakened them." Logan held on until she could get her feet beneath her. His gaze searched her face.

Though Mica felt rather foolish for her behavior, dread still caught in her throat at the thought of not being able to return to her own time. "My clothes? What did you do with my clothes?"

"Clothes? For pity's sake, is that what this is about? Leave it to a woman to screech about a simple skirt and shirtwaist."

"Don't go chauvinistic on me, mister, just tell me what you did with my things." Compelled to locate her key, Mica forgot to whom she spoke, or the simple fact that he couldn't possibly understand her words.

"Chauvinistic? I'm not familiar with that term. Does it have anything to do with the way you kissed me earlier?" He slid his arms around her waist and pulled her close.

His fresh male scent tickled Mica's nostrils, and she forgot what she wanted. His eyes mesmerized her, his breath caressed her, and his lips teased her senses. He kissed her, right there at the bottom of the stairs where anyone could walk in and see them. She didn't care, and apparently neither did Logan. He increased the pressure until she yielded her mouth, her tongue dueling with his.

"You've got to stop doing that," she gasped, searching her brain for a logical thought when he finally let her come up for air.

"Why?"

It wasn't the question he asked, but rather the heat of his hands and the passion in his eyes that backed Mica up a step. *Why, indeed,* she thought, taking in his dark, bedroom eyes, jet-black hair, and wicked smile. At that moment, she couldn't for the life of her come up with a reason to stop kissing him. She hadn't been this confused over a male since eighth grade. The fact of the matter was, he scared her. Or rather, *her reaction* to him scared her.

Think, she scolded herself. *Find some neutral ground.* As she stared at him, she realized nothing could be considered neutral about this man. He exuded sensuality, and she doubted he even realized it.

"My key." Finally, she remembered what had thrown her into a panic in the first place. She raised her brows in question.

Logan took her hand and led her along the hall to a set of double doors, which were opened instantly by the butler. Mica flushed, not recalling if the man had been standing there when she kissed Logan. The austere look on his face gave nothing away.

"We'll eat now, Simon." The butler nodded and disappeared through another door Mica assumed led to the kitchen. Logan seated her in a high-backed chair, then moved to the sideboard to dish up their breakfast. Thinking how pleasant it was to have someone wait on her, Mica felt she could get used to this.

Then again, she didn't believe in fairy tales or knights in shining armor. This could only be a brief mystical interlude in her sane, orderly life. That brought to mind her missing key.

"Logan, I really need my things." Mica knew she would never relax until she held the key in her hand again. No matter what she felt for the handsome man leaning over her with a plate full of hot, savory food, she could never stay in his world. She wanted the security of knowing she had an escape route.

Logan dug in his pocket and extracted a length of black velvet cord, which he hung around her neck. When Mica glanced down, she saw that her key dangled from the end of the thin ribbon. He answered her unasked question as he filled his own plate with food. "You did not have a reticule with you, nor any type of bag. When Mattie collected your clothes to have them laundered, your key fell out of a pocket. I assume it is the key to Sea Crest?" He came to sit beside her at the large table.

"Yes. I'm sorry I panicked, but it's the only key I have."

"It's just a simple key and could probably be replaced in town if need be. Regardless of what builders state about security, I doubt there are that many different combinations of keys around, and one may suit as well as another." He shrugged off the matter, delving into his breakfast.

Mica had the feeling she couldn't replace this particular key.

As they ate breakfast, she studied the large dining room, searching for something familiar now that she knew the connection with Sea Crest. Nothing appeared the same—not the paintings on the wall or the table at which they sat. While it could easily seat fifty people, Mica was glad Logan had chosen to sit next to her.

When Simon asked if she wished more coffee, she nodded then sat back, replete. Breakfast had always been her favorite meal. The fresh eggs, sausage and potatoes had filled her completely, though she didn't even want to think of the cholesterol level of the food she'd consumed. Instead, she took the time to study the man eating with gusto beside her.

Even in repose at the table, he held himself with an air of confidence Mica didn't see in many men. Perhaps the weight of responsibility had matured him, or perhaps it was just the way people grew up in this era. Along with his self-assuredness, Logan was a handsome man.

Where handsome men of the twenty-first century played on their looks and almost flaunted their bodies, Logan didn't appear to be aware of his effect on the opposite sex, specifically her. He was just Logan—a good-looking, well-muscled gentleman who could kiss as though he had taken lessons from the devil himself.

"Have you had your fill?" He had caught her staring, and she wondered if he realized the innuendo of his words.

She couldn't resist teasing him. As he rose from his chair, she allowed her gaze to slide up and down his frame before saying, "For now." Her smile brought an answering grin to his face.

"Let me know when you're hungry again. As a gentleman, I consider it my sincere obligation to appease *any* appetites you may develop." He executed a graceful bow before he moved to slide her chair out from the table.

"You're good, I'll grant you that," she taunted as she moved out of his reach.

"Just how good, my lovely lady, you have yet to discover."

Five

"Come. I must see the extent of damage from last night's fire." Logan pulled Mica toward the front door as he spoke.

The huge double doors loomed before her like the open jaws of some hideous monster, ready to gobble her up and spit her back out where she belonged. She jerked her hand from Logan's, clutching the key that hung around her neck.

"What's wrong?" Logan turned to her, and she knew he couldn't understand her hesitation.

She stared at the doors, wishing she could see through to the other side. Would she stay in this time if she walked through a door other than the one with the key? She had no idea of the rules governing this unearthly game she played and would just as soon stay inside, where she knew for a certainty she existed.

What if she just disappeared, or got caught somewhere between this century and her own? What if she could never go back to her own world?

"Michaela? Oh, I see. You have no shoes on." Logan unwittingly gave her the answer to her dilemma.

"That's right." She breathed a sigh of relief. "I couldn't possibly go outside and walk around without shoes."

"It didn't appear to bother you last night when you rushed headlong out the doors to the beach." Logan tilted his head to the side, one brow arched in question.

It suddenly dawned on her exactly what Logan had said. If she had gone outside last night and remained on this side, why couldn't she do so in the daytime?

"All right, I'll go." Mica conceded to his wishes, placing one hand securely in his, the other hand clutching the key.

She held her breath as she walked through the double doors to the sparkling sunshine of a summer morning.

She didn't disappear into a puff of smoke or get yanked back into the house by some invisible hand. Instead, she immediately fell in love. She had always been partial to her aunt's island, but the modern, semi-civilized state of Sea Crest and its neighboring resort homes were a sad parody on its original unblemished state. As Mica stood on the top step of the mansion, inhaling the clean, salt-tinged air, she gazed around her in wonder.

Lush foliage covered much of the area she could see right in front of the house. A wild abundance of colorful flowers greeted her. Unable to name the profusion of varieties, she could only wish this wild, natural garden had not been lost over the years.

The ocean roared off to her right and the entire island appeared to be wide open. There were no street sounds, no telephone poles and wires, and no electric lights on the corners. She loved it!

A circular driveway, covered with crushed shells, bent gracefully away from the house and disappeared beyond a grove of trees. Directly in front of her stood a small carriage pulled by two pretty bay horses that were patiently nudging the groom who held their lead harness.

"We'll take the curricle," Logan announced, pulling her down the steps and then lifting her high onto the seat before she could formulate a thought. "Once we have you properly attired, we'll ride." As he climbed in beside her and flicked the reins to set the horses in motion, he turned to her and grinned. "There's nothing quite like a sunrise ride along the ocean sands. The rising tide licks at the horses' hocks, and the spray stings your cheeks."

Mica was so caught up in the picture he painted, lost to the wonder of Logan's Indigo Bay. She felt as though a missing part of her had been found.

Settling back, she was content to enjoy the island in a way she could never have believed possible. As she absorbed Logan's words, she thought how wonderful everything he described sounded. His voice held such pride of ownership, she became curious.

"Why have you been away? I can tell from your voice you love this land." She glanced his way to find his eyes sparkling and the light breeze tousling his hair. "Your eyes light up, and you look like a little boy playing with his favorite Christmas toy. Why would you want to do anything else, or be anywhere else, besides here?"

"Michaela Marie, I do not expect you to understand. My family and my responsibilities are just that—mine. As a woman, I wouldn't presume to burden—"

"Whoa, right there! Let's get one thing straight, Logan Rutledge. I am *not* some wishy-washy miss who can't stand the heat or a little hardship. I can think past what to wear or how many courses to have for dinner. I happen to have a fine head for business. In fact, I not only have a law—"

He was laughing. She punched him in the arm, but he kept laughing, dropping the reins to cradle his stomach in hysterics. She sat dumbfounded as the carriage slowed to a stop, the horses bending their heads to munch grass that grew between the wheel ruts in the road.

"You are priceless," Logan gasped as he grabbed her by the shoulders to draw her near. So near, their lips touched.

Instant heat engulfed Mica, and she wondered how he did that. She didn't waste energy worrying about it, but instead enjoyed his kiss, returning his passion with her own. She slid her hands up his shoulders to curl her fingers in the hair that lay on his shirt collar.

Hungrily, her tongue touched his, savoring the heady male taste of him. She strained towards him, wanting more than he offered, but shy about how to proceed. After all, how did one go about seducing a gentleman who apparently put women on pedestals?

Logan was finding it extremely difficult to keep his hands still at Michaela's waist. As she strained towards him, he could feel the soft flesh of her breasts against his chest, and he swallowed convulsively.

He had no idea why she affected him the way she did.

He'd had his share of dalliances while in school up North, but never once would he have considered any of them serious. Now, based on only a few days' acquaintance, this woman had totally captivated him. He wanted to protect her, wait on her and shower her with gifts, revere her with all the honor and respect due her gender.

At the very same time, he longed to ravish her and share the delights of passion with her. He sensed in her a deep sensuality that triggered an identical response from his own body. He almost feared releasing his passion, for he realized if she in the least returned his feelings, he would never let her go.

While that seemed a logical objective for him to pursue, he had an innate sense of foreboding where she was concerned. Something held her apart from him, even as she eagerly responded to his kisses. He felt he should court her slowly and try to have patience, even when his body insisted otherwise.

"I thought I told you to quit doing that," Michaela whispered against his lips when he released them. The passion still sparkling in her sky blue eyes belied her words.

"I don't recall you saying that. I'm sure I would have remembered such devastating words." Ignoring his body's cries for satisfaction, he removed his hands from her waist and sat back against the curricle's leather seat. He cleared his throat.

"Well." He could think of nothing to say, and he couldn't gather the horses' reins until he could move his hands from his thighs without them shaking like some schoolboy's.

"Show me your island, Logan Rutledge." Her soft reminder of his promise straightened his spine and renewed his confidence. There would be time to continue his seduction, he thought, gathering the reins and clicking the horses into a trot once more. He would make certain there was time.

***

They passed through the grove of trees that lined the driveway, and the island opened up to a sea of green. Mica began to see what made Indigo Bay Plantation so unique to the area.

"Most of the island north of the house is planted in indigo," Logan stated, steering the small carriage along a dirt path. "As you have probably noticed, I have a small household staff. Almost everyone employed on the island works in the field or processing sheds. I find I can take care of my own needs fairly well, but I must have people out here." He glanced her way before adding, "I hope you'll not find it too inconvenient to tend to your own personal needs?"

"Don't worry about that. I've been looking after myself for a long time now." Mica wondered how shocked he would be if he realized she not only cooked and cleaned, but also worked and lived on her own. She knew for a certainty those traits were not on a nineteenth century woman's resume—at least not on a "lady's" resume.

Logan pointed to the fields of green plants, some growing as tall as four feet, and all covered with small, red flowers. "We plant several fields of indigo. This section is separated from the north fields by the processing vats and dye sheds. We harvested the first cutting in June and have finished the processing. The season's final cutting will occur in just a month, from the first to middle part of September."

Mica didn't want to think about September when she would have to return to her own work. Instead, she concentrated on Logan's voice, which attested to the pride he took in the land—his land.

"The flowers look like little butterflies," she said, marveling at the blooming plants which spread before her for acres.

"That's why they are poetically called 'butterfly flowers.'" His soft, Southern drawl, combined with a devastating smile, caused a different kind of butterfly to flutter in Mica's stomach. She clinched sweaty palms together in her lap to keep from reaching up and touching his gently curved lips.

She glanced around, still unable to comprehend this place as the same one she had visited as a child. Nothing reminded her of the island she knew. If she intended to stay awhile, she wanted to learn all she could about indigo and the way of life that had been created here. "Where did the fire start last night?"

Logan's brow furrowed in consternation. "In the northernmost fields, which is where we're heading. I still can't understand how a fire started among green plants. Hopefully in the light of day, I can determine the cause."

"We're going to the cliffs?"

Logan shot her a look of disbelief. "How did you know cliffs edged this end of the island?"

Mica stared ahead of them, her eyes searching wildly for a safe answer. *Damn,* she mentally cringed. How was she supposed get out of this one? Even if the buildings didn't look familiar, the lay of the land wouldn't have changed that much over a hundred years, and she searched for some way to save her from her faux pas.

"Well, you can see the rise of the land up ahead." She pointed vaguely off in the distance. To add credence to her answer, she smiled weakly at him. "Besides, don't all islands have cliffs, and sandy coves, and waterfalls, and..."

He laughed at her exaggeration, shaking his head. "It really is too bad they don't teach ladies something besides watercolors and menu planning. If you like, I will gladly give you some instruction in geography."

Mica had to grit her teeth and clench her fists beneath the folds of her skirt to keep from punching Logan in the jaw. She had purposely led him down this path to cover her blunder, but she hated his macho male attitude and longed to tell him as much.

However, in 1850, he was perfectly within his rights in a male-dominated world to express such thoughts. There would come a time, she thought, when he would be sorry for all the rude comments he had made. She would see to that.

She changed the subject, so she wouldn't forget what century she resided in and give him a lecture. "What are those?" She pointed to a series of large brick structures that stair-stepped down from each other in groups of three.

"Fermentation vats. They are used to create the dye that carries our name. The process is quite lengthy. Once the plants are cut, they must be placed in the largest vat at the top of the tier and covered with water. When the indigo leaves are saturated, the fermentation process begins. The liquid must be the right taste and color before it is drawn off into the lower vat where the process continues."

"The right taste?" Mica gave him an incredulous look. "Isn't dye poisonous?"

"Not at all. It must be exactly the right sweetness. An hour too long of fermentation could endanger the entire yield. Once the process at the vats is complete, the indigo is transferred to the building over there." He swung his arm to the buildings to the left of the road.

"The raw indigo is heated to remove impurities, then strained through linen cloth and formed into cakes, all of which bear our island stamp." He pointed to other buildings farther on. "That is the drying and storage shed, and farther along are the dyeing and weaving sheds. We not only grow and process the indigo, but we buy raw cotton thread which is dyed and woven into world famous Indigo Bay cloth."

Mica couldn't help being impressed at the work involved in such a venture, even though she had never heard of Indigo Bay cloth before. So used to ready-to-wear clothes, convenience stores, and electronic mail, she had no concept of the time and effort it took to create a product in this era.

"I am very impressed. You must be very proud of what your father and step-father have done."

An instant scowl crossed Logan's face, his dark brows coming together over menacing eyes. Mica leaned back, unaware of the blunder she had committed.

"Charles Seaton had nothing to do with the success of Indigo Bay. In fact, because of his incompetent dealings, the island barely survived." He snapped his mouth shut, and Mica realized he had said more than he intended.

Why was it men thought they didn't need anyone to listen to them, or to help out once in a while? That trait hadn't changed over the years. She placed a hand on his thigh and felt the muscle tighten beneath her touch.

"Logan, please. As I tried to tell you earlier, I'm quite capable of understanding business and economics." She smiled as she thought of her own tangled affairs. "And family."

She studied his profile as he concentrated on keeping the horses on the narrow dirt path, passing the buildings without further comment and leading them towards the northern end of the island.

"Logan?" She watched as his jaw tensed in aggravation. She added what she hoped was an element of trust. "You asked me to stay here and get to know you, to learn the legacy of your island. How can I do that if you won't talk to me?" She could feel the tension in his leg beneath her hand and knew the moment he let go of his frustration.

Logan glanced her way, and Mica could see the surprise in his gaze. "It's not considered polite to talk about family problems with outsiders. Besides, most women don't care about the land. Or economics or politics, for that matter." Somehow, Mica should have expected such an answer.

"I understand that, but as you have pointed out on more than one occasion, I am not your ordinary woman." She grinned at him.

He laughed in return, relieving the tension. "That is of a certainty, lovely lady." He concentrated on the horses, and she supposed it was because the path had narrowed. Indigo plants high enough to block the surrounding area gave Mica a feeling of seclusion.

He didn't speak, and she began to think he wouldn't tell her any more. When he did begin, his voice sounded far away, as though he pulled memories from the deepest part of his soul.

"The island has always belonged to my family, for as far back as anyone can remember. When indigo was introduced back in 1740, my ancestors decided the island was ideal for growing the plant. Thus the name Indigo Bay. My father learned from his father, and I from him.

"I never wanted anything else except to work the land, to be part of it. I understood at an early age that if I took care of the land, it, in turn, would take care of me and mine." He sighed. "But Father died when I turned only thirteen, and when Mother married Charles Seaton, he left no place for me in the scheme of things."

Mica could hear the heartbreak in his words and ached for a little boy's lost dreams. She gave his thigh a gentle squeeze. He chuckled, but she could hear no mirth in his voice.

"I tried so hard to take care of the island and Mother. But every improvement I wanted to make—every time I suggested a change—Seaton would have none of it. Neither my mother nor I could persuade him from his course. Over the years, he planted more and more, refusing to rotate crops or allow the fields to lay fallow. If he hadn't died when he had, he would surely have killed the land."

Mica realized how important family and this land had been to Logan, and she lost her heart to the boy who had been determined to take on a man's responsibility. Before she could say anything further, he gave a shout and jerked the horses to a halt. Tossing her the reins, he jumped clear of the still-moving carriage.

She glanced wildly around her, her hands automatically clutching the reins and pulling. She spied the source of Logan's aggravation at the same time he pounced, hauling a large man off a small African American boy.

Even as she tied the horses off and climbed down from the carriage, she could hear fists connecting with flesh. The boy appeared none the worse for wear and scooted backwards out of reach.

The two men continued to roll back and forth on the ground. Mica twisted her hands in despair, wanting to help, but afraid of getting in the way. She couldn't recall from her self-defense training just how to end a fight when it didn't involve her.

She needn't have worried. Within minutes, Logan had the other man pinned to the ground. Using his weight for leverage, he straddled the larger man, his hands still throttling his neck.

"Logan!" Her cry of appeal had no effect, and she rushed to his side to grab his arm. "Logan, stop it! You're going to kill him."

"I should kill the son of a bitch!" Though his voice was choked with anger, Mica was relieved to see him release the pressure on the man's neck. He rolled to the side and jumped gracefully to his feet all in one motion, but he never turned his back to the other man, who continued to lie breathless in the dirt.

"Get to your feet, Jacobs, and get off my land," Logan said, jerking the man up by the collar.

Mica watched in awe, for Logan stood several inches shorter and much leaner than the husky man he now handled so roughly. Yet he had shown no fear. He had acted on impulse, coming to the aid of someone unable to defend himself.

The man called Jacobs spat blood off to the side then rubbed the back of his hand across his mouth. "Those darkies need to know their place."

"These are people and work here because they wish it. They are no different than you or I."

Mica could see the anger build in Logan's eyes as he spoke, but she couldn't understand the reasoning behind his defense of the boy. After all, it was 1850, and everyone in the South owned slaves.

"They're niggers, Rutledge. Stupid nigger slaves. Mister Seaton kept them in their place and let me do my job overseeing them." The man balled his fists, and Mica feared he would throw a punch.

In the next instant, Logan drew a pistol from beneath his coat, leveling the barrel at the man's heart.

"Seaton does *not* own this land. I do, and I have been in charge for the past month. You have apparently forgotten who pays your wages, but that shall not be a problem any longer. You have one hour to be off this island. I will forward your pay, if I decide to pay you at all."

The surly man grabbed his hat from the edge of the road, knocking it against his leg to shake the dust. He refused to meet Logan's gaze, but as he turned to leave, he grumbled, "You'll be plenty sorry for this, I guarantee. You ain't seen the last of me."

As the man disappeared around a bend in the road, Logan breathed an audible sigh of relief and lowered the pistol to his side. He glanced around. "Where's the boy?"

Mica stepped to his side, lifting the corner of her skirt to wipe away the dust and blood from his face. “He ran away as soon as you freed him.” Her intense relief that Logan had come out of the fight unhurt turned to anger at his foolishness.

“You idiot! You could have been hurt. That man was twice your size. And why didn’t you just pull your pistol on him in the first place? Another thing, why do you even carry a pistol? They’re dangerous weapons.”

He silenced her with a kiss, his lips barely touching hers. But the instant fire was enough to squelch any further argument from her. When he lifted his head, she bit her bottom lip to refrain from picking up where she’d left off.

“I take care of what’s mine, Michaela Marie, by whatever means I need to use.” He tucked the pistol into the back of his trousers, took her by the elbow and guided her back to the carriage. “You would do well to remember that.”

Mica’s breath caught at the intensity of his expression, and the heat from his hands as he lifted her onto the seat. She subconsciously touched the key around her neck, wondering if she shouldn’t make a hasty retreat back to her own world. While his touch thrilled her beyond words, she wondered if a mere door between the centuries would ever be enough to keep her from wanting him.

He climbed aboard and released the horses, clicking softly to urge them forward. She turned her thoughts to other matters. “If you fire Mr. Jacobs, how will you manage your island?”

“I’ll do it myself, if I have to. They all think the same.”

Mica knew he referred to the slaves. “But the Afri…uh, Negroes are slaves.”

“Mine aren’t,” he lashed out, then softened his tone. “You wouldn’t understand.”

“Why? Because I’m a female?” Her statement brought a grin to his dirt-streaked face.

“You are definitely female, but that isn’t why. I guess because so many people don’t understand, I assumed you wouldn’t, either. I shouldn’t have jumped to that conclusion. I apologize.”

His sincerity touched a chord deep within her. In the short

span of a few days, she found she cared very much what Logan thought, not only about her, but also about his way of life.

"Tell me. I promise I'll try to understand. At least I won't judge you."

He rested his elbows on his knees, letting the horses find their own leisurely way down the path. "Many years ago, when Father still lived, we discussed freeing the slaves and paying them a wage for their labors based on the profits we made. It only stood to reason that if they had an investment in the work they did, they would work harder to make the island a success."

He snorted. "Father died before he could find a lawyer willing to draw up the necessary legal documents to make Indigo Bay a slave-free island. At that time, it amounted to the same thing as treason against the South, as you probably well know."

Mica understood better than he would ever know. Even in her time, prejudice and segregation issues were still very volatile topics to many deep-rooted Southerners.

"So how have you managed to free your slaves, especially when the abolition issue is beginning to heat up?"

He raised an eyebrow. "You have read about the abolition movement?" When Mica nodded, he went on to answer her original question. "I went to school to become a lawyer. I felt the only way to make changes was through legal avenues. I'm not the only one to feel this way, though most of the anti-slavery sentiment is in the Northern states. Just last year, Representative Lincoln introduced a bill to end slavery."

"Abraham Lincoln?" Her astonishment must have been clearly written on her face, but Mica couldn't help it. Her fantasy about jumping back two centuries had focused around Logan. Up until that instant she hadn't given a thought to the historical people who were alive and doing their incredible work at this very moment.

Logan misinterpreted her exclamation. "I see you have heard something about politics, then. Well, it did Mr. Lincoln no good, because our very own Senator J.C. Calhoun has blasted abolitionists at every turn."

Without thought, Mica stated, "It will lead to war, you

know."

"Oh, I doubt that." Logan countered. "The people of the United States are many things, but it would go against everything we believe in to fight against our own people, no matter what the issue. No, the President and the Northern constituents will eventually see that the South is capable of taking care of itself and will let us do so."

Mica realized she couldn't fault his logic, nor could she dispute what he said unless she gave him evidence to the contrary. Whatever the rules governing this adventure of hers, she instinctively knew better than to make a comment about his future that was her past.

"Damn! Look at that. Acres of lost crop. Why?"

Muttering to himself, he climbed down from the carriage and stormed off, kicking clumps of dirt and jerking the charred remains of indigo plants from the ground.

Left to fend for herself, Mica almost tripped over the cumbersome length of skirt before her feet hit the ground. Her training in law and associated work with detectives soon had her checking the ground for evidence as to the origins of the fire.

"Do you smell anything peculiar?" Logan asked.

Mica stopped and lifted her head into the breeze. "Nothing other than the burnt odor. What do you smell?"

Instead of answering her, Logan knelt by a plant at the edge of the field, rubbing his hand up the still green stalk. He lifted his hand to his nose, then swore in such colorful language Mica blushed.

"Lamp oil. This field did *not* burn by accident." As Logan rubbed his hand clean with his handkerchief, his eyes scanned the area for other signs of deliberate arson.

Mica watched his face, wary of his reaction. She didn't know him well enough to be able to predict how he would react to deliberate sabotage, and she was reluctant to stand in the way of his anger. While she waited for his reaction, she noticed the frown lines around his usually gentle mouth, and the dark shadows under his eyes.

She looked beyond his immediate outrage and realized

how tired he must be. He had been up half the night fighting a fire only to come home and have to chase her down the beach. Then he sat up with her for the remainder of the night while she slept peacefully.

"Come, let's go home. There doesn't appear to be anything more you can do here." She spoke softly, offering her hand in comfort.

He caught her hand, his fingers warm as they wrapped around hers. "You're right, of course. It's just that I didn't need a further financial setback. Damn! Someone ruined half the crop. Lives depended on that harvest."

"I thought the crop had already been harvested."

"Only the first cutting. It's necessary to get two good cuttings a season to make it through a year." His shoulders sagged, and she wished she could help him shirk the weight of responsibility for just a little while. He gave her a wan smile. "There is naught I can do about it now. I'm afraid your first day has not proven very entertaining, nor myself a very gracious host."

"Nonsense. I have learned a great deal about this island you call Indigo Bay." She added to herself, *And a great deal about you, Logan Rutledge.* The sensitive, caring man who led her back to the carriage was almost too perfect, and Mica hoped the dream would not end anytime soon.

***

Mica found the next week at Indigo Bay both enjoyable and frustrating. Logan had questioned the proprietor of the Belleview Hotel about her clothes, and since they hadn't arrived, he took the liberty of purchasing some gowns for her. She couldn't take exception to his forwardness since she had nothing else to wear. He hadn't questioned it when she said she had given Lana the message to take to the hotel.

It proved difficult for her to adjust to the layers of clothes required to dress, and she finally decided that one petticoat under any skirt would just have to suffice. She flat out refused to wear a corset. Even with those adjustments, she had to change her manner of walking so her skirts didn't bunch between her legs.

She began to enjoy her leisurely baths instead of a quick shower. She had to get used to a copper cistern holding heated water that sat at one end of the tub, while the pump for cold water was at the other end. The servants were responsible for keeping the holding tank full, along with lighting the small fire below to heat the water.

Mica had found no problems with this system until the day she tried to take a bath earlier than her normal time. She found the well water cold enough to turn her toes blue. While she had been trying to do away with schedules in her life, it appeared some things still required them.

Meals at Indigo Bay were pure pleasure. Not only did Annie cook scrumptious food, but Logan always joined her in the evening. Since her mother had always believed in dressing for dinner—and using all the forks, spoons and good crystal she could possibly get at one place setting—Mica felt quite comfortable, knowing her manners would hold up under scrutiny.

Time seemed the hardest obstacle to overcome. She would rise early, as she always had, but Logan would already be out in the fields or at the processing sheds. She didn't want to eat alone in the large dining room, so she would have breakfast in the kitchen as Annie worked.

Every day Lana fluttered about her, stating how unladylike it was for her to dirty her hands in the kitchen with the help. She had tried several times to press her point home by bringing Mica's breakfast to her room. Mica would always stay one step ahead, meeting her at the top of the stairs and carrying the tray right back to the kitchen to enjoy it with company.

However, eating in the kitchen and taking long walks on the beach didn't set aside her restlessness. As a lawyer, she maintained a busy schedule, and she felt useless here. One night at dinner, she tried to explain her feelings to Logan, but he refused to listen.

"You are not to work—it is not your place."

"To hell with my place. I need something to do." She scowled when he just smiled at her.

"What can you do, then?"

"I can..." Mica paused. What could she do? Though capable of cleaning and cooking, she couldn't take Lana's or Annie's jobs away from them. Mica felt inadequate when she realized all her education couldn't make her a competent person in this time.

"Can you test indigo? Or perhaps weave thread into cloth? Can you whip the fermented indigo froth for hours at a time until it is ready to settle?" Logan questioned.

"Of course not." She felt tears sting the inside of her eyelids and bit her bottom lip to stop its trembling. Logan rose from his chair and came to hers, sliding it away from the table and gathering her into his arms.

"I'm sorry. That was rude of me. As a lady, your place is not in the fields working, and I shouldn't have suggested it was."

"But..."

He touched a finger to her lips to silence her protest. "I guess I will just have to find a way to keep you busy, won't I?"

The next days passed in a whirlwind of activity, and Mica fell exhausted into bed each night, even though she never left the island. Logan had responsibilities he attended to every morning, but each afternoon, he took her exploring to a different part of the island. One day they rode in the buggy to the cliffs, just to stand and watch the waves crash against the rocks. She had laughed and danced around him as the ocean spray dampened their clothes and sat like angel mist upon their hair.

While she had not forgotten her former life, she preferred not to dwell on it, or the number of days slipping away. Unfortunately, it came back to her with crashing force the day Logan invited her to ride, and took her to the stables which were located to the south of the house. Upon rounding the corner on the path from the manor, she noticed the skeletal structure of an addition on the south side. She froze, her heart skipping several beats as she mentally visualized Sea Crest and its relation to Logan's Indigo Bay.

"Are you planning an addition to Sea...Indigo Bay?" She

unconsciously touched the key dangling from her neck.

Logan scowled at the structure. "Seaton had plans to expand the main house, sinking his money into that instead of the land. He died before it could be finished." His voice held no remorse.

Mica's voice shook as she questioned him. "How does it stand in relation to the inside?"

Logan pointed to the second story, which had few supporting studs and no floor. "There is a door. Do you see it?" At her nod, he continued. "The door at the end of the second floor hall would have led into this section. I don't even know where the key is at this moment, nor do I care. Perhaps some day, when I have righted all the wrongs done by my stepfather, I will complete the addition."

Mica heard hurt and betrayal in his voice, and again she realized how much he valued the land over material possessions. Honor and tradition bound him to the land, and she longed for a way to help him keep what was his.

A chill ran down her spine as she took one last look at the structure—to the Sea Crest that hadn't even been built on this day, yet somehow magically lay beyond that door. She hurried to catch up with Logan, determined to leave her fears behind with the ghostlike framework.

They rode that day down to the beach, racing their horses along the waves and playing among the tide like wayward children. She soon forgot her apprehensions as Logan smothered her with salt-tinged kisses every time she allowed him to catch her. As the sun set on the other side of the island, the last rays of daylight played off the rolling waves, creating a cascade of color. Logan twined his fingers with hers as they walked the horses back towards the stable. Mica wondered why every day couldn't be the paradise she had found here.

***

The next day, Mica sat on the verandah and stared out over the gardens, awed by what she had just discovered. Inside her, she had become aware of a new sense of self. She had found she was no longer impatient and could relax and take things as they came. Suddenly, she understood what a joy life could be without schedules and timetables to run her day.

She recognized and accepted the fact that her contentment rested for the most part on Logan's presence. She had found him very demonstrative—a hand on her elbow, a touch to her cheek. Even his eyes seemed to caress her when she'd look up to find his gaze on her. For someone used to independence and holding feminist viewpoints, she found Logan occupying more and more of her thoughts—and all of her dreams.

It had been so easy to fall into his world, accepting his attention and reveling in the wonderful sensations he caused inside her. He had done nothing more than kiss her, sometimes with intense passion, and sometimes with an equally erotic gentleness. Yet each night as he walked her to her bedroom door, bestowing a final kiss upon her cheek or brow, she longed for more—much more. She thought, perhaps, the time had come to return to Sea Crest and regain her perspective.

Silently, Logan observed Michaela from the door leading to the verandah. At times he felt guilty, as though he kept her prisoner on the island. They hadn't heard anything from her people at Sea Crest, nor had her clothes arrived. But instead of seeking word, he had played ignorant and continued to enjoy her company.

Everything about her fascinated him—from the way she tucked her hair behind her ear, to her laugh, to her avid interest in the work done on the island. She was quite unconventional in both language and manner, as now, when she had her feet propped on the seat of her chair, her knees tucked under her chin. All the qualities he desired in a woman sat before him packaged in one intriguing bundle.

She had a willingness to work and could carry on a lively discussion. She didn't appear to care about material possessions or fashion at all, for he often caught her without her shoes and stockings, and he knew from holding her that she wore no corset. The simple fact that she did not covet those things made him wish he could shower her with gifts to let her know he thought her wonderful. He had not known her very long, but Logan wondered if he had succumbed to love.

Just the thought sent blood pounding through his veins.

She made him feel alive and capable of doing anything. How he longed to take her in his arms and carry their passion beyond the kisses they had shared.

Sometimes, though, when she thought he didn't see, her face took on a dreamy quality, like she was a million miles away. He searched her face now and found her staring into space. Her distraction frightened him, for he didn't know how to reach her.

What if he woke up one morning and found her gone again?

Six

"You should be dressing." Logan spoke from the shadows, shaking Mica from her daydreams. "We don't want to be late for your official debut into Cameron society."

He strolled toward her, and for a moment, she dismissed what he said in favor of soaking in his image. Dressed in a dove gray cutaway coat, white shirt and cravat, and snug black trousers that showed the very outline of his muscular legs, he presented the picture of a perfect Southern gentleman. His dark hair was tied back with a satin ribbon, and Mica wondered if there could possibly be a more handsome man. His devilish grin told her he knew it, too.

She had to clear her throat in order to speak. "You didn't tell me we were going out. We aren't going to hear Miss Sophie Wainwright sing, are we?"

He laughed, his eyes twinkling with mischief. "I would not subject you to that."

"I can't possibly take a bath, do my hair—"

"Lana has your bath ready. If you hurry, we won't be more than fashionably late."

Excited at the prospect of meeting other people from this time, Mica shot up from the chair and scurried towards the door, Logan's laughter ringing in her ears.

She felt a twinge of guilt as Lana helped her slip a midnight blue silk dress over the several petticoats required for its bell shape. When her own clothes hadn't shown up at the hotel, Logan had come home with his arms piled high with boxes. They had contained dresses, shoes, petticoats and everything else necessary to dress her in style. She had protested, knowing he could ill afford to spend money on her, but he had insisted.

Since few of his mother's clothes fit her, she had relented.

Now, she was glad she had, because she felt like a fairy princess attending a ball. Her dress, draped off the shoulders with two ruffles of silk that created short sleeves, had a snug bodice and a pinched waist that made Mica feel dainty and feminine.

Though her hair was unusually short according to Lana, the maid had helped her pin it up in a simple twist. What wisps escaped their handiwork curled softly about her face and nape.

As Logan escorted her down the steps to the buggy, he complimented her on her attire, her hair, even the way her skin glowed. But all the while his eyes didn't strayed far from her cleavage.

Finally, she kissed him to shut him up. Then he threatened not to take her out at all, but keep her prisoner and ravish her until the sun set one hundred days from now. Though he spoke in a joking manner, Mica decided it wouldn't take much for her to take him up on his suggestion.

As they crossed the causeway linking Indigo Bay with the mainland, he spoke in a neutral tone, and she decided she would have to settle for a night on the town instead of a night of passion.

"I would beg your indulgence tonight and ask that you not mention the fire nor the damage it did to my crops," he said.

She turned to him in surprise. "Why? Don't you discuss business with your friends?"

He smiled in the moonlight. "We speak only of success, not of failure."

"In other words, you brag." It appeared the male species had not evolved much in the last hundred-plus years.

"You are correct." He leaned over and quickly kissed her cheek. "Tonight I will be the toast of the party and have much to brag about, for I will have on my arm the loveliest woman in the county."

"Only one county?" She couldn't help teasing him, though she blushed at his compliment.

"Several counties, then." He laughed and clicked to the

horses, speeding up their arrival at the party and agitating the butterflies that had taken up residence in Mica's stomach.

Curiosity made her want to meet Logan's friends, but she was deathly afraid they wouldn't accept her, or she would embarrass him in some way. Seeming to read her thoughts, he patted her clenched hands as they arrived in front of a huge mansion set back from the road and surrounded by a lush lawn.

"You will be a smash. I promise. Just follow my lead and be yourself." He jumped down, tied the horses to the hitching post, and returned to the side of the buggy to lift her down. His hands lingered at her waist, and his gaze held hers captive for an instant in time. She parted her lips in a gasp as she read the desire and passion deep in his gaze. Obviously, her gasp seemed invitation enough, because Logan stole a kiss before he released her with a sigh.

"It will have to wait until later, for I fear our arrival has been noted," Logan said, for someone called his name—a man's voice inviting them to join the festivities.

Judith and Gray Cavanaugh, their hosts for the evening, welcomed Mica with warm smiles. Judith confided that Gray and Logan had known each other all their lives and had remained friends even when Logan went north to school.

"And just how did you come across this jewel, Logan? Your brashness usually doesn't attract such beauty." Gray slapped his friend on the back, and they both laughed good-naturedly.

"She's visiting her Aunt Theodora Josephine Ashley, but, unfortunately, her aunt came down with a chill," Logan replied. "Not wanting to spoil her niece's evening, she insisted I bring her along."

Mica opened her mouth to protest, but Logan's wink reminded her of his earlier comment—follow my lead.

"Ashley? Any relation to the Ashley's of Charleston?" Gray frowned in concentration, and Mica worried she would be found out.

"Very good, Gray. You're not as senile as they keep accusing," Logan remarked before she could answer. The gentlemen laughed once again.

As soon as they moved aside to allow new arrivals to greet their hosts, Mica couldn't help questioning him. "Why on earth would you tell them my aunt is indisposed? Is that a polite way of saying *dead?"*

Instead of answering right away, Logan tucked her arm in his and walked her around the fringes of the large room. Ornate furnishings, beautiful flocked wallpaper, and high ceilings lent the room an air of elegance not found in modern homes. Not yet comfortable with the hoop skirts she wore, Mica feared she would break something, for bric-a-brac sat everywhere—on pedestals, shelves on the walls, and even the backs of the sofas contained varying sizes of fragile figurines.

While decorated in what she realized must be the current trend, she much preferred Indigo Bay's more simple style, and the uncluttered look maintained throughout Logan's home.

Logan's soft voice near her ear brought her back to the subject at hand. "Why would I tell them you are visiting an aunt, instead of announcing you are staying with me unchaperoned? Somehow, I doubt you are that naive."

About the 1850's, I am, she longed to say in answer to his mocking comment.

"Look around you," he continued. "There is a great need in our society to appear proper. Strict rules of etiquette give them all a feeling of order and control. Some of our generation still cannot grasp the changes that are occurring, with the new inventions and all, so they try to hide their insecurities behind a moral facade."

"You mean they're really not so righteous?"

He grinned and whispered. "I can give you names. Or better yet, you try to guess which ones are a step or two below sainthood. For every one you miss, you owe me a kiss."

Ever the dangerous male animal, his breath was hot against her neck. Mica's blood heated, and soon her heart pounded twice as fast as usual. Still, she decided to play his game.

"And what if I guess correctly? What do I win?"

"In that case, I owe you a kiss." His smile so dazzled her that it only occurred to her later in the evening that their bet was one-sided.

The party had been planned as a simple get-together, so guests were free to mingle and visit instead of sitting to be entertained by a pianist or singer. Mica laughed at the stories told her about Logan in his youth. She enjoyed the people she met—politician John Greenwood and his wife, Elizabeth, the Applegates, and of course, the Cavanaughs.

Nicholas Westfall, an attorney in Cameron, intrigued her. She tried repeatedly to engage him in conversation regarding the law, if only to find out how far statutes had progressed to this point. Every time she initiated a conversation, however, he would either change the subject or speak directly to Logan, as though she were not there.

She came to realize Logan was unique in his regard for women. He actually conversed with her and he listened closely to her responses. Most of the men here, from what she could gather, felt women were frivolous attachments to be used for social status. How sad for the women, she thought, and how sad that the men didn't realize what they were missing.

She finally left the circle of men and wandered about the room, letting the atmosphere soak into her like the champagne she drank. As she did, conversations flowed around her. From the snatches she overheard, she realized her earlier nervousness had been unnecessary. Socializing in this century varied little from the twenty-first century country club set. Women gossiped about children, fashion, decorating and the latest scandal. The gentlemen's conversations focused on business, money and politics. She had to smile, for each was intent on besting the other's story.

She leaned down to place her empty glass on a side table when she had the eerie feeling someone watched her. Her gaze quickly scanned the room, and she saw him. Standing off by himself, his handsome features distorted by the sulky droop of his mouth and his hard green eyes, Neil Seaton glared at her. They hadn't been properly introduced, but she recognized him from the day he'd knocked her off her feet as he'd stormed out of Logan's library.

He looked as though he wanted her dead, and she had no idea why. Perhaps he thought she would interrupt his dealings with Logan. Hoping she could say something to help mend the feelings between Logan and his stepbrother, she moved in his direction, but a hand on her elbow stopped her.

"Ready to eat?" Logan had come to claim her for a late supper, and when he didn't mention seeing Neil, she decided she wouldn't bring it up.

"Thomas, come sit by us." The greeting came from Mr. Applegate, and Mica was surprised when Logan pulled her in his direction. She could not contain her astonishment when the man repeated the name and Logan responded.

"Thomas, good to see you back. My condolences on your mother's death. Both she and your father were good friends of ours."

"I appreciate your concern, William," Logan answered.

He held a chair out for Mica, and she all but fell into it. William had apparently misplaced his wife, Susan, and he hurried off to locate her, giving Mica the time she needed.

"Who the hell is Thomas?"

"Tsk, such language," he said with a grin and she blushed.

"My father's name was Thomas Logan Rutledge, and I'm named after him. In order to avoid confusion, I asked to be called Logan. All my friends refer to me as such." He glanced in William's direction. The latter now had a short, plump woman in tow. "Some of Father's friends still refer to me as Thomas, or Thomas Junior." He wrinkled his nose in apparent distaste.

Mica felt faint. A memory swirled in her head that was too incredible to believe. Again, as her aunt lay dying, she heard her –say, "Thomas needs you—go to him. You're the only one who can save him. Thomas can make you happy."

Because of her aunt's bequest, she had come to Sea Crest and found Logan, whose name was actually *Thomas.* Was Logan the Thomas she'd been referring to?

"Are you all right? You look as though you've seen a ghost." Logan leaned toward her, his hand touching her knee beneath the tablecloth.

Mica wanted to laugh at his choice of words, but the arrival of the Applegates, and the serving of the meal, saved her from having to make a response. She sat in numbed silence through most of the courses, telling herself that it had to be a coincidence.

She managed to answer questions and commented in turn on the delicious food, though she couldn't have told anyone what she ate. She couldn't initiate a conversation, however, and wanted nothing more than to get Logan alone and question him further.

Following the meal, the women retired to the sitting room while the men smoked their cigars and enjoyed their drinks. When they joined the ladies again, Judith Cavanaugh organized several tables of cards. Logan asked Mica if she played, and when she shook her head, he suggested a walk in the gardens while the others engaged in the games.

"You were exceedingly quiet during supper, and your color appears quite pale. Are you sure you feel all right?" Logan asked, voicing his concern as he strolled beside her.

"May we sit?" Mica asked, pausing beside a stone bench. At Logan's nod, she arranged her full skirts so she could be comfortable. He remained standing, one foot propped on the bench and his arm across his knee, his gaze intent on her face.

During their meal, Mica had sorted and discarded several options with regard to his real name. Now, she wondered how to broach the subject of her aunt without triggering too many questions in his mind. Perhaps it would be better not to say anything at all.

"You have a question." When she glanced up at him, he said, "Don't look so surprised. Your beautiful face is very easy to read."

His comment caused a flush to creep up her neck. She shifted her gaze away from his, afraid he would read things better not known. "It's just that...my aunt mentioned someone named Thomas once."

"Perhaps she meant my father. They would be closer in age, I would think." His gaze never left her, but Mica could tell he reflected on her question. "Now that you have made me think on it, I do recall Aunt Margaret speaking of a friend of hers, but the name was only Theo."

Mica leaned forward. “I called her Theo, though she always *said* she preferred Theodora Josephine. May I speak to your Aunt Margaret?” It didn’t seem possible that two women from different centuries would have known each other, but Mica was living proof that strange things did happen at Sea Crest.

“I’m afraid that won’t be possible. My aunt died several years ago.”

Mica hung her head in defeat. She didn’t honestly know what she had hoped for. Perhaps she wanted to find some small piece of evidence to explain why she had been allowed to come here.

Logan turned and sat beside her, his arm curving around her shoulders and pulling her close. “Why would you want to dig up old ghosts? I can think of better ways to occupy your time.”

The instant his lips grazed hers, Mica forgot everything and reveled in the taste of him. The heat from his kiss sizzled in the already sultry night as her arms circled his neck to pull him closer.

“Hold me. Touch me.” She didn’t realize she had begged until she heard him groan low in his throat. He kissed a feverish path down her throat to where her breasts pushed up against the fabric of her dress. She ached to have him closer—longed for nothing to be between them except the heat she felt in his touch.

She slid her hands down the inside of his coat, searching for the buttons of his shirt. Her hands trembled trying to undo the tiny studs even as his own hand slipped into her bodice to capture her breast, his thumb rubbing her nipple to a tight peak.

“Heaven help me, I want you in the worst way,” he rasped against her ear, and she leaned into his hand.

Unable to work his buttons open, she quit her attempt and slid her hand down his chest to his waist, then lower to caress the bulge in his trousers. He jerked, grabbing her wrist and bringing it to his lips where he planted a heated kiss to her palm.

"Woman, you will have me embarrassing myself in an instant, if you don't quit." Though he said the words, the passion in his voice and his heated gaze told Mica that he didn't want her to quit.

"Take me home, Logan." A request—a command—and they both knew it meant much more than a simple ride back to Indigo Bay.

Logan had wanted Michaela for so long he wasn't about to ignore her request. He made their excuses as rapidly as possible, keeping her in front of him to hide his arousal as they bid good night to Judith and Gray. The instant he lifted Michaela into the buggy and climbed in next to her, she picked up where she had left off by sliding her hand up the inside of his thigh. His hands trembled as he tried to control the horses and set them a course for home, but Michaela made it impossible for him to concentrate.

Holding the reins with one hand, he slid his free hand around the back of her neck and pulled her close. He turned to kiss her smiling lips with a hunger he had never felt before.

"You are a she-devil." Though he longed to do otherwise, he returned his gaze to the road, steering the horses around the last curve before they came to the causeway leading to Indigo Bay. "Now behave yourself, or you will cause me to drive my horses right off the road and into the water."

The moon caught a twinkle of mischief in her eyes, and before he could stop her, she had slipped her hand between the buttons on his shirt to touch his bare chest. A lightning bolt of heat sizzled through him, and the pleasure-pain throbbing in his groin intensified as he savored her caress.

With more control than he thought he had left, he urged the horses to a trot, hoping he could last long enough to get them to the house. He misjudged his control—badly—for when Michaela leaned over and tickled his ear with her tongue, he thought he would explode.

"Whoa!" He jerked on the reins, bringing the horses to a swift stop the instant they crossed the causeway. In one movement, he jumped clear of the buggy and turned around, grabbing Michaela by the waist and lifting her clear of the wheels.

"Logan, what in the world..." Her question hung in the air between them as his long strides took them away from the road.

He stopped beneath a small stand of trees that fringed the edge of the bank, their leafy shadows hiding the two of them in the night. Logan allowed her legs to slide to the ground but kept his arms around her to pull her against him.

His heart pounded rapidly, and he wondered at his ability to still speak. "Never in my life have I allowed anyone to control me. Never—until now." He tilted her head, his mouth crushing hers in a hungry kiss. When her lips parted to his questing tongue, the passion she had ignited swept through him.

Mica felt an urgent ache deep inside and knew only Logan could appease it—had known long before they almost let themselves go in the Cavanaugh's garden. And even while she recognized the danger of depending on this man for her happiness—to care for him far more than she logically should—she wrapped her arms around his neck and gave herself over to him.

"Logan, I want..." His kisses drove her wild, and he wouldn't stop long enough for her to speak.

"Shh, my love, don't waste your breath speaking. Show me what you want." As he spoke, he nibbled his way to her ear, his breath warm and erotic against her skin. He bent his knees and pulled her with him until they sprawled on the soft grass, clinging to each other.

Mica jerked his shirt out of his trousers as his hand slid up her leg beneath her skirt. Her hands were a wild frenzy of motion as she tore at the shirt's buttons. His touch left her trembling, and she couldn't get close enough to him. She moaned when his lips left hers to trace a path of fire down her throat. She wrapped her leg around his thigh to pull him closer. Momentarily gratified to feel his manhood hard against her, she soon began rocking erotically against him. Mindless, she told him what she wanted him to do to her, whispering her licentious desires against his ear as he bent to nuzzle her breasts.

Logan kissed her with abandon, and then lost touch with reality as she wantonly rubbed against him. Nothing in his experience had prepared him for this woman's erotic response to him, nor the very colorful suggestions she whispered in his ear.

"God, sweetheart," he moaned against her skin, jerking the bodice of her gown even lower until her breasts sprang free. Hungrily he savored first one then the other, his hand cupping her buttocks to pull her tighter against him. She rocked her hips, nearly sending him to premature ecstasy. He rolled her onto her back, his hips settling into the cradle of her thighs. While she pulled his coat and shirt off to caress his back, he bent his head to nuzzle her breasts, the nipples puckered tight and jutting up in invitation.

She writhed beneath him, moaning his name, while her hands found his flat nipples and teased them to hard peaks. She arched her back, silently begging him for more, and though he wanted to gladly oblige her, he knew if they didn't slow down the end would come too fast.

He slid to her side, keeping one leg across her hips, and his manhood snug against her. He kissed the side of her neck, her ear, and the hollow behind. Her hands slid frantically down his chest to the waist of his trousers. His breath caught, but he took her wrists in his hand and stilled her movements by pressing them against his chest.

"Logan, please." Her breasts heaved with her ragged breathing, and he feasted on the sight of them in the shadowy moonlight. Her pleas tugged at his heart and created a sweet agony in much lower regions.

"Shh, love, be still a moment. You're causing me the greatest distress." He growled the request, having a difficult time not letting her have her way with him. But he wanted to proceed slowly, to savor each moment he had dreamed about constantly since her arrival at his door.

"You'll think distress, if you don't finish what you started." Michaela gazed at him, her eyes flashing in the moonlight.

He fully intended to see their lovemaking through to

completion. However, he could not resist teasing her, even in the throes of passion.

"I don't believe I started this delightful interlude, dearest. I really think—"

"I don't want to talk, damn you."

His laughter rendered him helpless as she pushed against his chest. He rolled to his back, bringing her with him. Her breasts dangled at a level just above his mouth, and he couldn't resist taking the rosy tip of one, sucking gently. She arched her back above him, her hands propped in the grass at his head.

He marveled at the beauty of her face, tense with sexual delight. Her luscious black hair fell forward to curtain her face, and her skin was iridescent in the silver moonlight. Long, sooty lashes rested against her cheeks as her eyes closed in ecstasy.

Wanting to view the rest of her, Logan quickly unfastened the buttons down the back of her dress. She helped him slide the remainder of her clothes over her head, flinging then to the ground. Without shame or embarrassment over her nakedness, she straddled his belly and looked down at him, passion gleaming vividly in her eyes as her hands slid in a slow, sensuous pattern across his chest. Time and again, her thumbs flicked his nipples, her hips rocking against his skin, igniting more fires where he feared he would already go up in smoke.

He reached up to cup her breasts, but suddenly found his arms pinned to the ground beneath her knees. Astonished at the aggressive role she had assumed, he looked up to find her lips curved in a seductive smile.

"You, Mr. Rutledge, are far too slow. But then, perhaps that is all you are capable of, being a man of such advanced years. Maybe we should forego this game. I would hate to give you a heart attack at some crucial moment."

He could take no more of her taunts and instantly rolled her over and came down on her, crushing her breasts beneath his chest, his lips silencing any further words. Her tongue came out to tease his own, and her hands at his waist helped unfasten his trousers.

The instant his manhood sprang free, she caressed the length of him, causing him to cry out in pure ecstasy. He grabbed her wrists and held them above her head, thrusting his hips forward. In one tumultuous surge, he buried himself deep within her.

Mica cried out as Logan came into her, sensitive to his every touch. She wrapped her legs around his waist, refusing to allow him to move while she reveled in the passionate sensations shooting throughout her. Never had she experienced the tremendous hunger he created in her body—the desire to crawl into his skin and become one being. He released her wrists and braced himself above her, and she hugged him tighter as he began to move in and out. He withdrew almost to the brink of her, only to slide back in, his slow movements more erotic than the faster pace she would have set.

Again and again he came into her, each time pushing her closer to orgasm. While all her senses focused on his hips joining hers, he continued his caresses to her face, kissing her lips, her damp brow, whispering sweet love words and tickling her ear with his tongue.

She clawed at his bare back as he increased his pace, his thrusts shooting electric currents throughout her body. He surged forward once more, this time melding his hips to hers. His release triggered her own, her body shattering into a thousand pieces, throbbing sensations squeezing her tightly around him.

"Sweet, merciful heavens," Logan exclaimed, his breath exhaling hotly against her neck as he collapsed on top of her.

"Yeah." Mica could think of no response. She didn't want to think, period.

Logan slid onto his side, his head propped on his hand. In the silence, Mica could hear his raspy breathing, which matched her own irregular gasps. The longer the silence lasted, the more uncomfortable she grew. Almost afraid to look him in the eye, she hoped she wouldn't see disgust written on his features.

In all probability, she had committed a major faux pas by

being so forward with him. When she heard him chuckle, her eyes popped open, and she jerked her head toward him. Before she could curse him for laughing at her, he bent down and gave her a quick kiss, his lips still hot and moist from their lovemaking.

"I am sorry to laugh, sweetness, but you had your face screwed up in the worst expression, as though you'd eaten a persimmon. Was it that terrible for you?"

"Oh, Lord, no. Don't ever think that. It was awesome—heaven, in fact. It's just, well, I have the feeling you're going to think I'm a terrible, loose woman to act the way I did."

"That I do, my dear. In fact, *wanton* would describe you better, I believe."

She couldn't bear his twinkling eyes, or the grin on lips she still longed to kiss. She buried her head in his shoulder. "Oh, God, I'm so sorry."

"Michaela Marie, listen to me." His hand caressed her cheek before cupping her chin and raising her face until they were practically nose-to-nose.

"Nothing that happens between us shall ever be construed as wrong or in need of an apology. You are the most sensuous, beautiful woman I have even known, and I am extremely gratified you reacted as you did." He paused, and Mica raised a brow, sensing he had more to say.

"However, I do take exception to your comments regarding my age, and I guess I shall just have to show you that age builds not only character but also stamina."

***

The sun washed the sky in the palest pink of dawn by the time Mica and Logan returned to the house. Mica wasn't at all sure she had her clothes on straight, but knew for a fact she didn't *have* all her clothes, because Logan kept sliding his hand up her skirt, and her bare bottom still tingled from his caresses.

They managed to stable the horses and sneak into the house without alerting Simon or Mattie, and Logan walked her to her bedroom door as he had on previous nights. She thought this ridiculous, but she supposed propriety still had a hold on him.

"I'll have Lana bring you up a tray." He brushed her hair away from her face, his hand warm on her flushed skin. "I doubt you want to dress for breakfast, do you?"

"No." She whispered her answer, and then bit her tongue to keep from telling him what she really wanted. She turned to enter her room.

"Michaela?" The hesitation in his voice caused a shiver of apprehension to snake down her spine. Slowly, she turned to face him.

"I know I said that nothing in our relationship could ever be considered wrong, and I hope that you can confide in me and trust me, even if it is a dark secret."

She squinted at him, her brow furrowed. "What on Earth are you talking about?"

"When we made love...you acted with a good deal of experience." She couldn't believe it, but sure as the world, Logan blushed. It didn't take a Ph.D. to figure what he hinted at.

"Logan, I'm twenty-nine years old. Of course I'm not a virgin." At his look of astonishment, she softened her tone. "I was married before."

He instantly stiffened. "Married? I told you...is he dead?" She realized he wanted to give her the benefit of the doubt.

"No, I divorced him." She sighed. "I can't believe we're having this discussion in the middle of the hall."

"What?" His voice sounded incredulous. "How the devil could you divorce him?"

"Richard was irresponsible."

"You can't divorce a man because he's irresponsible." Logan shook his head, and Mica realized not knowing the rules of etiquette might be one thing, but apparently there were morality rules during this century that were not taken lightly. She tried to explain.

"Look, he went through his inheritance and bankrupted three businesses. Then he started in on my money."

"He would have been perfectly within his rights to use that money. When you marry, what you have belongs to your husband."

"Not under South Carolina law, it doesn't."

"We're in South Carolina, sweetheart, and although I haven't taken the bar exam for this state, I doubt seriously the laws have changed since I finished law school."

"Changed? They..." She realized the hole she had dug. To distract him, she changed the subject. "When did you finish law school?"

"I graduated two weeks after my mother died." His tone hadn't varied, but Mica could see the pain in his eyes.

"She would have been so proud. Why haven't you taken the bar?"

Logan braced his feet and crossed his arms over his chest. He couldn't understand how she had managed to turn the tables on him, putting him on the defensive.

"When Mother died, I learned my father's will had been entailed, and Indigo Bay became mine, not Neil's. People depend on the plantation for their livelihoods, and that had to take precedence. With the fire and other problems I've incurred, I don't have time to practice now, anyway."

Michaela's face lit up, and again Logan's body tightened. "You have time. We'll make time. I can help you study."

"It's dawn. We haven't slept, and I'm exhausted!" Even as he said it, his body responded to the wiggle of her hips as she dragged him down the hall to the library. Just inside the door, which he closed, she left him and hurried across the room to light the lamp.

Struggling for some control over the situation, he stated, "Don't think I've forgotten why we argued. I'm not so easily distracted."

"Is that so?" She cocked her head to one side, lips curving into a seductive smile.

He should have known better than to issue her a challenge. His hands clutched the doorknob as she reached behind her and undid the buttons of her dress, letting the garment slide from her shoulders to pool at her feet. Logan swallowed hard—she wore nothing underneath. He forgot his exhaustion, his mind blank to everything except the beauty who graced him with her smile and her quite naked body, glowing in the lamplight.

As she glided across the space separating them, Logan realized he had fallen in love. Always one to scoff at the idea of love at first sight, he had fallen fast for this unpredictable, unconventional, wanton woman advancing towards him. He would allow her to assault his person, for she had already captured his heart and stolen his soul, even before he had tasted the nectar of her body.

***

Mica woke up in bed later that day, smiling as she recalled Logan carrying her to his bedroom after they had made love in his study. When she stretched and rolled over, she caught the scent of flowers. Forcing her drowsy eyes open, she found the bed strewn with a colorful array of fragrant blossoms. She spied a sheet of paper nestled among the blooms and reached for it, thinking how romantic of Logan to shower her with flowers. They meant more to her than if he had given her a priceless gift.

Sitting cross-legged on the bed, she sniffed a rose as she unfolded his note. Her eyes widened and her breath came in short gasps the further she read.

"My Dearest Michaela Marie,

"Please do not think I have abandoned you, but urgent business has taken me from your side for a few days.

"What I did abandon was my self control, but I cannot even apologize for that. The hours makinglove to you were the most exquisite of my life, and I shall be eternally grateful for the gift you gave me last night.

"Upon my return, we shall discuss a date to marry. I consider myself an honorable man, and even if we had not relinquished ourselves to passion last eve, I would want to make you my wife and keep you by my side forever.

"Keep me kindly in your thoughts until I can hold you in my arms once more.

"With sincerest regards, T L R"

"With sincerest regards?" Mica sputtered as she crumbled the paper and flung it across the room. She didn't *want* to get married again, not that he had bothered to ask. Lord, men didn't change, no matter what century they were from.

As she bounced off the bed and began to dress, she admitted she was at blame. What had she thought? That she could waltz in and out of his life and not suffer the consequences? Given the times, and a gentleman of Logan's period, Mica could understand his feelings on the subject. Honor and family meant everything to him, and she had no right deceiving him.

However, from her twenty-first century viewpoint, if she were to marry again—and that was a big if—she would only do so for love. No more of this honor and respectability and family tradition crap. And *sincerest regards* didn't sound like love to her.

She tugged on her own clothes, knowing she had to leave Indigo Bay. When she turned and her gaze caught the flowers on the bed, however, she wanted to weep. She took a single rose and the note she had crumpled and left the room.

She entered the door to Sea Crest. She realized she cared too much for a man on whom she had no claim, and there appeared to be more distance between their views than she knew how to bridge. As the door closed silently behind her, her rose turned to dust in her hand, and Logan's note faded until the words were almost illegible, but they had already been branded on her heart.

Seven

On previous occasions when Mica had visited Logan, no one knew she was gone because it had only been for a few hours at night. However, this morning when Mrs. Harris had casually asked her whereabouts over the past several days, Mica realized that Sea Crest and Indigo Bay ran on exactly the same timetable. To avoid having to explain her disappearances, she had mentioned vaguely that she was working on a case and not to worry if she was gone days at a time.

Now, she sped towards Charleston, knowing she had to put some distance between herself and Sea Crest because the temptation to stay near Logan had been so strong it had made her physically ill. She stopped at a convenience store for antacids, but they did little to dispel her anxiety. Just as the gloomy rain battering the windows did little to improve her mood. It was ridiculous to feel that way, especially after getting so angry when she first read his note.

Because of the time in which Logan lived, she could understand his overbearing attitude toward marrying her, even if he had *told* her instead of asking. What made her so upset was that, for a very brief time, she had actually thought about doing it.

As soon as she got in her apartment, she called Katie and asked her to come for lunch. She hoped a visit with her friend would get Logan off her mind.

"Katie, you've known me all your life, right?" Mica turned to her friend, who now sat in an overstuffed chair, legs curled under her.

"Yeah, why?"

"Have you ever known me to do anything not sensible? Have I ever strayed from the straight and narrow plan for my life?" Mica couldn't quell the foreboding that something terribly wrong might occur because she had traversed time and ventured into the past.

From the misgivings she had, she wondered if she had somehow upset history. Perhaps her longing for adventure had disrupted time waves, or ripples, or whatever science fiction writers called them.

Katie looked up from the magazine on her lap. "What is this, a cross examination?" She gasped. "Oh, Mica, have you been picked up for speeding and need a character witness?"

Mica had to smile at her friend's theatrics, but it was true. She had never broken a law or done anything irresponsible. "Come on, help me out here, will you?"

Katie scrunched up her face in thought. "Well, what about that time we smoked cigarettes out in the pool house after your parents went to bed?"

"Katie, be serious! We were fourteen."

"I'm thinking...I'm thinking."

Mica went on as though Katie hadn't spoken. "I mean, I always did what I was told. I had good grades and studied hard. Why would this happen to me?" She looked at her friend. "I'm a lawyer, for God's sake. I believe in fact, not nonsense. Proof, not some long-dead apparitions or a machine that signals when ghosts appear."

She had explained just a little about the strange people in residence at Sea Crest, but she had not mentioned Logan. Yet somehow, she sensed his life was connected to Professor Bigley and the Barkers as much as Indigo Bay was connected with Sea Crest.

Katie moved to the window, taking her hand. "Who are you trying to convince—me or yourself? Like you said, the man's a quack. Did you do a background check on him?"

Mica realized Katie thought she was upset because of the Professor. She decided not to alter that belief, because Katie would never comprehend the enormity of what Mica had done—even if she believed it, which was doubtful.

"I asked around town, since he said he has been there several years before. He is what he says—a professor on sabbatical from Columbia, investigating paranormal phenomena."

"And he thinks there are ghosts at Sea Crest?"

"Apparently. Look, I might go back. Come with me and see for yourself." Perhaps if Katie went with her, she wouldn't be tempted to cross that invisible line into Logan's world.

Logan's image flashed in her mind, and her stomach plummeted. His kisses had fired her passion, and when they had made love—Mica silently moaned, her feminine core heating in remembrance of the exquisite torture he had put her through. She tried to focus on her friend's voice.

"I don't know if I can get away. Matthew might not like it."

"Katie, show some independence! You slave away for Matt and the kids every day. You deserve some time to yourself." Katie truly believed in her calling as a mother and wife, and chair of the Country Club Charity. She never did anything without Matt's permission. Mica liked Matt, and Katie was a dear, but sometimes...

"I'll ask Matt." Katie spun around and headed for the door. "Gotta run—school PTA is this afternoon. You will come for dinner tomorrow, won't you?"

"Do you promise not to serve up another Mr. Right?"

"Honestly, Mica, just because Richard didn't work out, don't give up on men. We'll find you one yet." She waved and dashed out the door before Mica could tell her she had probably found the right man, but from the wrong century.

Thomas Logan Rutledge—she must have been out of her mind to stay with him. Now, what could she do about the untenable situation she had created? Several easy solutions came to mind—seal the door at Sea Crest, never go up there again in this lifetime, or sell the place.

Since Logan had no idea where she actually lived or the peculiarities regarding her arrival at Indigo Bay, she would never have to answer his questions. But Mica realized it wouldn't be that easy. The fact was, she didn't know if she could let him go.

She grabbed a basket of dirty clothes and headed for the laundry room as she thought about the man whose life she had interrupted and who now wanted her to become a permanent part of it. Scared would be an understatement for the sensations gnawing at her middle and muddling her brain. She was terrified by the fact that she was even *contemplating* going back in time again, and her mind refused to dwell on the idea of actually *staying* back there.

If Logan were a twenty-first century man living across town from her, she still would have hesitated before marrying him. She wasn't sure she could give up her newfound independence for a man again, even for a man like Logan, who epitomized all the best qualities she could dream for in a life partner.

His gentleness towards her, his sense of fairness and justice towards his freed slaves, and his humor and love of life were ideals Mica held close to her heart. That didn't even take into account the way her heart catapulted whenever he was near, or the sensuous heights they had traveled that last night together. He symbolized everything she wanted and couldn't have, all due to a breach in time.

"Damn it all, anyway." She let the lid to the washer bang down, the sound satisfying to her frustrated frame of mind. Her cell phone rang and she grabbed it off the counter.

"Hello." She didn't care if she sounded bitchy. That was exactly how she felt at the moment.

"Michaela, dear, you are home. I tried to call you at Sea Crest, but a nice woman named Anna said she hadn't seen you in days. When did you get back?"

"Hello, Mother. I'm not staying. I just came down to do a few things." Mica knew she should have packed everything and come back to the city and to work, but she had time left—time to figure out what she wanted to do.

"Well, as long as you're in town, be here for dinner at seven. You know how your father detests late meals."

"Mother, I really don't think I can make it."

"Michaela, I refuse to let my only daughter ruin her life."

"If you invited Richard to dinner, you won't see me step foot inside the door." Mica couldn't understand why her mother wouldn't let it go.

"Now, dear, I don't see why..." Mica heard a sigh on the other end of the line. "Please, come for dinner. I've found some old letters of your Aunt Theo's."

Mica couldn't resist, even knowing her mother would no doubt manage to bring Richard into the conversation at some point. "I'll be there."

***

Dinner proved more pleasant than she expected, most likely because Richard hadn't been invited. Since her mother refused to allow her father to discuss business at the table, Mica visited with him in the study after the meal. Trials had been scheduled and were being handled efficiently by junior executives, though her father reiterated his desire for her to return early.

"Thirty days, Dad. That's what you gave me, and that's what I need." The whole idea of taking time off had been to come to terms with her life and make the necessary adjustments to being a divorcée and career woman. So why did she now have doubts as to whether she really wanted that life any more? She seemed no closer to a resolution than when she had started her vacation.

Even though her sensible, responsible side nagged her to return to work tomorrow, deep inside her woman's heart she wasn't ready to let go of Logan. She gave her father a kiss on the forehead and left him to his work.

"In here, Michaela." Her mother's voice reached her from the parlor, and Mica shook off her own misgivings about delving into her aunt's past.

"As I told you the last time you popped in, most of our family's historical documents have been given to the Society. When we sorted through things, Aunt Theo must have set aside these personal letters." Her mother handed Mica a small bundle of letters, the yellowed envelopes addressed in a flowing script. "I tried to read them, but they don't make much sense."

Mica carefully removed the ribbon tying the bundle together, lifting the first to examine the words. As she glanced down at the stack, she noted the envelopes were addressed to Theodora Josephine Ashley, but there were no street addresses or stamps on any of them. "Who are they from?"

"Someone named Maggie. She must have been a friend."

Mica's gaze snapped to her mother then back to the first letter that she now held in shaking hands. *Maggie—Margaret.* Could there be a connection?

The first letter made reference to Theo's ride in an airplane. It seemed Maggie found that incredible, since she had been frightened to death when George (her husband?) raced his trotters with her in the curricle.

Those words didn't seem at all odd to Mica considering her aunt's age and the fact that many older families in the area still maintained a stable, even if they also had automobiles and traveled in jets.

Mica read through more letters, but none mentioned anything she could connect with Sea Crest and Indigo Bay. She also noted none of them contained the year in which they were written. The writer began with the month and day, giving no indication when, in her aunt's eighty-nine years of life, these letters were written.

She silently read on. *Thomas continues to study very hard, but, oh dear, how that boy misses his father. He doesn't return home as often now that Elizabeth has remarried, for he doesn't deal well with his step-father, Charles.*

The parchment fluttered from Mica's nerveless hands onto her lap. Her vision blurred until the script ran together, and she couldn't see any of the words except the first—Thomas. Could it be?

Had her aunt somehow discovered Sea Crest's secret and gone back in time to make the acquaintance of Logan's aunt? How did they manage a correspondence through time? Why had her aunt never told her anything about this? And how could she jump to such incredible conclusions based on the appearance of a name that had, no doubt, been very popular throughout history?

Luckily, her mother had begun her embroidery and paid little attention to Mica. She placed a hand to her chest in hopes of stilling the heart palpitations that thundered clear up to her ears. She swallowed several times and blinked her eyes against the pictures her mind conjured up.

Instead of blocking out the images, Logan's face came to view, his dark hair gleaming and a frown bringing his brows together. She could almost hear him say something like—*Leave things be, Michaela Marie. Don't question fate. Just enjoy each day to the fullest.*

"Easy for you to say. You don't have to figure out which century—"

"What did you say, dear?" Mica's mother looked up from her sewing.

"What? Oh, nothing. Just something I read." Mica hadn't realized she had spoken aloud. She took a breath and willed her hands to quit shaking as she pulled the last letter from the envelope. The writing was the same, but the message proved incriminating.

Dearest Theo,

Poor Thomas. I fear there will be nothing left of his legacy, for Neil and his father are bent on destroying Indigo Bay. If only my poor brother-in-law were still alive. While I love dear Elizabeth, she just is not strong enough...

The script faded to nothing, water stains blurring the rest of the message, but it had been enough to make Mica's hand tremble once again. She very gently folded the letter and returned it to its envelope, half afraid it would disintegrate before her eyes.

So there was a connection between her aunt and Indigo Bay. Did she dare return to Logan and tell him that *his* aunt had written to *her* aunt, and the letters indicated Neil spelled trouble? What if he questioned her about her aunt? How could she ever begin to explain that the two ladies had somehow carried on a correspondence even though far more than one hundred years separated their lives?

Mica hung her head, rubbing her forehead with her fingers. Logan's aunt could have written the letters, but in actuality, they didn't prove a thing. They didn't point to any facts that weren't already clear. The only supposition Mica could make was that her aunt might have known about the door at Sea Crest and had tried to tell her about Logan, whom her aunt had called Thomas, so that she could help him in some way.

At the moment, she couldn't begin to imagine how she could be of help in an era where women were not acknowledged as having the ability to do much of anything. The most she could accomplish by going back would be to warn Logan of Neil's plans to destroy Indigo Bay. And that wasn't even very clear since everything alluded to in Maggie's letters had already happened in Logan's life.

By returning, she would open herself, and Logan, to more hurt. It had been hard enough to leave when she had. Given the circumstances and progression of their relationship, she could only imagine it would be twice as hard the next time.

Was it fair to Logan to return when she knew she couldn't stay? Oh, God, she thought her life had been complicated before. The whole idea of going to Sea Crest had been to resolve her conflicts, not create more.

"Michaela, dear, it's getting late. You'll stay in your old room, won't you?" Her mother's question gave Mica something else to focus on.

"I really should return to the apartment. I left clothes in the washer. Besides, I'll probably return to Indigo—Sea Crest—early tomorrow." She let out a sigh. "Mother, was there anything else, any other correspondence?" Mica didn't know what she wanted to find, but her mind refused to relinquish its quest.

"What are you looking for, dear? Didn't those letters contain any useful information about whatever it is you're trying to learn?"

"No." Mica refused to disclose even the slightest tidbit of the strange coincidences. Her mother would have her committed to the nearest padded room.

"I'm afraid I don't have anything older than those letters," her mother said "During the War Between the States, many family records were either destroyed or hidden and never recovered. I remember when we worked at the Society more than one woman commented on the tragic loss of family history. And, too, so much of our past was lost during the fire."

"What fire?" Mica asked, her heart beginning to pound again.

"Oh, heavens, dear, I don't recall the date. Long before my time. Probably even before Aunt Theo's time. I do recall, though, something about lost stock certificates. I'm not sure what happened, but Aunt Theo did say once if the stock had remained in the family, there would have been no need to sell off most of the Sea Crest land after the war."

Mica filed that information for future reference since she had no idea whether stock certificates played a part in this game or not. She gathered her aunt's letters, replacing the faded ribbon to hold them together. Then she rose from the chair and flexed her shoulders to relieve her tension. So much to think about.

"I need to go, Mother. Thank you for the scrumptious meal." She bent to kiss her mother's cheek, anxious now to leave and mull over all she had learned.

"Oh, by the way, Lucy has your clothes mended. You really should be more careful. She said she had to completely replace your zipper."

"Yes, ma'am." Mica waved as she exited the parlor. Grabbing her clothes by the front door where Lucy had left them, she headed back to her apartment. As she drove, she plucked at the new buttons Lucy had put on her pajamas.

Now she understood what happened when she went through the door, and she wondered if there weren't certain rules that had to be followed. She recalled the flower that had turned to dust when she returned from Indigo Bay. How could she play by the rules when she didn't know what they were?

That night, even though she stayed at her apartment, she dreamed of Logan, waking herself when she cried his name out loud. She pawed through the medicine cabinet for the sleeping pills she had depended on after her divorce. As the capsules tumbled from the bottle into her hand, she hesitated.

She hadn't taken the pills to Sea Crest with her and hadn't needed them. Why start up an old habit?

Because the answer to her question was the source of her current sleeplessness—Thomas Logan Rutledge. She hated that he had made her feel again, much deeper than she wanted to admit. Besides that, he had unknowingly teased her with a life and freedom she couldn't have in her own time.

But she didn't want to dream about him. She didn't want to recall his sensuous lips on hers, or his gentle voice and caring nature. She didn't want to remember, and yet his allure remained so strong, she felt the tug on her heart even though centuries separated them.

She contemplated her aunt's dying words and the most recent discovery of her letters. Before she had to return to work, she still had time to return to Sea Crest and try to help Logan in some as yet unfathomable way.

She couldn't deny the whole situation intrigued her. Was her aunt talking about Logan when she had mentioned a man named Thomas? Why hadn't Aunt Theo told anyone about the door or her correspondence with Maggie? Who started the fire at Indigo Bay? The questions piled up, intensifying the sense of mystery surrounding Sea Crest.

Mica packed her bag for the trip back up the coast to Cameron Island. She shook her head ruefully, knowing that by returning to the bed & breakfast, she might lose her heart. Yet the memory of Logan sent her senses into a tailspin.

***

Mica hadn't tried to pass through the door during the day. She no sooner slipped the key into the lock than a horrendous alarm sounded from somewhere behind her. She jerked the door shut and whirled around, her heart erratic and her skin instantly damp with nervous perspiration.

She passed a shaking hand over blurry eyes as she tried to focus. Even when she recognized the intruder as Professor Bigley, jittery sensations still rippled along her spine.

He stood by the door to his room, his ghost machine clutched to his chest and his eyes wide with disbelief. As his gaze came to rest on her face, his mouth turned down in a frown, and his bushy gray eyebrows lowered to show his disappointment.

But his infernal contraption kept ringing in her ears.

"Professor, can you shut that thing off?" Mica yelled to be heard over the racket.

His hand dropped to the box, and within seconds, silence again shrouded the halls. "I don't understand..." The confused professor concentrated on his device. He flipped a switch as he walked over to Mica, and the alarm instantly filled the air with squawking.

Before Mica could open her mouth, he adjusted the volume to a high-pitched beeping. Though tolerable, it still grated on her nerves.

"Professor Bigley, you scared the wits out of me! I suggest if your machine isn't working, you keep it turned off so you don't disturb the other guests."

"But Miss Chadwick, it *is* working. In fact, for several days I picked up random signals from the north end of the house, but I have been unable to locate the exact source. Two days ago, the signals quit. Now they've started again and appear to be very strong right around you." He eyed her suspiciously.

Two days. She'd returned to Sea Crest two days ago before leaving for Charleston. Now she was back, and the professor's signals were back. And he was inspecting her as though he thought she was a—

"Professor Bigley, I am not a ghost." She laughed outright even as the hair on the back of her neck prickled. She slowly stepped away from the door to move down the hallway. The professor followed, and as he did, the intensity of the alarm faded. When they reached the top of the stairs, it quit altogether.

The professor's face scrunched into a frown again. His fingers adjusted knobs as his gaze darted from the machine back to her. "How odd. I thought I finally found…" He stopped mid-sentence and looked up at her again. "I am sorry. Of course, you're not a ghost. It's just the last week has given me such hope of a discovery."

While his words were apologetic, Mica sensed he still

considered her a spectral suspect. She started down the stairs, knowing she could never attempt to enter the door now. "If you would like my birth certificate—"

"No, no." He laughed good-naturedly. "I'll just have to keep trying, that's all." He turned towards his room, and Mica had a sinking sensation in her stomach.

"Professor?" When he stopped and turned back to her, she continued. "Is there a way to attach a bell to your machine, instead of that awful alarm?" She could tell he was already lost in thought, for he murmured something incoherent as he shuffled towards his room.

Mica's stomachache continued as she walked down the stairs to the main floor. What if the professor's machine really worked? What if he had been picking up vibrations of life from Logan's side of the door? Now he had apparently picked up phenomenon from her because she had been there.

She would have to be more careful the next time she attempted to cross the threshold into the past. Under no circumstances did she want the professor or anyone else to find out what lay beyond the door that supposedly didn't open.

Mica ran into Mr. Barker at the bottom of the stairs. He turned guiltily at her approach, his pudgy hands hidden behind his back. Papers were strewn across the reception desk. Mica knew Anna wouldn't leave such a mess, and she began to suspect Mr. Barker of mischief.

"Uh, well, Miss Chadwick, you're back." He made it sound as though she shouldn't have been there, and Mica wondered what he was trying to hide from her.

"Of course, I'm here, Mr. Barker. I live here." He backed away from the desk. Mica raised a brow, glad to be in the offensive position instead of being the guilty party as she had with the professor. "May I ask what you're doing here?"

"I...uh," the man sputtered, glancing anywhere but at her.

Mica's investigative nature kicked into fast-forward. She stepped quickly around him before he had a chance to back further away. His hands clutched a leather bound book, but Mica couldn't see the title before he swiveled to face her again.

"What do you have, Mr. Barker?" she asked, suspicious

of the rotund little man who thought to find buried treasure.

"There is no call for concern. The journal belongs to us." He clutched the book to his chest. "And you have given us permission to search." His pathetic look almost made her feel guilty. Almost.

"The permission didn't mean you could intrude on other people's privacy or property, Mr. Barker." Mica cast a pointed glance towards the reception desk.

To defuse the situation and shed some light on the mystery that seemed to surround Sea Crest, Mica flashed her friendliest smile. "Perhaps if you allowed me a glimpse of the journal, I could help you. After all, I've been associated with Sea Crest much longer than you."

Mr. Barker handed over the journal without a qualm, his round face glowing with enthusiasm for her support. "Why, that would be very thoughtful of you. Not many people would be so kind toward helping another find a treasure."

Mica had serious doubts about any treasure, but she did question why the Barkers thought there might be some here on the island. She surveyed the book as quickly as possible, because she knew if Mrs. Barker happened by, both of them would be in trouble.

The entries were not dated, nor could she find the author's name inscribed on the front or back cover. The script proved almost impossible to read, written in black ink with little regard for legibility.

She squinted as she read out loud. "*...I shall rename the isle after myself, instead of some damned crop, which will yield him no money after I have my way.*"

Apparently whoever had compiled the journal felt a tremendous anger, for the sentences Mica could make out were forceful and the language abusive. She continued to read silently.

The bastard refuses to acknowledge what is rightfully mine. Not only does he have the land, but now the gold as well. I shall endeavor to return when ghosts haunt the land and a raging inferno consumes all he holds dear. Then I shall have my revenge!

More ghosts! Mica thrust the book back into Mr. Barker's hands. She rubbed sweaty palms up and down her jeans, trying to brush away the negative vibrations she sensed while holding the book.

She took a deep breath and called on her years of training to state the facts. "There are no names in the book. Nowhere does it remotely mention Sea Crest. Although gold is mentioned, what makes you think the journal is about this island?"

Mr. Barker gave her a smug smile. "You obviously have not studied it as we have. There are references to the Cameron Islands, and indigo, a crop grown in this specific area before the Civil War. The journal tells a story of family strife, also common during that period when one brother had what another coveted."

"How weird," Mica mused. " May I see that again? " *It sounds just like Logan and his stepbrother,* she thought. She held out her hand, only to have the book snatched away by red-tipped talons.

"Certainly not!" Nadine Barker grabbed the book, her lacquered nails beating an angry staccato on the leather cover as she clutched it to her chest.

Her husband visibly melted under the heat of her glare. His face reddened as his shoulders slumped. Mica might feel sorry for him, but *she* wasn't about to wither beneath the woman's haughty manner.

"I was telling your husband that perhaps I could be of assistance since I've known Sea Crest all my life." Her smile froze the instant the other woman spoke.

"I'm sure you would be more than willing to help *my husband,* Miss Chadwick." The snide undertone in her words could not be mistaken.

Mica bristled. "Surely you don't think—"

"I think you'd better leave my husband, and this journal, alone. What's mine is mine." The woman stepped between Mica and her husband, and if Mica hadn't been so angry, she would have laughed outright.

"I have the same rules, so please confine your search to

public areas only." Mica's gaze swept the reception desk before she looked the taller woman straight in the eye. "Just so we understand each other."

A winner in any confrontation got in the last word and left first, so Mica sailed from the room, back straight and head high.

***

Much later that night, she still chuckled when she thought about Mrs. Barker's preposterous claim that she might have amorous intentions towards Mr. Barker. If the woman only knew where Mica's intentions lay, she would have heart palpitations of her own!

She closed the overnight bag she had packed and grabbed the key from her dresser. Locking her own door behind her, she crept through the house barefooted, confident all the guests were asleep. Having no idea whether Logan had returned yet from business, she could only hope she would beat him back to Indigo Bay. Trying to explain where she had been would not be easy. It became more and more difficult to disguise the truth.

The instant she crossed over and tossed her bag onto the bed, she felt as though she had come home from a very long trip. Home—she smiled at the idea.

She saw lights glowing from below and followed them down to the kitchen where she found Mattie just finishing the dishes. She had a cup of tea with the housekeeper and visited like old friends—another nice feeling. Even though Mattie didn't question her whereabouts over the past couple of days, Mica mentioned having returned to Sea Crest on estate business since Logan was gone.

"Master Logan is expected later in the evening," Mattie said as they cleared away their teacups.

"Then I may wait up for him," Mica replied. "Good night, Mattie."

As Mica climbed the stairs, she contemplated her strategy. It wouldn't do any good to postpone telling Logan about Neil. After all, that *was* the reason for her return. Mica kept telling herself that, even as she donned her most becoming dress and brushed her hair until it shone.

She glanced longingly at the big poster bed and decided she'd better not wait for him in her bedroom. She wandered into the music room, recalling the time she had come upon Logan as he played the piano. Even then, he had captured her heart with his soulful music and his magnetic smile. Her fingers caressed the keys. It had been ages since she had played, though music had been her passion when younger.

***

Logan watched Michaela from the doorway. His brow smoothed, and his tense muscles relaxed as the music swept away the business worries he had confronted in Charleston over the past several days. He sighed deeply, aware it wasn't the music at all that made him feel this way, but her presence.

He didn't question how or why she had appeared in his life. He only rejoiced in the fact that she had. She was so beautiful, her graceful hands caressing the ivory keys with tenderness. Yet he remembered how those same hands had touched him with urgent passion during their last night together. God, how he had missed her!

She must have sensed his presence, for her fingers never faltered as he laid his hands on her shoulders, bending down to kiss the nape of her neck. Possessed by an urgent physical need to carry her off to his bed and love her passionately, he forced himself to be content savoring the smooth, fresh taste of her skin.

From the time his mother had died, he had withdrawn into himself, trying not to need others. He cared for his people and the land, the only thing he could call his own, but he took pains to keep his own needs deeply buried. Since Michaela had come into his life, however, he found his needs taking precedence over his other responsibilities.

He wanted to claim her for his own. She had an inner strength that would allow her to stand beside him instead of depending on him as did so many others. That didn't insult his sense of manhood, for his soul searched for a mate to compliment his own passion and strengths.

At present, however, he felt shy and unsure how to proceed

with their relationship. He sat down beside her on the bench, speaking to her as she played. "I don't recognize that melody. Is it Chopin or Beethoven?"

"No—Kenny G."

"I'm afraid I'm not familiar with his work."

"He's contemporary." Michaela gifted him with a smile. "Welcome home, Logan."

Her words melted his heart. He wrapped an arm around her. Replacing her fingers with his on the keyboard, he began the melody he had heard her play.

She turned startled blue eyes to him, her breath a sweet whisper against his cheek. "How can you do that?"

He shrugged, bringing his arms closer together, which shifted Michaela closer to his chest. He kept his hands on the keyboard even though he would have rather caressed her.

"It's a gift, I'm afraid. My mother insisted on lessons, but I hated them. I found, though, if I played without fault for my instructor, I could be done that much faster and be allowed to ride my pony. So I concentrated very hard, or thought I did, but apparently it didn't take much effort on my part."

"You are truly gifted. Did your instructor push you to play professionally?"

"Oh, yes, as did Mother. But my professor was... effeminate, you might say." Logan glanced down at her and batted his eyelashes. Her responding laughter created a melody of its own in his mind.

"Even at eleven years of age, I wanted to be considered a man, not a child. I became deathly afraid if I continued to play, I would turn into another Mr. Weathersby. So I quit. I faked sprains to my wrists and fingers, colds and coughs, until Mother finally decided it wasn't worth paying a music instructor *and* a resident doctor."

A murmur of agreement was all he heard from Michaela, but she snuggled closer to his chest. He forced his fingers to remain on the keys, changing the melody to one as happy and carefree as he felt at the moment.

"Entertaining people is all well and good," he continued, "but only the rich can afford to attend a concert or the opera.

I needed to feel more useful than that. I needed to make a contribution."

"I feel the same way."

Her remark gave him one more reason to love her. He responded musically as his fingers caressed and cajoled to bring forth a melody with softness like the wistful beauty in his arms before blending the sounds into a strong and commanding finish.

He tried to tell her how he felt with the music he played, his heart pounding in time with the beat. When she swayed in rhythm against him, he forgot the music and let his body tell her what he needed. He turned her in his arms, his lips crushing hers in a kiss of hunger and need—caring and passion.

She answered his request by opening her mouth, her tongue dancing with his to a melody that throbbed through his very blood, reaching in to capture his soul.

Unlike the first time he had encountered her in the music room, tonight Michaela didn't protest when Logan waltzed her to the door then swept her into his arms and carried her to bed. He felt he couldn't get close enough to her.

All day long he had felt a restlessness, like a storm was brewing, but it focused inwardly rather than on the land around him. Something untoward was about to happen, and Logan had the irrational fear that he might lose Michaela in the process.

Eight

Logan didn't leave her bed that night as he had before. Instead, his magical hands continued the rapture he had started in the music room, carrying her time and again to a majestic crescendo of love.

But now, as dawn nudged aside the night, Mica unexpectedly shivered. She curled closer to Logan's warmth, her bare back snug against his hard chest. She had done it royally this time—tumbled headlong into a situation from which she could see no way out.

She turned to study Logan's profile, softened in sleep. How had she thought to turn her feelings for him on and off like a switch? She could never stop caring for this passionate man. A smile curved her lips. Passionate didn't begin to describe the exotic pleasures he had showered on her last night.

She had thought to come back and help him without becoming more entangled, but now she knew she had lied to herself. She hadn't come back for Logan's sake, but for her own. With every waking breath, her need for him grew. And yet it proved an impossible situation.

He sighed and reached for her in his sleep, his warm hand gentle on her breast.

"Oh, Logan," she whispered, "I only wanted to help, and now look what I've done." She kissed his brow and savored the tender emotions that welled up inside her. In her mind's eye, however, she could already see the inevitable. Before she created more trouble for herself, she needed to complete the mission she had come here to accomplish.

"Logan?" She caressed his bare shoulder. "Logan?"

He turned slightly. "Michaela." He mumbled her name,

his breath warm on her skin, and Mica's heart twisted.

"Did your Aunt Margaret and her husband live here at Indigo Bay?"

"For a while." His answer came out muffled, for he had snuggled closer and his hot lips nibbled incredibly erotic patterns on the side of her breast.

Determined to keep her mind on the task at hand, she took a breath, but that only pressed her closer to his lips. "Did she know your brother? Do you think she realized how much Neil wanted your plantation?"

Instead of answering, he nuzzled her, then his tongue traced sizzling circles around her nipple.

"Oh-h-h," she moaned, then groaned when he withdrew his mouth.

Seconds later, his lips moved down her belly, planting butterfly-light kisses against her sensitive skin. Mica had forgotten what she had asked by the time he answered her.

"Neil is headstrong, but he'll come around. Why all the questions?" He pursued an unerring path back up her stomach, nipping her skin then licking with his hot tongue. His movements remained unhurried, his voice sleepy, but Mica knew he realized exactly what his tender forays were doing to her.

She squirmed beneath his assault, determined to finish before her body betrayed her and succumbed to his expert lovemaking. "Just...just one more...question." She squeezed her knees together in a weak attempt to stop his hand that slid from her knee closer to the aching core of her body.

She tried to recall the Barkers' journal entry in order to make some connection with Logan and Indigo Bay. "Gold. Is there reason for someone to believe gold is buried on the island?"

"Ah-ha!" His head came up so quickly Mica's heart skipped a beat. He rocked back on his heels beside her, planting his hands on his hips. His actions drew her gaze to his hips, and sent heat spiraling through her fast enough to set the bed on fire. While passion throbbed through her veins, he now seemed completely unaware of his effect on her.

"Here I thought my other fine qualities were what drew you, and all this time you're a fortune hunter." He attempted a frown as he spoke, but his dark eyes twinkled.

Though he no longer touched her, his gaze seared her body, making love to her with eyes turned dark with desire. He licked his lips as his gaze lingered on her breasts before sliding down her body to the juncture of her legs leading to her feminine core.

Mica watched his hands clench and relax on his thighs, and she marveled at his control. Why didn't he touch her? She tried to capture his gaze—to beg him with her eyes for what her body craved, but he kept his gaze averted as he spoke.

His voice, husky with need, aroused her even more. "My father told me pirates never ventured to islands this close to the mainland. Even so, when I was a boy I looked for buried treasure. Now I realize how foolish that was."

Her voice quivered in response. "Why would a boy's dream be foolish?"

"Because I realize my treasure awaited me as an adult." His gaze drifted up her body to capture hers. Finally, he reached out, his callused fingers sliding up her oversensitive skin. Instead of releasing her tension, his touch only increased the sweet agony her body experienced.

"No amount of gold or jewels can equal what I have right in front of me. There is nothing on this Earth of greater value to me than what we share." He entwined his fingers with hers to pull her into his embrace. "Now, come here. Nothing else matters except you and me."

Mica shut her mind to everything except his hot touch on her skin. As his hands tenderly cradled her body, she relished the feeling of being cherished. But being cherished didn't mean he thought her fragile, and their lovemaking swiftly escalated into a ferocious tumble. He captured her lips in a torturous kiss, appeasing some of her need, yet leaving her hungry for more.

Her nails scratched across his muscle-ridged back as she rubbed her breasts against his chest. Her nipples were tight and puckered, aching for his touch. As though he read her thoughts, he released her mouth as he laid her back on the bed, but before she could complain, he lightly nipped the tip of one breast before capturing it fully in his hot, wet mouth.

Mica cried his name out loud, enthralled with the sight and musky male scent of him, enraptured by his taste as she nibbled on his shoulder. His hot male length against her hip inflamed her senses, and she opened her legs in welcome. Skyrockets roared in her ears, and fireworks flashed behind her closed eyes as he entered her with one tumultuous plunge.

"More. Give me all of you." He rasped the urgent command even as he lifted her hips to drive deeper, plundering her very soul. Relinquishing her entire being to his safekeeping, she wrapped her legs around him, raising her hips to meet his.

"Yes!" The word ripped from him as he thrust deeper, then stopped, their bodies fused intimately together. She felt him swell and throb within her, and for the first time in her life she knew what completeness meant.

Logan didn't give her time to analyze her thoughts. The tempo his body set soon caused sweet ecstasy to spread through her like wildfire. She tightened her legs, drawing him inward, arching to meet his thrusts, willing him to take her with him over the precipice.

"Look at me!" The words hammered through her with each thrust of his hips. His face spoke of his passion. His chiseled features were covered with a fine sheen of perspiration, his black hair in disarray.

His eyes, darkened almost to black, captured her attention. In them she saw the reflection of her deepest thoughts. *I love you, Thomas Logan Rutledge.*

"Heaven help me," she moaned as he sank deep within her then stopped. The throb of his release triggered hers, sending them both spiraling through a vortex of electrifying sensation.

***

Though reluctant, Logan left Mica's room, promising to return for her later in the day. He insisted she stay in bed and rest while he saw to the final preparations for the first shipment of indigo to market.

"The auction will be held in Charleston, and we must have the crop ready. With the first of September so near, I can't leave anything to chance." He kissed her cheek and hurried off, unaware of the turmoil his words had caused.

September! She promised her father she'd go back to work after Labor Day. How could she possibly return to work when things were still so unsettled here, and especially since her heart-wrenching discovery while making love to Logan? She was in love with him!

Determined to push aside her emotions in the interest of helping Logan, Mica pulled on a wrapper and grabbed her bag from the armoire. She really wished she had more than just a few letters with which to convince him his stepbrother meant trouble.

As she pawed through her belongings, setting aside the bundle of letters, she began to doubt what had been on her mind at the time she packed. Her peasant-type cotton skirts and blouses where there, as were her silk teddy and slip, but where were her hairbrush, her bras and stockings? All that remained of her sandals was a handful of leather straps, and she couldn't find any of her cosmetics. She plopped down on the bed and stared at the strange assortment of items.

Rules—everything in life had rules, even if they weren't always understood or followed. Mica remembered Uncle Gene telling her that once. Apparently even time travel had rules, and Mica could only guess at them as she surveyed the remains of her belongings. She plucked at the ribbon tying together her aunt's letters. If there were one more mystery tied to this adventure she had created, she would go mad.

"Miss Michaela?" Mattie stuck her head through the doorway, drawing Mica's attention away from her musings.

"Good morning, Mattie. What can I do for you?"

"I was just wondering, Miss, if you would care to go to town with me and the Mister. It's time to restock the pantry, and the fish is always best if you get there early."

"I would love to come with you. Just give me a few minutes to dress." A change of scenery might be just what she needed to get her thoughts in perspective.

The morning flew by as Simon and Mattie pointed out various sites while they traveled by buggy through the small town of Cameron. Mica was amazed at what had survived through the years. Not only the Belleview Hotel, but two churches and the market area remained very close to the structures of her own era.

On the pretense of seeing if her clothes had arrived at the hotel, Mica separated from the Browns when she saw a boutique. At first she hesitated. She didn't have any money, but she decided to take a chance that some things never changed.

"Charge it?" She questioned the clerk once she had picked out a few dresses and a small valise.

"Of course. To whom shall we send the bill?"

Mica exited the shop quite pleased with herself. When she spied the Browns, she informed Simon her bag had arrived. After eating a light lunch, they stopped by the hotel before they returned to the plantation.

Logan had left her a note indicating he would be tied up the rest of the day at the processing sheds. Mica thought about walking out to see him, but concluded if he were busy, now was not the time to interrupt him. She could wait until dinner.

As she prepared for her bath, she toyed with the ribbon on the letters lying on her desk. How could she broach the subject of the information they contained? How could she express her concern for Logan without letting him know exactly where she had gotten the information?

Should she even bring up any relationship between their aunts? After all, she had already decided that in itself didn't spell danger for him.

The journal had her stymied, though. The Barkers felt certain whoever wrote it had connections with this island. Mica had begun to think it was a hoax. After all, no names were mentioned, and she felt certain many other plantations grew indigo. However, there was just enough information in what she had read and what Mr. Barker had said to give her pause.

On the positive side, however, Logan was not a wealthy

man. If he had any gold, she felt certain he would use it to help his people, not hoard it in some hiding place.

She just couldn't conceive of any way to help him. Perhaps she just needed to be here for him, to provide some kind of emotional support during his transition as rightful owner of Indigo Bay. She sighed. If Aunt Theo had only realized what sort of predicament Mica would embroil herself in, she probably would never have bequeathed her Sea Crest.

She dressed with care in the new emerald-green silk she'd purchased in town, brushing her hair into a French twist. She glanced in the mirror, pleased with her reflection. She felt rather wanton. Even when attending a country club gathering, she had never worn dresses this elegant.

Perhaps it was that she'd never wanted to appear seductive before. As she stared at her image in the mirror, she saw that her cheeks glowed, and her eyes twinkled. Already her pulse was accelerating knowing that Logan waited for her downstairs. Determined not to think beyond this night, she slid into matching slippers, leaving the room and all thoughts of the future behind.

***

Mica watched Logan's eyes widen when she entered the dining room. Her hands trembled when he offered her a glass of wine. His magnetic smile told her he appreciated her attire, yet his eyes gave no clue to his thoughts.

"You look magnificent." His whisper feathered her ear as he kissed her throat where her pulse beat a rapid cadence. He trailed a finger from her shoulder down the scooped neck of her dress, his touch causing her to shiver. "In fact, you look quite good enough to eat." His eyes smoldered, and his touch was hot and electrifying.

In that moment Mica realized that she wanted something more from Logan. While sex must surely be part of the appeal in any relationship, she couldn't bear it if all they had was a physical attraction. After all, he hadn't repeated his earlier marriage proposal, and although Mica might not want to answer such a serious question, she did need reassurance that their relationship existed beyond the bedroom.

"Do you find me sexy, Logan? Is that all we have?" Silverware clattered to china, and she heard Simon's discreet cough behind her. She clapped a hand to her mouth, embarrassment flushing her cheeks with warmth as she dropped her gaze to the floor.

"There are several meanings for the word *sexy,* but in your case, it must have to do with a woman who's outspoken in the extreme." Logan chuckled, his voice the gentle tease she had come to love.

When she raised her eyes, she found his gaze lingering on her chest where the cut of her gown revealed plenty of breast. Without taking his gaze from her, he gave Simon orders in a shaky voice.

"Simon, I believe that will be all." He sucked in a ragged breath as he removed the wine glass from her hand and gave it to the butler. Mica gave Logan her most seductive smile. "Yes, I'm sure that will be all—for the rest of the evening, in fact."

Once Mica heard the doors close behind the servant, she allowed herself to breathe again. Would she forever put her foot in her mouth, voicing things better left unsaid? She opened her mouth to apologize, but Logan put a finger to her lips to silence her.

He stood close, and she could hear his harsh breathing in the quiet of the large room. Her gaze remained locked with his, even when his finger left her lips to trace a fiery path down her chin and across her throat to her bare shoulder. She trembled beneath his touch, the heat from a single finger burning her skin while sending rapid signals skittering along her nerve endings to her heart.

"Sexy, hum?" Just the sound of the word, enunciated in his slow, husky drawl, caused erotic images of their lovemaking to flash before her eyes. "By being sexy, do you mean a woman's allure?" His finger continued its forays, pausing along its path to dip beneath the silk and brush the tip of her breast.

Her body reacted instantly, her nipple tightening and jutting against the constraints of the fabric. A now familiar ache collected at the very center of her being. She answered with a moan low in her throat.

"Michaela Marie?"

She had to struggle to remember the question. "Yes, I guess that's what I mean." She shrugged just as his finger slid beneath the shoulder of her dress, her action causing the material to slide down her arm. He kissed the exposed skin.

"Ah, then I would have to say allure is a female's scent." He brushed his nose against her as he sniffed. "She must smell of fresh air and sunshine, and taste of lemon." His tongue licked her shoulder before his hot breath dried it.

"What about her...figure?" Her voice, quaking as though his answer meant life and death, broke the spell.

Logan laughed as he caught her around the waist and twirled her in a circle. "Michaela Marie, every woman has breasts. You surely cannot think that would be more important to me than other things?" His eyes twinkled, and Mica ducked her head at the foolishness of her question.

"Well, most men don't think the way you do. What other things?"

Logan stopped dancing and took a step back as he placed his hands on her shoulders, his eyes searching her face.

"You are serious, aren't you?"

At her nod, he stepped away, breaking contact, as if touching her interrupted his train of thought. Mica knew his touch interrupted hers. He stood, legs braced and hands on hips, his expression that of someone ready to impart great knowledge.

"A woman's allure is much more than surface beauty. For example, I have never had much use for beautiful but empty-headed and giggly females who only know how to plan a party and give orders to a staff of servants. I also cannot tolerate women who would leave the rearing of their children in the hands of nannies, instead of being active in their development."

He raised a hand to silence her when she tried to interrupt. "On the other hand, I find great appeal in a woman who is intelligent and able to hold a conversation on something other than the latest fashions. She must be caring and willing to share in every aspect of my life. Above all, she must be passionate—about the land, about people, and," he arched his brows as he grinned wickedly, "about me."

Mica wondered if she measured up to his ideals. Lord knew she had searched for someone of his character. Someone who looked beyond the surface to the person within and who didn't regard one's family tree and annual income as the prerequisites for a marriage. Before she had a chance to question him further, he began to stalk her, his heels echoing on the polished hardwood floors.

He clasped his hands behind his back and lowered his brows to a fierce frown as he eyed her up and down. Mica stood her ground, hands at her side as he continued to take her measure, strolling around her in decreasing circles until he once again stood close in front of her. He crossed his arms, tapping a finger to his rigid chin.

"Do I pass inspection?" She tried for a lighthearted tone, afraid her defenses would crumble if he found her lacking.

"Perhaps," he drawled, the smile that started at his full lips reaching his eyes in an instant. "But tell me, Miss Chadwick, what you look for in a man." He postured for her, jutting out his chin and puffing up his chest as he placed his hands on his hips and turned this way and that. "Must he have bulging muscles and pockets full of money?"

Mica realized in a heartbeat he was the man she had always searched for, but could she find the right words?

"I want compassion and kindness. A commitment to principles, and the strength to stand up for them. I want someone to care for me as I am, and not try to mold me into something I'm not. I need someone who won't judge me... and find me lacking."

Logan quit posturing and entwined his fingers in hers to draw her close. With her free hand, she brushed an errant curl of black hair from his brow then slowly traced his aristocratic features.

Her voice deepened, because only her heart knew what she needed. "I need someone of average build, so I'm not overpowered. Someone with black hair and dark brown eyes that make my heart melt when he looks at me."

As her gaze captured Logan's, his eyes smoldering with tightly leashed passion, she whispered, "Above all else, he must be able to love me with all the exuberance of youth, but with the patience and experience that comes with age."

Logan gathered her in his embrace, kissing her with an exotic tenderness. She pulled back just enough to whisper against his lips. "Make love to me, Logan...only to me. Always me."

She could hold the future at bay just a little while longer, because at that moment she couldn't live without Logan's love. In fact, she wondered how she had managed to live until now without knowing of his existence. She succumbed to his drugging kiss because deep down inside her it felt right. Not because there was any sane reason for it, and not because life or death might depend on it. She accepted his love and returned it twofold because...just because.

Their tongues danced, mating in a ritual that transcended all time barriers, and she accepted the fact that their spirits belonged together, despite the difference in their times.

"Marry me. Right now—tonight." His words were punctuated with hard, hot kisses on her neck, and Mica thought she would die from the pleasure. Until his words penetrated.

"Oh, Logan." Her heart, still fragile with awakening love, shattered.

"Mister Logan! Mister Logan!" She was saved from having to answer when a small boy burst into the room with Simon close behind. Logan released Mica and turned, almost falling as the youngster catapulted against his legs, grabbing hold for dear life.

"I am sorry, sir," Simon said, standing red-faced at the door, apparently distraught for allowing a small child to get past him. "I tried to stop him, but he got by me."

"It's all right, Simon," Logan said as he knelt beside the boy.

Mica could see the child's shoulders shake as he gasped for breath, and large tears streaked down his cheeks. Wide, frightened eyes peered starkly white from his small, black face.

"What is it, Robby?"

"Fire! There be a fire in the sheds. Paw sent me to fetch you." The boy's arms waved in wild circles, smearing Logan's white shirt with soot.

Logan stood and raced to the door. "Simon, sound the alarm. We'll need every available body. Robby, you did well. Stay here at the house and take care of Miss Chadwick."

Mica wasn't about to be left behind. "I'm coming with you." She gathered her full skirts and ran out into the hall just as Logan reached the front door. He turned, piercing her with a gaze so intense it stopped her.

"Stay in the house, Michaela. You'll only be in the way, and I don't have time to worry about you."

Her mouth dropped open at his comment, but he was gone before her numb mind could form a reply. So much for letting her stand by his side. Fuming, she turned on her heel and ran up the stairs to her room.

By the time she changed and arrived at the scene, fire had consumed the better part of the processing shed. She had dressed in a simple skirt and top, minus her petticoats and shoes to make it easier to maneuver. She quickly joined the bucket brigade, though she doubted their paltry efforts could salvage anything.

As she grabbed bucket after bucket of water, passing it to the next in line, hot sparks singed her arms and clothes. She didn't stop or slow her efforts. The men who were closest to the blaze used shovels and hoes, even blankets, in an attempt to smother the flames.

Her gaze flew across the open area, frantically searching for Logan. Her heart pounded painfully when she finally spotted him shouting orders from the very edge of the fire. *God, please look out for him. He's too close.* She saw his frantic wave towards the west side, and realized his intent.

"Over there," she yelled over the crackling of the flames. Nudging those next to her, she grabbed two buckets and raced for the side as yet untouched by the rapidly spreading blaze. They had to keep the fire contained to just one building. The line soon shifted, and water poured against the remainder of the building, preventing the flames from leaping across the narrow opening and catching another building on fire.

Unmindful of the heat, unaware of the regard of those around her, Mica hefted gallons of water. Each time she released one container, another was thrust into her aching hands. Her shoulders bowed, her eyes and throat burned from smoke, but she refused to give up or take a break. She lost track of time, knowing only that she had to help Logan save what they could.

"Ouch!" She shook her hand as the rough handle of yet another bucket rubbed her raw blisters. She bent and ripped a piece from the bottom of her skirt to wrap around her hand, then grabbed the bucket to pass it on.

She saw Logan disappear around the corner of the building. Although she worried about his safety, her mind was numbed to all thought. Her arms swayed to the rhythm established by the constant forward movement of the water buckets.

She reached back for the next bucket, only to have her hand clasped by the person behind her. She lifted tired eyes to find kind black ones staring back at her. A white grin flashed against a soot-covered face.

"You did good, Missy." The older, stooped-shouldered man gave her hand a gentle squeeze.

"Is it out? Are we done?" Without waiting for a response, Mica collapsed to the ground. Her tattered skirt swirled around her. Her blouse, black with soot and beyond repair, clung damply to her sweaty body. She crossed her legs beneath her, resting her elbows on her knees as she dropped her head into her hands. Her arms felt as though someone had tried to jerk them out of the sockets. Never had she felt so drained.

"Michaela!" She heard Logan shout her name and managed to raise her head as he streaked across the yard towards her. He was as black as the rest of them, but the minute he dropped to his knees in front of her she could see the anger in his eyes.

"What the hell are you doing out here?" he shouted at her.

It wasn't a question, but Mica couldn't summon the energy

to argue with him. Instead, she reached out to touch his bare shoulder, thankful to see him unhurt.

"Where's your shirt?" Somewhere in her hazy brain she recalled how handsome he had looked in the pristine shirt, black jacket and trousers. Now he knelt before her bare-chested.

"It caught fire." He shrugged off her concern, catching her hand in his before she had time to hide it beneath her skirts.

"What's this?" His fingers plucked at the makeshift bandage before his gaze again seared her, his brows pulled together in a frown. Before she could defend herself, he pulled her to her feet. "Can you walk?" At her nod, he tugged her towards the house.

Mica couldn't determine whether he was concerned for her safety or just plain angry because she had disregarded his orders. He didn't give her a chance to explain, and he didn't speak to her. He just kept a death grip on her wrist, walking fast enough that she had to trot to keep up.

Just as they reached the drive, Logan stopped abruptly, and she slammed into his back. He still didn't look at her, but instead gave orders to his foreman.

"Ezra, post some men to keep watch and find out if anyone saw anything. This fire, just like the first one, was deliberately set."

Mica sucked in her breath at his words.

"Mister Logan, I knows who done it," Robby said.

Mica had seen him running down the drive when his father, Ezra, and the others approached. He now pulled on Logan's pant leg to gain his attention.

"Robby, boy, not now," Ezra quietly reprimanded his son.

"But, Paw, you seen 'em, too." Robby wouldn't be put off, and Logan finally released Mica to squat down in front of the youngster.

"All right, Robby. Tell me who you saw."

"Ghosts." With a vigorous nod of his head, Robby solemnly pronounced the word.

"Robert Ezra, you listen here. There be no such thing."

Ezra caught the child by the shoulder and spun him around.

Mica touched Robby's curly head and gave him a weak smile to reassure him. But his next words caused her to jerk back in dismay.

"But I seen 'em! Big white creatures, hauntin' and floatin' all around, with huge black holes for eyes and fire 'stead of arms." The small boy gestured wildly, his eyes wide with the horror of what he had witnessed.

Logan watched Michaela race for the house. Why hadn't she stayed there in the first place? He would no doubt find his hair gray beneath the soot. She had scared him half to death when he looked up to find her fighting his fire.

Even though she had disobeyed him, he had found it hard to maintain his anger in the wake of teary, sky-blue eyes peering at him from a soot-streaked face. He sighed, anxious to reach the house and confirm she hadn't been seriously injured. At the same time, he wanted information.

"Ezra?"

"Some folks says they seen *somethin'*, but I don't believe in no ghosts, Mister Logan." His foreman firmly shook his head.

"Then who?" Logan scanned the area, but the dark of night obscured all signs. The light from the fire no longer illuminated the grisly scene. *Why?*

He had no answers, but he knew the people who worked for him would do anything to keep Indigo Bay alive. They had proven that with their efforts tonight. Too tired and too upset over Michaela's actions to worry about what he couldn't change, Logan shook his head in frustration.

"Keep an eye out," Logan ordered. At his foreman's nod, he turned towards the house.

Once he had washed off some of the soot and donned a clean shirt, he searched for Michaela. He found her in the downstairs study, pacing between the desk and bookshelves. She had washed and changed. Her skirts swirled as she moved, and her dainty feet padded soundlessly across the carpet.

God, if anything had happened to her—

His heart swelled with pride at the way she had pitched in

to help, mindless of the danger to herself. Even so, his anger rose right along with his love.

"Look at you. Don't you realize you could have been hurt out there?" He heard the anger in his voice but couldn't help it. Horrid scenes flashed across his mind, all of them ending with her hurt in some terrifying way he could not stop. He grabbed her hands to still her movements, his eyes tracing the red spots dotting her arms where sparks had singed her fair skin. "I told you to stay in the house."

"I'm perfectly capable of helping."

From the icy tone of her voice, he realized she had misinterpreted his reasons for saying what he had. He lifted her injured hand, turning it over to inspect the blisters. She had been hurt fighting his fire and trying to help save his crop. He raised her hand to his lips, tenderly kissing the raw flesh. She cared so much, had been willing to sacrifice as much as he.

He watched her stormy gaze as she struggled to control her anger at his careless words. His throat constricted, and his eyes hazed with unshed tears, for at that moment Logan loved her more than life itself.

He pulled her roughly into his embrace, burying his face in her hair. The faint scent of lemons wafted even over the stench of smoke. Sweet, just like the woman who brought such joy to his life and helped him forget the difficulties.

"My dear, adorable, Michaela Marie. Never believe I doubt your capabilities." He pushed her to arm's length, hands on her shoulders as he gazed into her sea mist eyes. "Seeing you so close to the blaze frightened the hell out of me. Can you understand how devastated I would be if anything happened to you?"

His hands shook with the force of overwhelming emotion. He watched her eyes cloud with tears. She tucked a strand of hair behind her ear, refusing to meet his gaze. He caught her hand and kissed the injured palm.

She pulled away from his embrace, her shaking hands shuffling papers needlessly on the desk. Logan realized something was amiss, but he couldn't put his finger on the source of her disquiet.

"Michaela, what is it?"

"I...I may know who started your fire." Her words were muffled, her head turned away from him.

"What?" He couldn't believe what he heard. Surely she didn't have anything to do with this. She had appeared in his life just before the first fire, not long after he had come home to Indigo Bay. No, he refused to believe she could—

"I said—" she repeated.

"I heard what you said," he shouted. She winced as though he had struck her, and guilt lowered his voice. "What do you know?"

She turned then to face him, her cheeks streaked with tears, her eyes betraying the same wretchedness he felt. How could something so wonderful dissolve right before his eyes? Why did his gut twist as though she drove a knife through him? Surely whatever she had to say could not kill their love.

"There's a journal. I don't know whom it belongs to," she began. "I haven't even read it all, but clear reference was made to 'ghosts haunting the land and fire destroying all he holds dear.'"

She looked at him, pleading with her eyes, but for what? Logan couldn't comprehend the meaning of her words.

"Where is this book? If you don't know who owns it, how do you know the writer means to destroy me?" Her story was almost as preposterous as Robby's ghosts, but something in her voice told him she wasn't weaving a fanciful tale.

"Would you recognize Neil's handwriting if you saw it?"

"Damn it, Michaela, why do you keep bringing him up? Leave him out of it. You don't know anything about Neil, so how can you judge him capable of doing something like this?" Logan lashed out, knowing his words stung with the force of a whip, but he couldn't retract them.

He knew Neil was still upset over his father's will and realized the man he had always called Brother harbored ill feelings. Regardless of the arguments they had, Logan refused to believe Neil capable of burning Indigo Bay to the ground just to spite him.

"I can prove it." Mica said at his disbelieving look. "I'm sorry, but I can." She turned towards the door, tears obscuring her vision as she almost tripped over the leg of a nearby chair. *God, it hurts so much.* She hadn't known it would be this hard.

She had only wanted to warn him. She looked back. He stood there, hands clenched and shoulders rigid, his eyes telling her he refused to believe her.

Or perhaps he believed that she had something to do with the fires. Her heart screamed—*No, don't destroy our love by thinking that.*

"I'm so sorry, Logan." She sobbed, her words echoing across the chasm that had opened between them. "I do love you." She didn't know if her whisper reached him, because she turned and fled.

It had been useless to think she could help. Instead of retrieving the journal to show Logan, she would just lock herself on her own side and never bother him again.

"Michaela, wait. I'm sorry." His voice reached her down the length of the hall as she climbed the stairs.

"Oh, God, why did you make me fall in love with him?" Another sob caught in her throat as she raced to the extraordinary door that would provide her safety.

Tears spilled down her cheeks and obscured her vision as she tried to fit the key into the lock and remove herself from Indigo Bay. She swiped at her eyes with one hand, willing the other to quit trembling so she could make her escape. She could hear his boots on the stairs, each step pounding louder than her heart.

"Oh, no! Please let me be gone before he gets here." Mica couldn't bear the thought of having to tell him good-bye. Coward though that made her, she knew she couldn't face him and say the words. She turned her head and glanced down the hall as the lock gave beneath the flick of her wrist. She could see his shadow grow as he topped the stairs. Any second he would see her.

The door swung open, but she couldn't get the key out of the lock.

"Michaela? What are you doing? Don't go through there!" The panic in Logan's voice and his heavy footsteps as he sped towards her spurred her into action.

She jerked the key out just as Logan caught her wrist. As she lurched through the doorway, her forward motion propelled both of them over the threshold.

"Damn it to hell, woman! This section isn't..." His voice ended in a strangled whisper as she watched him gaze around, "...finished."

Mica felt the familiar tingle shoot up her arm as Logan released her wrist. In the dim light of the hallway he appeared almost transparent.

"Oh, Logan, you can't be here. It's just not possible." Mica had deduced some rules about the passage through time, because things had a habit of disappearing when she went through the door. And when she brought his flower back to the present, it had turned to dust.

"I can't be here?" His voice sounded incredulous. "What the hell are you talking about? Where is here? This section of the manor hasn't even been built."

Mica saw his eyes flicker about, trying to absorb what he saw, and she didn't know how to explain.

"What's going on out here? Who's making all the noise?" Mrs. Barker stepped into the hall, dressed in a pink ruffled nightcap and a pair of men's striped pajamas. Mica groaned as she watched the woman's husband pop his bald head out by her side, curiosity clearly written across his sleepy face.

"Mrs. Barker, there's nothing to worry about."

"Who the hell is that?" Logan's voice boomed in the silence, and Mica knew he couldn't possibly understand what was happening.

"Please, just be quiet a minute, and I'll explain."

"I most certainly will not be quiet, young lady." Mrs. Barker's voice rose an octave. "You have no right to talk to me like that considering the amount we pay for these rooms."

Mica glanced from Logan to Mrs. Barker in astonishment. "I wasn't speaking to you, I—"

"Squawk—ERK, ER-er-erK!"

Mica jumped a foot at the sound. Shock waves ricocheted through her body, and she glanced down to see Logan's hand clasping her elbow.

"What in the name of Satan is that?" Logan gasped.

Mica thought hysterically that she couldn't remember ever hearing him swear quite so much as he had in just the last few minutes. Her world was falling apart, and all she could think of was Logan's sweet nature turning irreverent because of her. She giggled, glancing helplessly from the Barkers back to Logan, wondering why Mrs. Barker didn't comment on his appearance at her side.

"Michaela, answer me." Logan's stress-filled voice reached her.

She tried to formulate a reply, but Mrs. Barker swept around the corridor and pounded on Professor Bigley's door, demanding he silence his infernal alarm. Before the woman could beat the door down, the professor appeared in a knee-length nightshirt, his gray hair standing on end.

Demonic bleeps, which escalated into a continuous, ear-piercing screech, emanated from the silver box he clasped to his chest.

The incredible noise bounced against the shadowed hallway walls. As everyone shouted at once, their voices covered Mica's strangled whisper.

"Oh dear God, the ghost machine."

Nine

"This is it! Pictures—I'll finally have pictures!" Professor Bigley shouted as he fumbled with a switch on the side of the box.

Mica watched in horrified silence as he shuffled towards her, his ghost detector positioned in front of him. Buttons flashed and alarms blared over the others' yelling.

Her arm tingled, and she knew without looking that Logan still clutched her elbow. For some inexplicable reason, she felt the need to protect him. She stepped in front of him, hoping to block the professor's view.

"Turn that damned thing off!" Mrs. Barker barreled down the hall after the professor, and Mica saw her chance to get Logan away.

She turned her head to whisper, "Stay behind me, no matter what happens." Before she could move, he quickly stepped in front of her.

"It's my responsibility to protect you." He reached out to push her behind him, but all Mica felt was the continuous tingle.

"No!" She yelled to be heard above the clamor. Stepping back in front of Logan just as the flash of a camera momentarily blurred her vision.

"This is no time to go chauvinistic on me, Logan. Just stay close," she pleaded as she scooted along the wall, moving as quickly as she dared.

She flipped the first switch she could reach on the box as she came abreast of the professor. The sudden silence echoed as loudly as the noise had.

"Thank you so much, Professor," she said. "I'm sure you

have what you need now that you've interrupted everyone's sleep." She shouldn't really blame him, but at the moment, she needed a diversion.

"But," the professor stammered.

"Please, everyone, go back to bed. Hopefully there won't be any more disturbances tonight." Mica had reached the top of the stairs and started down, careful to keep herself between the patrons and Logan. She collided with Anna, who apparently had heard the commotion from her room below.

"Get everyone back to their rooms and soothe any ruffled feathers, please," she pleaded with the inn's manager, but she didn't wait to see if her instructions were carried out.

She had to get Logan out of sight, because she could sense the tension building in him. It would be difficult to explain his presence to the other guests if he decided to react to his strange circumstances.

She hurried down the short corridor to her apartment door before she realized she had no keys. "Damn!" She pivoted, raced back to the registration table and yanked the extra set out of a drawer.

Logan followed her into the apartment, and she slammed the door behind them. Only then did she dare breathe easy. She slumped against the door, hanging her head in resignation.

"Would you care to tell me what the hell just happened?" A see-through Logan stood before her, hands braced on hips. A dark scowl marred his handsome features.

"I don't know." She shook her head in wonder, thinking the light was playing tricks on her, because he looked like a faded out photograph. Even so, she couldn't believe he stood there in her twenty-first century apartment.

"What do you mean, you don't know? You walk through a door to a section of Indigo Bay which doesn't exist, talk to people I have never seen before in my life, and move through this house as though you've lived here all your life." He threw up his hands in despair and began pacing.

"Oh, I thought you meant about the professor," Mica hedged, trying to figure a way to explain their circumstances.

Logan stopped pacing to turn in a circle, staring around

the apartment. In slow motion, he moved from the couch to the dinette table, over to the TV and then to her desk, where yesterday's newspaper lay.

She rushed over to grab it, but the expression on his face told her it was too late.

"That year can't be real, can it?" He croaked as his head swiveled wildly around.

Mica empathized with him. She hadn't been ready for the difference in time when she first entered his world. She reached out to touch him, wanting to reassure him. Her hand passed right through his shoulder.

"Oh, dear God!" Her hand flew to her mouth.

Logan turned back at the agony in her voice. When he reached out, Mica could feel the tingles of his touch, but couldn't feel his warmth. Rather than become angry, he tried again and again to touch her, but she could tell by his expression he felt nothing.

"Michaela?" That single word echoed all his frustration and fear.

She took a deep breath to calm herself before she blurted out the truth of their circumstances. "The door—the one we came through—is somehow a time passage. The year on the newspaper is correct, and this is Sea Crest." She gestured to encompass the inn.

"The door leads from Indigo Bay?" His voice doubted her words even as his eyes still surveyed the room.

"Yes, well, Sea Crest *is* Indigo Bay. A descendant so to speak."

"This—this is what's left of my plantation? Who are those mad people above stairs? Surely not descendants of mine?"

Mica almost giggled at his incredulous tone. "No. Actually, this building is a bed and breakfast—an inn where people come to stay on vacation."

She knew this conversation didn't make sense. Of course, nothing about her relationship with Logan had made sense from the beginning, but why was he taking this so well?

Logan plopped onto the couch, or rather seemed to be absorbed by the couch. When he sat, the patterns shimmered through his shirt, and it became harder to see him. Mica panicked, wondering if the rules she had only guessed at could somehow make him disappear at this end of the time spectrum.

"I am normally a logical man, as any lawyer should be, but this is all beyond me." Logan shook his head in disbelief. "You say you live in the future, and you traveled back to the year 1850, to Indigo Bay, by going through that door? Why did you lie about who you were?"

His accusation stung, and Mica felt the need to justify herself. "I never actually lied. I am from Sea Crest, and that's all you ever asked me. Remember when I asked you about your Aunt Margaret and whether she knew anyone named Theodora?" At his nod, she continued. "My great-great-aunt was Theodora Josephine Ashley. She has letters written by someone named Maggie—letters that identify Indigo Bay, you, and Neil.

"On her deathbed, my aunt told me to help *Thomas,* and when she died, she bequeathed me Sea Crest," Mica continued before he could respond. "I didn't realize that you were that person until I heard you called Thomas."

Instead of ranting or raving, or refusing to believe her, Logan listened without comment to her faltering explanation. She moved to the French doors that led to the garden. How had her aunt expected her to help him?

She spotted the Cupid statue, flooded with moonlight, and recalled her aunt's comments about a romantic man in Mica's life. Perhaps her aunt and her friend, Maggie, had known all along that she and Logan would fall in love if they met. Perhaps that had been the reason for her bequest—not for Mica to help, but to have a chance at romance. But how could she have known? There was no indication in the letters that she'd actually met Logan.

She turned back to face him. She'd known from the start that she played a dangerous game. Not knowing the rules had proved disastrous. "I didn't understand what my aunt meant about helping you until it was too late."

He came to stand in front of her, reaching out before he remembered his transparent state. His hands dropped uselessly to his sides. "Too late for what, Michaela?"

She sobbed into her hands, aching for his touch. "It was too late, because I had already fallen in love with you."

"As I have with you, sweet one."

She gasped at his pronouncement, then sobbed all the harder, cursing the fates for her misfortune.

"We have really entangled ourselves, haven't we?" His voice faded, and when Mica glanced up, she found he had moved to the windows. "You picked a fine time to declare your affections. All I want is to drag you off to the closest bed and make passionate, consuming love to you, and I'm unable to even touch you." He gave a snort of disgust as he held his hands up where the light appeared to filter through them.

He shook his head in disbelief before continuing. "For the moment, I'll assume what you say is true. How is it possible for *you* to travel back in time where I can touch you and make love to you, but I cannot do the same? I'm like a ghost."

"Dear Lord." Mica's hands fell away from her face as understanding dawned. The professor's machine really did work. A horrid thought struck her. The machine had taken pictures—photos of Logan and her after they came through the door. Now she understood why she had felt the need to protect him when they had been in the hallway.

"Make me understand, Michaela," he pleaded, and her heart ached for his situation.

Since little could be done about the professor and his pictures, she concentrated on Logan. Actually, he was handling this very well considering his circumstances. How much could she tell him, however, without further disrupting the flow of history?

"I'll try to explain what I've learned about the rules involved in traveling through time. If a present-day object exists in some form in 1850, it can go through the passage. If not, it disappears." She looked around the room for something to prove her theories. "The letters from your aunt, for example."

"And where are these letters?" He arched a brow in disbelief.

Mica groaned. “They’re still in my room at Indigo Bay.”

“What about me? Why did I change? Don’t men exist in your time?”

Mica ignored his sarcasm. “I haven’t quite figured out your end of it. Perhaps since the future hasn’t happened yet for you, you can’t visit it. Whereas the past has happened, and therefore it’s possible for me to go back.” She saw by his expression he still questioned her explanation.

“Look, I’ve found out some things don’t travel well. For example, my silk and cotton clothes remain the same, but zippers and plastic buttons just evaporate. Probably because they haven’t been invented yet.”

His inquisitive gaze swept her figure. “That’s why you were dressed so strangely at times.”

“Yes. All I know is I’d better not wear polyester.”

He stepped away from the window and became a little more visible without the strong light shining through him. As he moved closer, Mica could feel the energy emitting from his body, the body she longed to touch and caress once more. His eyes deepened to a dark brown.

“And what would become of this...this Polly Ester?” He spoke the word as though it were a name.

Captured by his gaze, and wrapped in the electrifying aura that bound their spirits if not their bodies, Mica stammered, “It’s a fabric, and it would ... disappear.”

He grinned at her. “Then I would definitely like to see you in polyester.” As quickly as his smile formed, a frown replaced it. He took the final step toward her so their chests touched and lifted his arms to wrap around her.

“Can you feel me, Michaela? As we stand here touching, and yet not touching, do you have any idea how much I want to make love to you? Can you understand how desperately I want to claim you for my own, regardless of all you have said?”

Mica felt the heat and vibrations of his body even if she couldn’t see him very well, and she craved his hard, solid presence. Unable to voice her heartbreak, she shook her head in denial.

Logan's arms dropped back to his sides as he sighed. He glanced once more around her apartment, then walked toward the door.

"I have no purpose here. I have no existence. I must go back to my people, to my own time." He turned to her, his glorious brown eyes full of misery which reflected her own.

"I love you, Thomas Logan Rutledge," she whispered on a sob.

His shoulders lost some of their rigidity as his gaze caressed her. "I know," he answered quietly, but remained at the door, waiting.

"I'll take you home," she sighed in resignation. Grabbing the key, Mica prayed her guests were once again safely tucked away in their beds.

This time when they reached the second floor, Mica turned to walk down the hall farthest away from the professor's door. She motioned for Logan to move in silence before she realized he couldn't make any noise. Her heart beat double-time, scared that if the machine was on, the alarm would start any instant.

"Damn it to hell!" She had reached up to insert the key only to find someone had jimmied the lock. Rough grooves dug into the wood around the doorknob, and the flat metal plate on the doorframe had been bent. The key wouldn't turn in the lock.

"It won't work," she whispered, frantic that someone would discover them. Whoever had tried to open the door might still be awake and watchful. She threw a furtive glance over her shoulder, imagining the Barkers with ears up against their door, ready to pounce at the slightest noise.

"Here, let me try." Logan reached around her to grab the key only to have his hand pass through the metal. She could see the panic in his eyes this time. "Do something. I don't exist here."

"I can't." Her voice broke, her nerves raw from all she had been through. In the distance, she heard a soft bleep-bleep-bleep and realized they didn't have time to stand in the hallway and argue.

"Come back to the apartment. I'll have to call a locksmith."

Since she couldn't touch him to move him away from the door, she made shooing motions with her hands.

Immediately upon entering her apartment, Mica raced for the phone book. Her hands shook as she thumbed through the Yellow Pages, praying a locksmith lived in Cameron. The only number listed rewarded her with an answering machine. The voice on the message assured her he would get back to her as soon as possible. Mica practically shouted her name, number and address into the receiver, never thinking how odd her actions were until she hung up and turned to face Logan.

His expression was one of disbelief. "What is that contraption?"

"A telephone." She glanced from the phone back to him. All the marvelous inventions of his future couldn't take him back to his own time. She sighed. "It won't be invented for another twenty-five years or so."

"Telephone." He sampled the sound of the word. "If the telegraph means written words over a distance, then telephone—*phone* coming from the Latin for sound—could mean sound over a distance."

He raised both eyebrows in surprise. "Do you mean it's possible to send your voice over a wire, like the telegraph, and someone hears it at another place and time?"

"In another place, yes, but not another time." *Not unless you count Pacific Time,* Mica thought, but decided not to try to explain that to him.

Logan spun in a circle. "This is incredible. You are living in an age of wonder. What other machines have been invented? Tell me what will become of my plantation." His face showed a sense of awe, as though she were a fortuneteller.

Mica knew she must be cautious. "How much should I tell you, and how much do you really want to know?"

If it were possible for a ghost to turn pale, Logan did. Barely above a whisper, his voice frightened her with its intensity. "You know when I die?"

"No, I don't know that. It's just that you're talking about more than one hundred years of history. Suppose I tell you something I shouldn't, and when you return to your time, you inexplicably change history? What do you think might happen?"

As if to emphasize her dire prediction, the clock on the wall chimed—four dainty tinkles that sounded more like a death knell. She shifted her eyes to the clock, unable to meet Logan's direct gaze.

"Michaela, talk to me." His insistent voice caused Mica to glance over to find him sprawled on the couch as though he belonged there. He was taking this entirely too well.

"How can you just sit there as though nothing is wrong?" she questioned, holding her stomach against the panic she felt.

"I long ago concluded there are certain things over which I have no control. In such cases, it is better to adapt until a solution presents itself. Is there something else I can do about my predicament before your voice person answers your shouted message?" His voice sounded concerned but not desperate as he glanced at the phone. "He will somehow contrive to answer you, won't he? Once the operator relays your message?"

Mica refused to explain answering machines and the instantaneous method in which telephones operated. She was a lawyer, not a technological wizard. "Yes, he'll return my call." Defeated for the moment, she slumped into a chair opposite him.

"I'll tell you something of my life and the twenty-first century, but I *will not* explain anything remotely close to your time in history, okay?" She had to make sure he understood.

At his nod, she commenced with a fascinating overview of the time in which she lived. For two hours she talked, and Logan listened avidly, only interrupting for details on inventions and other technology. She spoke of world trade, automobiles and airplanes. Fast food restaurants and inventions such as microwaves and computers. She showed him how the TV worked, but oddly enough he seemed more interested in the stock market concept.

Mica knew there were numerous things she could share with him, but it was difficult. She was so used to the conveniences in her life, they didn't seem that awesome to her. Finally, she quit talking and leaned back in her chair.

She refrained from even hinting at the devastation of the War Between the States, Lincoln's assassination, or what would eventually happen to his precious Indigo Bay.

"What role do you play in this incredible, fast-paced world of yours?" Logan questioned when she paused for breath. "Do you manage this inn you call Sea Crest?"

"Actually, no. Aunt Theo bequeathed Sea Crest to me, but I only came here for a vacation. I'm a member of a law firm in Charleston with my father and my uncle."

"You're a secretary for your father?"

"No, I'm a lawyer."

Logan shot upright from the couch to stand over her, hands on hips. "Women do not pursue careers, especially not a career in law," he stated emphatically.

She started to protest, but he held up a hand. For the moment, she decided to allow his nineteenth century chauvinistic ego to spout off.

"Judith Cavanaugh enjoys the latest inventions and often has gatherings at her home. She invites scientists and inventors to expound upon their work in front of her friends. That does not make *her* a scientist." He paced around the room as he instructed her, waving his index finger in the air to punctuate his remarks. Mica noticed that even in his outrage his body still had little more substance than a shadow.

Mica couldn't keep quiet. "This is too much. We're talking about more than one hundred fifty years from your time!"

"Nevertheless," Logan continued, "principles regarding women are unbendable. Elizabeth loves to grow things. She and John have the largest hothouse in Cameron. She often supplies her friends with flowers for winter balls when there is no other way to get the variety." He spun around to pierce her with his gaze. "That in no way makes her a tradesman." He said the word with such a condescending air, Mica refrained from correcting him by saying *tradeswoman.*

"In other words, if I work at a law firm, you think I can only be a secretary?"

"If you are to convince me you have an occupation in this

time, then yes. A secretary would be, if not believable, at least more plausible than being a lawyer. How could your father allow you to pursue such an *unsafe* profession?"

Logan appeared adamant about this, and Mica wondered if his thinking had more to do with the attitudes of his day than he was letting on. "I thought you were more progressive than that, Logan," she said.

Her comment seemed to surprise him and he looked chagrin. "I will admit I admire your choice of careers and your desire to help the downtrodden, but surely you don't want to associate with the dredges of society?"

Mica frowned. There were definitely things she would change when she returned to Indigo Bay, and Logan's attitude was just a start. As quickly as the thought came, her anger deflated, knowing their love could never be untangled. It wasn't just a difference in attitude.

Logan must have sensed her inner struggle, because his voice calmed as he said, "Michaela Marie, you should not *have* to work. You should be taken care of, pampered, given your heart's desire."

"You don't really believe me, do you?"

"I believe you are the most desirable woman I know, and the most beautiful. I believe the mystery surrounding you is part of your appeal, but I doubt I would desire you less if I knew every detail of your past."

It was probably fortunate the phone rang at that time, startling Logan and giving Mica time to collect her thoughts.

"Mr. Whitney? Yes," Mica glanced at the clock. "I didn't realize you worked so early. No, it's an inside door, but it must be repaired immediately. Fine, I'll meet you at the front door." She turned to give Logan the news, but found his gaze intent on the phone that sat on the table.

"Amazing. You talked into that...telephone, and the locksmith will come and do as you request?"

"Well, he'll come, anyway, in just a few minutes. He was on the way to work when he got my message, so will stop here first. We'll have to keep our fingers crossed that he can do what needs to be done."

"Keep our fingers crossed?"

"Just an expression. Look, I'm going to make some coffee." She glanced his way while heading for the kitchen, but then stopped and stared. The first pale light of morning streamed through the French doors, and for a moment she couldn't see him at all.

"Logan?" His name caught in her throat as she watched the shimmering light particles move to the side of the doorway.

Even with the wall behind him, his shape was less defined and much more transparent than it had been earlier. She had no trouble reading the depth of anguish on his face. Panic squeezed her heart that they may not have enough time to return him before he became only a memory.

He turned to the light for an instant, then back towards her. "Michaela, I must go...soon. I want to feel the wind in my face and the rich earth sifting through my fingers." He held out his hands, pleading with her to help him.

"I know." At that moment, the outside entrance buzzer sounded, and Mica silently said thanks that the locksmith must have been close by, perhaps answering her call from a cell phone. "Please, stay here. I can't take a chance the professor's alarm will sound again." She paused with her hand on the knob. "I'll be back as soon as I can."

She couldn't say that perhaps the door couldn't be fixed and he'd be stuck on this side—the side where she was alive but he couldn't exist.

Luckily, Anna hadn't awakened with the buzzer. Mica quietly let the repairman in and guided him upstairs.

"If you could work quietly since it's still so early, I would appreciate it. We have guests, you know."

The locksmith nodded his gray head in agreement as he knelt to examine the lock. "It doesn't appear to have damaged the lock itself. Someone mostly dug at the surrounding area a bit."

"Can it be fixed, exactly as it was before?" Mica's nails dug grooves into her palms as she waited his answer.

"Why *exactly as it was?"*

"Well, because it has to be the same...to..." What? To allow her to use a key that opens a door to the past? She remembered what Anna had told her. "Everything is of the Georgian period. It must be the same to keep the symmetrical appearance of the house."

"That's what your Aunt said when she had the same problem some forty years ago." He shook his head and turned back to the door, digging into his toolbox. "Must be where all the family skeletons are kept." He chuckled to himself as though he had made a great joke.

Mica gaped at the back of his head, unable to form any kind of reply at all. Aunt Theo had known forty years ago?

"I see the key is missing now, too, just like back then. Don't see why a door needs fixed when there's no key, but I suppose you know the answer to that." Without waiting for a reply, he concentrated on his work. "I don't need nobody looking over my shoulder when I work, Miss, so I'll just knock on your door when I'm done."

Mica returned to her apartment, sending up a silent prayer that the locksmith could repair the damage before it was too late. She entered quietly to find Logan staring out the window, unaware of her return. She had done what she could. Now all they could do was wait. She slipped into her room, grabbed some clean clothes and started a shower.

"How novel. I thought we had progressed as far as possible with indoor plumbing." Logan commented from close by.

Mica squawked at the sound of his voice. "I swear you'll be the death of me," she commented, sticking her shampooed head around the edge of the shower curtain.

Logan stood, arms crossed and leaning against the doorframe, looking terribly masculine and out of place in her aunt's dainty bathroom, even in his current indistinct form. His heated gaze steamed the tepid water that ran down her back, causing her temperature to rise.

She knew he couldn't see through the opaque curtain, but she still felt his energy caress her slick skin. Knowing there was nothing she could do about the sensations which coursed through her body—at least not until they were back at Indigo Bay—she jerked the curtain closed and rinsed her hair.

"I'd offer to share my shower, but in your condition I don't think it would do any good."

"I'm afraid I have more than one condition which requires attention, but it will have to wait until your telephone man has fixed the lock." His voice, clearly frustrated, still carried enough sexual innuendo to make her shiver with anticipation.

Mica's thoughts ran along similar lines, so she could understand his frustration. She changed the subject. "He's not a telephone man, he's a repairman," she said as she pulled her wrapper on behind the curtain then stepped out of the tub.

"He talked through the telephone."

"Everyone does that." She shook out her hair and stood before the mirror to brush it, looking for Logan's shadowy reflection in the glass.

"Just like everyone drives these automobiles and airplanes you spoke of?"

"Automobiles, yes, but not airplanes."

"Why not?" His brow lifted in question. Before Mica could formulate a reply, the doorbell rang.

"Good, he's done." She hurried past Logan. While his ghost-like existence meant she couldn't touch him, she still felt his presence as she moved to the door.

"Could you fix it?" she asked even as she swung the door open. Her shoulders sagged when she saw who stood on the other side, and she tried to slam the door shut. But it bounced back open.

"What are you doing here, Richard?" Her voice a monotone, she realized she had overcome all her feelings for the man except anger.

"Why, I've come to see you, darling." Richard moved quickly into the apartment before Mica could again slam the door in his face. He wrapped his arms around her as though happy to see her, which Mica knew was not the case. There could be only one reason he would travel to Sea Crest, which he confirmed the next instant.

"You closed our accounts, Michaela. That wasn't very nice."

She wiggled out of his embrace only to turn straight into

Logan. The amazement on his face registered as quickly as her fear of Richard's discovering him there. Richard appeared unconcerned, as though he couldn't even see him. Mica tilted her head to the side, considering that possibility.

"Say something," she whispered to Logan.

"Who the hell is that?" he snarled as Richard reached for her again. She spun around and sidestepped, searching Richard's face for any sign that he'd heard Logan. All she saw was anger at her evasiveness.

"Where'd you put the money?" Richard grabbed her arm and squeezed, but she stood firm, a smile lifting the corners of her mouth.

"He can't see you," she said over her shoulder to Logan.

"Who can't see me? The banker?" Richard shook her, his tone belligerent.

Mica clinched her teeth, her mind reliving all the horror of their last year of marriage.

Logan growled, "Whether he can see me or not, if he doesn't let you go this instant, I'll find a way to kill him."

He stepped forward and surrounded her with his energy. Suddenly Mica felt warm and protected, his strength seeping into her and giving her courage.

"Richard, let go of me," she said in a firm voice. "Regardless of whether we're outside of Charleston, I'm sure you remember the judge's warning." His hand dropped to his side, and she breathed a sigh of relief.

She had managed to keep the abuse factor out of the divorce hearing, but she had had a private conversation with Judge Wilson. He had assured her he would relay to Richard what would happen if he ever touched her again.

Richard ran his hands through his hair. The action caused Mica to become aware of things she had missed when he first burst into her home. His clothes were disheveled, his hair needed a trim, and his face looked puffy.

"Look, Mic, the restaurant went under, and I need funds. You're the one working for your father and getting a great salary, so why won't you share?" His tone pleaded with her for leniency, but his eyes still held the anger she remembered.

Richard never could understand how hard she worked for what she made. He actually thought she was just a figurehead and her father gave her money whenever she wanted it.

"I'm already paying you plenty. There is no more." She tried to keep the quiver out of her voice. Taking deep breaths, then exhaling slowly, she also tried to control her fear.

Richard moved slowly around the room, eyeing the furnishings and fingering the draperies. Mica began to shake, the breathing exercises not working this time.

Logan whispered in her ear. "Shh, take it easy. This man is all bluff."

"I'm afraid even though he looks kind of scruffy, he's anything but bluff." She leaned back into Logan, aching for the comfort she knew he could provide. Forgetting that he had little form, she lost her balance and almost fell.

Richard turned back to her. "Perhaps I'll just take a cut of this nice little business. No, maybe I'll just take it over for you."

"Sorry, but the divorce was final six months ago. You have no claim to anything I acquire after that."

"Always the lawyer, aren't you?" His voice escalated as he stalked toward her.

Logan's voice came from the area of her desk. "Can't you use this telephone to contact the authorities?"

"Yes." Relief flooded her. She had forgotten everything except the menace her ex-husband posed.

"So, you're seeing the light," Richard said, giving her a sinister smile.

"What?"

"You just said yes to a cut of this enterprise."

"Like hell," Mica swore as she moved to the phone.

"Michaela, such language." Logan grinned as she stomped towards him.

Mica looked from Logan to Richard and back, unable to keep track of two conversations at one time. Especially when one of the people talking didn't know the other existed. Men! Why had she ever thought she needed them? When her gaze came back to Logan, though, she knew why.

She gave a snort of exasperation as she pointed to Richard. "You. Sit down and stay put."

Turning to Logan, she hissed, "You, follow me," then stomped off to the tiny kitchen.

"Get me a beer while you're in there," Richard called after her.

Mica's eyes narrowed to a glare, but she bit back any retort she considered making.

"Will you please be quiet and let me handle this?" she chided Logan, her anger more about Richard's appearance than Logan's comments.

"He hurt you. I could see it in your eyes." When she offered no response, he continued, "No gentleman has the right to abuse a lady in any manner. Especially a lady of quality such as yourself. I understand now why you divorced him."

"Look, I'll get him to leave, somehow."

"I would prefer dragging him through the door with me, and then shooting him for what he has put you through."

His words were exactly what Mica needed to hear. By offering her assurance and comfort, even though he contemplated violence, he expressed his love and concern for her. It gave her the courage to return to the living room.

With her hand on the phone, she said quietly, "Richard, you will leave now and never return. If I have to, I'll call the police and have you removed."

He stood and took a menacing step towards her. She picked up the receiver, her finger poised to punch 911. She saw his hesitation before he gave a casual shrug and turned away.

"You've changed, Mic, and not for the better."

"Get out of my life." She kept her voice quiet until the door swung closed behind him. Then she added in a loud voice, "I hate being called Mic!"

"Now what?" Logan questioned from the other side of the room.

Mica watched as he raised a ghostly hand to the early morning sun streaming through the window. He turned his hand this way and that, a scowl on his face. She couldn't begin to imagine what he thought. When she crossed the time barrier, she could still feel the sun on her face and could touch his bronze skin. She cursed her stupidity in not making sure Logan was away from the plantation when she tried to return.

As she rushed to her bedroom, she said, "I'll dress and see how the repairman is doing. Surely he's done by now."

She'd no sooner pulled on shorts and a top then the doorbell rang for the second time. But as before, it wasn't the one person Mica needed to see.

"Katie, what on earth are you doing here?" Mica wedged herself between Katie and the door. Momentarily forgetting he couldn't be seen, she frantically waved at Logan, hoping he would take the hint and step into her bedroom.

"Is that any way to greet a friend who left her children and husband quietly sleeping and sneaked away like a thief in the night?" Katie tilted her head to the side, and Mica knew she had to think fast.

"Of course not. I'm sorry. It's just that things have *not* gone according to plan this morning." Mica glanced back into the apartment to see Logan move toward her bedroom. For the first time since his ghostly arrival at Sea Crest, a mischievous smile darted across his face.

He stepped out of sight but his voice clearly reached her. "It has come to my attention that I can neither be seen nor heard. Do you recall my telling you I try to make the best of any situation?" He popped his head past the door and graced Mica with a wicked grin.

"This situation could prove *very* interesting."

Ten

Mica's gaze jumped from Logan back to Katie. She should be glad to see her friend, but it would only complicate things if Katie stayed too long. While Logan might pretend to be amused by harassing her in front of her friends, she knew it was just a cover-up for his not having control of the situation.

She sighed. Deciding for the moment to do as Logan suggested and adapt, she pasted a smile on her face. She wondered what Katie would say about Logan and felt a twinge of regret. Her best friend would never meet the best thing to ever happen to her.

Inspiration struck as she opened the door wider for Katie to enter. Perhaps, as her closest friend and confidant, Katie might be able to see Logan. Perhaps Richard couldn't because of his animosity towards her.

As Katie plopped on the couch, Mica signaled for Logan to come out of the bedroom. "Katie, I want you to meet someone special."

"I'm glad you've finally met someone. It's time you forget Richard and get on with your life." Katie looked up as she spoke. Mica saw no surprise register, even though Logan now stood at her side. Her friend continued, "Now tell me about this new guy. Is he that handsome hunk you mentioned last week?"

Logan laughed.

Mica groaned.

"His name is Thomas Logan Rutledge."

"Nice name. What does he look like?" Katie asked, tucking her legs under her on the couch.

"Katie, can't you see?" Mica asked in exasperation.

"See what?"

"Logan."

"Michaela Marie, I thought a vacation would do you good, but you're sure acting strange. How could I have seen him when I haven't met him?"

Logan laughed as he said, "I thought this would be interesting. I just didn't realize how much. Please tell Miss Katie that though she can't see me, I am flattered to make her acquaintance."

Disheartened, Mica spoke to Logan without thinking to lower her voice. "It doesn't matter now. I guess you can leave."

"Leave? I just got here." Katie straightened from the couch, her brow furrowed.

"I didn't mean you. I..." Mica frowned as she looked from Katie to Logan. "Excuse me a minute. I'll get us some coffee."

As she walked towards the kitchenette, she whispered to Logan, "Come here!"

Once she had the safety of a wall between her and the living room, she turned, only to find Logan so close she yelped in fright. "I wish you'd quit sneaking up on me. You might as well stay in here or lie down in the bedroom. She can't see you, anyway."

Logan had the audacity to grin. "I think I'll stay. What else did you say about me besides being a *handsome hunk?* And I'm assuming that *hunk,* whatever it means, is a compliment."

Mica moaned. "I should have added conceited and arrogant." She picked up two mugs of coffee and turned toward the door. "If you insist on staying in the same room, please don't talk to me. It's confusing holding two conversations at once."

"What did you say?" Katie shouted from the living room. "I can't hear you in here."

Mica gave Logan a *see-what-I-mean* look. Pressing her mouth in a firm line, she struggled for the determination to ignore him.

Mica really did try to concentrate on Katie's chattering as they sipped their coffee. From the corner of her eye, she noticed

Logan wander past the windows, then pause at the desk and study the telephone. At least he was respecting her wishes and being silent.

Katie had just finished regaling Mica about last weekend's country club dance when a flash of white sailed across Mica's vision to land at her feet. Startled, she turned to where she had last seen Logan, only to find he had moved directly across the room from where she sat. Her eyes widened. His naked chest, though pale in his ghost-like state, radiated heat even from this distance! She jerked her gaze to the floor to find his translucent shirt in a puddle.

"Quit that," she said loudly without thinking.

"You don't have to yell at me. I know I shouldn't bite my nails," Katie said, hands fluttering to rest in her lap, "but you know me. Old habits are hard to break."

Mica tore her gaze away from Logan. "What?" she squawked as she heard a thunk. Logan's belt landed on top his shirt. She squeezed her eyes shut.

"My nails. Mica, you don't look well. Are you feeling okay?" Katie reached over to pat her hand.

"I'm...fine." Mica could barely swallow as two consecutive thuds sounded from Logan's vicinity. She didn't think she could bear to look, but she couldn't bear not knowing.

Logan stood across the room, clad in only his snug black trousers. His bare chest glistened in the early morning light. He wiggled his bare feet.

Mica had never considered a man's feet sensuous, but as part of the whole sexy package parading before her, they almost caused her to hyperventilate. She dragged her gaze up his form, her insides churning and her blood pounding. He looked pretty real at that moment, not like a phantom at all. She held her breath and counted to five before slowly exhaling. It didn't help.

He had respected her wishes and hadn't spoken, but the taunting smile on his kissable lips was hot enough to turn everything around them to cinder. She squeezed her knees together, the ache inside reaching fever pitch, and still she couldn't tear her gaze from him.

In slow motion, he slid his hands from his hips to the very center of his belly and then down. His gaze locked on her face, and her gaze locked on his hands as they leisurely unbuttoned his pants. One button—two—

Mica groaned out loud, her head falling back against the couch as heat flashed through her. She just knew she had been struck by lightning.

"You *are* sick, Mica! Your face is flushed, and you're trembling." Katie jumped up and immediately swung Mica's legs onto the couch. She propped a pillow behind her head.

Hurrying toward the kitchen, she said over her shoulder, "I'm going to fix you some herbal tea and then let you rest. I swear, I don't know of anyone but you who could exhaust themselves on vacation." Katie's voice trailed off as she rattled around in the next room.

Mica fully expected Logan to complete the striptease he had started. His expression told her he was aware of her anticipation, but the minute Katie disappeared, he quit undressing and moved towards her. He knelt beside the couch.

"Are you ill? You look quite flushed." His voice expressed concern, but his eyes twinkled, and the corners of his mouth twitched.

"You know perfectly well exactly what's wrong with me. Just wait until I get you back to where you're solid enough to smack. Of all the low-down, rotten—"

"I want you – desperately." His whispered entreaty made the ache at her core worse.

"You're shameless."

"You're beautiful when you're all hot and flushed. I think I should like to keep you that way for an extremely long time." Though she couldn't feel his hand when he touched her cheek, the exotic sensations she always experienced in his presence suffused her with color once again.

"First, we have to get you back home," she said just as Katie entered from the kitchen.

"I know I need to get home. I have no doubt Matthew will be upset, even though I left him a note saying I came up here." Katie set a steaming cup of tea on the table by Mica's head and bent to touch her forehead with the back of her hand. "You don't feel hot, though your face is still flushed. I suggest you rest and not do anything strenuous. I'll call tomorrow."

Mica started to rise, not nearly as overheated now that Logan had started putting his clothes back on.

"Now don't get up. I can see myself out," Katie said as she headed for the door.

"I'm not sick, really." Mica said, though her legs wobbled slightly when she stood.

"Mica...Now who can that be?" Katie asked as a knock sounded at the door. "I'll get rid of them on my way out."

"No," Mica and Logan shouted at once, though Mica's voice was the only one echoing through the small apartment. She rushed forward as Katie opened the door.

"Mr. Whitney, have you managed to fix the lock?" Mica asked as soon as she saw the man standing in the hall.

"I've done what I can, but without a key, I don't know if it will work." The gray-haired locksmith stood to one side as Katie exited the apartment.

"Mica, don't be worrying about some door." Katie gave her a final hug.

"I'm fine, Katie. Give Matthew and the kids a kiss for me."

"There's just over a week until the big Labor Day celebration. You'll be back in Charleston by then, won't you?" Katie kept talking even as she walked down the hall toward the outside entrance.

Labor Day! Mica didn't even want to think about that. Already she was thinking about asking her father for an extension. "We'll see. Bye, Katie."

In the next breath she turned to Mr. Whitney, who had stood patiently waiting. "Thank you for responding so quickly to my call. If you'll just send me a bill, I'll see that it's paid promptly."

"Don't you want to see if the lock works first?" He frowned, and Mica knew he didn't understand why she had made the job sound so urgent if she wasn't going to check out the door.

"I'm sure you've done your best, and I'll pay you regardless of whether or not the door works." Mica prayed the man would leave. She only hoped no one else came calling before she could disappear upstairs with Logan. She glanced at her watch—less than an hour before Sunday brunch. Hopefully all the guests would still be sleeping or already out of their rooms. She certainly didn't need Mrs. Barker interfering right at this moment.

"I guess that does it then. I'll send you a bill." Mr. Whitney left, and Mica breathed a sigh of relief. As soon as the door closed behind him, she hurried to her bedroom to retrieve the key.

Logan waited by her apartment door. She thought it strange that he had not tried walking through doors or walls. She supposed that even though he was transparent to her, he still felt himself whole and unable to perform such feats.

"Ready?" she whispered, though no one was in sight.

"I've been ready to return since this nightmare started. I don't understand how you can enjoy this world where everything moves so fast. People fly into and out of your life with rapid irregularity, and there's such an incredible amount of noise."

Mica moved swiftly up the stairs as she mulled over what Logan had said. He was right. Modern life did have its drawbacks, but if she had gotten stuck back in his time without the key, she would miss—what would she miss? Except for Katie and her parents, Mica couldn't think of a thing she couldn't live without if she had to.

She held her breath as she inserted the key in the lock and turned it. A soft click brought her breath whooshing out. "It works." She experienced the familiar tingle as she turned the knob and swung the door open.

Logan stepped quickly over the threshold. She hadn't consciously thought about returning with him and she tentatively reached out to touch his arm. He grabbed her wrist and jerked her through the doorway, his grip unbearably tight.

"Hey! What are you doing?" Her question and rising anger at his proprietary attitude melted away when his lips crushed hers. His arms circled her in a bruising hug, and yet Mica understood exactly what he needed. She had felt incomplete during his stay at Sea Crest—moving about the same rooms, talking, yet unable to touch. It had been torture for her, too.

"God, you *are* real." Logan clasped her to his chest, his breath harsh in her ear as he moaned her name again and again. He couldn't seem to quit touching her, his hands roaming the contours of her back. He kissed along her hairline, down her cheek and across the bridge of her nose, punctuating each word with yet another kiss.

"I thought I was losing my mind. I've never felt so helpless." He clutched her shoulders and pushed her away enough to search her face, frowning.

"What an incredible nightmare. Thank God I'm awake now, and you didn't really fall through that door."

"But Logan, it wasn't a dream." Mica had wondered how long it would take before his initial reaction of wonder wore off.

"I don't want to discuss it. Just stay here by my side and let me touch you—let me know you really exist and that the past weeks haven't been an hallucination." Logan swung her up into his arms, his grip possessively tight but no longer crushing.

Mica pulled away from his embrace as much as she could, dread creeping up her spine at his expression. He stared past her to the door, the look of disbelief still clearly written on his features. She could tell he really didn't believe they had visited the other side. "Logan, you can't just wish away what happened."

His gaze returned to her face, the haunted look fading. He spun on his heel and carried her toward her bedroom. "I have only one wish," he stated as he kicked the door closed. "That is to make love to you until we're both too breathless and exhausted to think of anything else."

***

Logan watched Michaela sleep, curled against his side, her warmth radiating against his own bare skin. He idly turned the brass key over and over in his hands.

It was far too late to save his heart—they'd gone beyond the point of no return. And yet he didn't know how to convince Michaela she belonged to him, not to some far-fetched time as she would lead him to believe.

He fingered the key. He had known there was something unique and special about her. She had come to him in the night, with no clothes and no reason, and he hadn't questioned her.

He snorted. He had definitely known better than to question her. He hadn't wanted the dream to burst—hadn't wanted to admit he'd fallen in love with an illusion. But as he gazed on her now, warm and soft against him, he realized she was no phantom in his time.

Different from any other woman in both manner and dress, she stood up to him and spoke her mind. She willingly participated in the concerns of the plantation. Other women would have fainted rather than fight a fire or be seen barefoot with soot covering their faces. Michaela had shown him her passionate nature and her feminine side. She'd shown him her compassion and her practicality. And he had fallen in love with every facet of her being.

He marveled at her willingness to adapt to his way of life. While he felt comfortable with his lifestyle, she must think it crude and backward, given all the modern inventions in her time.

She wiggled against his side, sighing his name in her sleep.

"I love you," he whispered as he bent to kiss her cheek. He was driven by a desperate hunger for the softness, the goodness, and the faith she brought to his world of hard work and little reward. His fingers folded tight around the key. He would do anything—*everything*—in his power to keep her here.

***

Mica woke with a smile early that evening. Logan had disappeared, yet the scent of him lingered. She reveled in being back in his arms and back at Indigo Bay.

He had refused to acknowledge the time spent at Sea Crest. Mica realized eventually things would have to be put to rest, but for the moment she was content. She would *not* let it interfere with her happiness.

It had taken the absence of his touch to make her aware of her need for him. Though they had still talked during his foray into the future, it was the physical manifestation of their love that fused their souls as nothing else could. Touching, kissing and making love could only be achieved here at Indigo Bay. Mica spent less and less time thinking about her life before meeting Logan.

She enjoyed the elegance and leisure of Logan's time. Since others did the cooking and cleaning, the lack of modern appliances didn't bother her. She had become accustomed to the clothes, the lamplight, and the isolation. More than any luxury, though, she enjoyed long carriage rides with Logan, either up to the bluff or down along the beach.

No doubt corruption and poverty and most of the problems of modern day Charleston had already started in the towns. As a lady in Logan's home, however, she wasn't expected to know about such things, much less deal with them. That suited her fine, because she was tired of trying to solve everyone else's problems. In 1850, the responsibility lay elsewhere. She didn't regret not having to make those decisions.

Her relationship with Logan also left no regrets. Though he leaned towards arrogance and possessiveness at times, his arrogance suited him for the era in which he lived. Even his protective nature touched a chord deep within Mica. It was nice to feel protected instead of always being the protector. Though possessive, Logan allowed her the freedom to speak her mind and even question him.

Unwittingly, she compared Logan to her ex-husband. Logan possessed all the traits she had wanted to see in Richard, but which had never materialized—honesty, responsibility, gentleness, and a willingness to share his life and be concerned about her own.

She smiled as she recalled how upset Logan had been when he learned she often visited the jail. He finally admitted he admired her choice of careers and her desire to help the downtrodden, but it outraged him that her father would allow her to pursue such an *unsafe* profession.

She heard the downstairs clock toll the hour as she dressed. Mica refused to spend any more time reflecting on her past. She needed to make new memories—enough to last her a lifetime once she returned to Charleston in less than a week.

"Don't think about that," she chastised herself, not wanting to face reality. The time would go fast enough without constantly thinking about it. Tonight she would not allow herself to brood.

Logan greeted her at the top of the stairs with a kiss that she returned with equal fervor. He held her at arm's length. "If you keep that up, I'll sweep you off your feet for a repeat of our earlier magic." Brown eyes twinkled at her as he spoke. His lean finger traced the line of her jaw upwards, where he tucked her hair behind her ear.

Mica shivered, but not from the tickle of his finger. She recalled with vivid clarity the desperate passion Logan had exhibited. If he believed they had visited her time, he never said so. Instead, he had possessed her by making love to her in exotic ways, as though that were his talisman for anchoring her in 1850. She only wished it were that easy.

She linked her arm through his and turned him towards the stairs. "As much as I liked your attentions, I'm starved now."

"Liked? You merely *liked?"* Logan stopped mid-stride on the stairway, jerking Mica to a stop before she tumbled headlong down the rest of the steps. "If *that* is your reaction to my heartfelt endeavors, I most definitely will have to try harder." He tugged on her arm as though intent on propelling her back upstairs.

Mica laughed, enjoying the sexual banter. "Come here," she whispered in her most seductive voice. When he stepped closer, she lowered her voice further, employing all her Southern charm. "The exotic paths we traveled enraptured my heart."

"That's more like it." He grinned as they resumed their descent to the main floor.

She leaned closer to whisper as they entered the foyer, "I

was enthralled with your marvelous expertise and profuse performance." Logan's arm quivered beneath her touch, but she wouldn't relent. "My skin still tingles from the erotic pleasures we shared. I get hot all over just thinking about taking you in my—"

"Michaela Marie!"

Logan actually blushed, and Mica was delighted to find him passionate but not perverted. She released his arm and sailed through the dining room door. That would teach him to beg a compliment from her.

"Good evening, Simon. Please give my greetings to Mattie. It seems an age since I last saw either of you." Simon smiled to her as she spoke. She waited at the table for Logan to seat her, but when he did, it was with an unexpected challenge.

"You win this round, sweet one," he whispered as he bent close. Before she could turn, his tongue flicked around the shell of her ear, sending goose bumps down both arms. "But be forewarned. You will have to beg me to make love to you the next time."

Simon had the audacity to interrupt their intimate conversation by serving their meal, but Mica couldn't really blame him. He had no way of knowing how she ached inside, both from her own comments about their lovemaking and from Logan's dare. While there were definite characteristics about Logan she liked *other* than his magical physical prowess, that alone might have made her a slave to his desires.

Her mind searched for a sensible topic of conversation as she ate her fruit compote. Though it seemed an age ago, she recalled the fire that had occurred just last night.

"I assume you've been out to survey the fire damage? Was the crop salvageable? Were any of your workers hurt?" She fired questions at him as Simon served the next course.

Logan smiled at Michaela's innocence. Unaware of the social dictates against discussing business during a meal, and in front of servants, no less, she expressed genuine concern for his plantation.

"Once the indigo's processed and pressed into blocks, it's moved to the drying sheds. The majority of our first harvest is at the drying stage, and the second harvest won't occur until mid-September. That didn't leave a tremendous amount of dye in the processing shed which burned." He frowned as he sipped his wine. "Regardless, I'm stymied as to who started the fire, and why."

Logan glanced at her, but she remained silent. She had spoken out against his stepbrother, but once he had refuted her argument, she hadn't brought it up again. For that matter, he had not seen Neil for several days and assumed he remained out of town on business. He felt sure that in time Neil would find his own way in the world.

As for himself, he found he enjoyed discussing business with Michaela. She had a level head on her shoulders, and he could voice his concerns and feelings freely, knowing she would be honest and forthright with him. He hadn't realized how much he missed the interaction of other people when he cut himself off from his friends after his mother died.

Michaela incorporated all he could hope and dream of. From a concerned friend to a passionate lover, she exhibited a tenderness rare in Logan's world. He still didn't quite understand the one rather large gap in their relationship. Unless she brought it up, he was determined not to mention the inevitable.

Instead of expressing his emotional thoughts out loud, he spoke only in fact, saying, "Money will be tight, but the indigo market is good, and we should get a top price for our crop. The Indigo Bay imprint has stood for quality since the plantation began production over one hundred years ago."

"Imprint?" Michaela asked, and Logan realized he had never taken her through the entire process.

"It's difficult to explain and much easier to show you. Would you care to take a stroll after dinner?"

Her glowing smile made his heart ache. "I'd love to."

They shared coffee on the front porch before walking down the lane arm in arm, beneath the arch of trees lining the drive. No words were needed for Logan to know how Michaela felt. Her sea blue eyes spoke of her love. Her possessive grip on his arm told him she wanted to remain close by his side.

Her lips quivered ever so slightly when she glanced up at him, and Logan knew the thoughts left unspoken were not words he wanted to hear. He drew her close to place a gentle kiss on her soft lips. His own silence begged her for a reprieve from the unknown future over which he had no control.

Glowing lanterns from the low-roofed drying shed afforded enough light to show them the way. He didn't speak until he led her inside.

"This is the last of a very long process in preparing indigo for market." He surveyed the room with pride, knowing Indigo Bay was well on the way to regaining its status as a leader in the dye market, regardless of the losses he had experienced.

As he explained, he took her hand and led her between long wooden trays, each containing racks of the dark blue cakes. "The cubes must be protected from direct sunlight. If drying is too quick, the cubes will split or crack, fetching a lower price on the market.

"The dye is compressed into lumps of twenty-two pounds, then later cut into handier cubes of four ounces, which are impressed with our stamp, very similar to the way tea is produced." He held up a block to show her. The imprint showed the delicate Indigo flower surrounded by an outline of Indigo Bay Island.

"This stamp is known world-wide, and it stands for the quality of our dye. It's our reputation. Because indigo is expensive and most sought after, there have always been those who have tried to falsify the process. While large trading houses and dye-works can test new parcels in their own laboratories, smaller concerns have to complete costly test dyeing.

"With our stamp, they know they can rely on quality, and this saves them time and money." Logan couldn't help the pride in his voice. The long, strenuous process of producing this dye was worth the effort. The best textile mills in the world would use his product in their fabrics.

"Don't you have to worry about the stamp wearing off, or getting wet and dissolving?"

"Indigo is insoluble in water. When the plant is subjected

to fermentation a substance present, particularly in the leaves, produces indigo. When combined with an alkaline reduction it turns into a solution in which dyeing can be achieved.

"However, when the textile-materials are lifted from the dye-bath, the oxygen in the air transforms it back into its original insoluble state. It's one of the few dyes that is absolutely fast."

Logan glanced down to find Michaela's gaze fixed rapturously on his face. He flushed. "I seem to have expounded far beyond what you really wanted to know. Your eyes are glazed over."

"I love the sound of your voice. Tell me more."

Her compliment fed his ego, but he longed for something other than talk. "If you desire, sweet one, step outside into the darkest night, and I'll share more than my voice with you."

It took little persuasion for Michaela to latch onto his arm. He escorted her from the drying shed, only to hear thunder rumble in the distance. Thoughts of a torrid interlude beneath the trees fled when huge drops of rain splattered the dry ground.

"We'd best get back before we're soaked to the skin." Transferring his grasp to her hand, he tugged her along the path, anxious to regain the house before it rained harder.

They didn't make it. Warm summer rain poured from the sky, forcing them beneath the shelter of the trees. Even there, water seeped through the branches, affording them a rather leaky shelter. The house, obscured by the storm, formed a distant shadow. Lights from the windows were only a pale glow.

Logan sucked in a breath of fresh air—a combination of earth and sky—clean and refreshing. He stood behind Michaela, hugging her close to his chest. Life was good. His crops would see his people through another year, Michaela loved him as he did her, and the Lord above provided rain to sustain the Earth that in turn provided his livelihood. He smiled with contentment, even as the steady downpour trickled water down his back beneath his shirt and plastered his hair to his head.

"Have you ever made love in the rain?" Her question

startled him from his silent reflections.

"I am a properly brought up gentleman, Michaela Marie. I wouldn't think of doing anything of the sort outside the confines of the bedroom." Even as he spoke, he ached with longing and pulled her tighter against him.

Michaela turned in his embrace, nipping his chin with her teeth. "I do recall, sir, one particular night when we didn't quite make it to the bedroom." As she spoke, she rubbed against him, her hips sliding across his groin. His manhood, already in a state of arousal, throbbed in response to her suggestive movements.

Logan leaned against the tree in a stupor as Michaela stepped from beneath its protection into the rain. Unmindful, she spread her arms outward and twirled slowly in front of him, the rain turning her blouse transparent and molding her skirt to her hips. While he knew she could not command the heavens to rain, he realized she must have premeditated her seduction, for he swore she wore nothing beneath the thin cloth of her dress.

She lifted her hands to her head, slowly brushing her wet hair from her face. Her movements tugged the material of her blouse tighter, the rosy tips of her nipples jutting out in invitation. He reached for her, but she stepped back. She licked the rain from her lips, her gaze fixed on his face. Slowly, erotically, she undid her buttons and shrugged out of her blouse, letting it fall to her waist.

Logan thought he would explode. Rivulets of water caressed her breasts, making her skin shimmer. He ached to kiss away the rain—to lick the water from her skin.

"Do you want me?" she whispered across the distance.

Logan moaned. His breath came in shallow gasps. His hands clutched in need, and still she tortured him.

"Do you ache for me with every breath of your being? With every second that passes, do you long for me in your arms?"

His voice rasped with longing as he said, "You won the last round, and I swore you would have to beg me the next time. But I will gladly lose this time, also, for you create a need in me too great to take slowly."

He unbuttoned his shirt, jerking it from his pants. The warm rain caressed his skin, but when she stepped close to rub her breasts against his chest, he knew steam rose in their wake.

"There are no losers. In this, we both win." Her lips, wet and hot, touched his. They needed no words, for a flood of desire shook them even as the thunder shook the heavens.

Michaela's fingers threaded through his hair as she kissed him, and Logan sensed her desperation. Wanting to prolong their passion, but unable to withstand the hunger, he fumbled with the buttons on his trousers, jerking the wet fabric open. Bunching Michaela's skirts up around her waist, he found the hot, moist center of her, unimpeded by undergarments. One touch told him she was more than ready. He slid his hands over her bare buttocks as she kissed a fiery path across his jaw and down his neck.

"It is your fault I've lost my control and forgotten all my manners, but we will discuss it later." With total abandon, leaning against a tree in the rain, Logan lifted her hips to his and thrust upward.

"Logan," she cried against his neck, biting him in her passion. She then arched back, legs clutching his waist as his hands supported her weight against him. Unleashed passion consumed him as her body clutched around his. He bent to capture her slick breast in his mouth, the contact inciting a frenzied reaction.

"More, please, I beg you," she cried.

Her hips arching against his punctuated each word as she created a whirlpool that pulled him deeper and deeper into her depths. Her eyes widened, her face glorious as passion swept through her. Her release triggered his own explosive climax.

"Love me, Logan, as though there were no tomorrows. There's only now—this fragment of time we've been granted."

In that moment of his deepest need, he couldn't discern whether the moisture shimmering in her blue eyes was raindrops, or tears.

Eleven

Drenched to the bone and exhausted, Mica and Logan sneaked into the house just as the clock struck midnight. Logan insisted she dry off and crawl beneath the warm covers. He promised to return to her later.

"There are business matters I must see to before market day." He sat on the edge of her bed, bending to place a gentle kiss on her lips.

Mica wanted him to stay, and almost begged him. But she bit back the words. In a few short days, she would be gone, and Logan would have to conduct business and provide for his people. She had no right to claim his time, no matter how she ached to keep him with her throughout the night.

He smiled mischievously. "Though my business intentions were good prior to dinner, it seems I became slightly distracted."

"Only slightly?" Mica teased.

His warm lips trailed a breathless path up her cheek to her ear. "Your wanton behavior will keep my dreams warm through the coldest night."

"That's better," she replied, willing to let him have the advantage.

It seemed Logan had other ideas, though, and continued to test her limits. "The next time we need rain, I would prefer you dance completely naked, for surely the rain god could be no less pleased with your luscious form than I. The way the rain caressed your bare breasts, and the taste of it on your skin—"

Mica clamped a hand over his mouth, but couldn't conceal his laughing eyes.

When she removed her hand from his mouth, he said, "Never fear. In just a short while I shall return to make sure you're completely dry."

Mica couldn't see him leave through the mist of unshed tears. The instant the door closed behind him, she burst into sobs, stuffing the corner of the pillow into her mouth to muffle the sound. But nothing could stop her heart from breaking.

"Aunt Theo, I will never forgive you."

Although she cursed her dear aunt soundly, she knew the fault to be her own. Only a month ago, she had laughed at Katie's foolish idea that she might find the man of her dreams at Sea Crest. Now, within a matter of days, she would have to give up that dream to pursue her life—her responsibility-filled, dull life.

***

Much later, as the moon broke the cloud cover to wash across the bed with silvery light, Logan watched Michaela sleep. Her pale face, streaked with dried tears, tore at his heart. A moonbeam glinted off the key that lay on the table beside the bed. Again he considered insuring she remained by his side, but he knew the choice must be hers.

He shrugged out of his clothes and slid into bed, pulling her tight against his heart. If his love couldn't bind her to him, he would be lost forever. He didn't even know how much time they had left. She had never said, and he feared asking.

It was like stumbling across your own marker in a graveyard. Your name and birth were clearly written. The only fact lacking was the date on which you ceased to exist. Logan was positive his heart and soul would leave with Michaela.

"Trust in the Lord," his mother had always told him, even on the heart-wrenching day of his father's funeral. Somehow, Logan didn't think the Almighty had planned on Michaela Marie finding a breach in His grand scheme of things.

He thought of waking her and making love to her again to prove she belonged with him. Although he realized she already knew of his love and returned it wholeheartedly, he feared it wouldn't be enough in the end.

The night passed, but Logan didn't sleep. The moon

disappeared from view and cast the room in total darkness. Still he held her close, memorizing her face, caressing the silk texture of her dark hair. He recalled how she'd tuck it behind her ear, not even aware of the endearing gesture. Though her eyes were closed, he could visualize their vivid blue twinkling at him in laughter as she teased him, or turning dark with passion as she loved him.

"I love you so much," he whispered against her hair.

"I know," she answered, her voice sleepy, as she turned in his arms. Her warm, naked body slid against his with perfection. "And I will love you until my dying day. My heart will remain here with you always, even when—"

"Don't!" Logan refused to allow her to say the hurtful words out loud. With unerring precision, he molded his lips to hers.

He worshipped her body, kissing every part of her, bringing her to a crest of passion. Only when she sobbed his name in her ecstasy did he enter her, driving deep to mesh their bodies into one. Hoping to get her with child, if that were the only way to bind her to him, he climaxed, hot and throbbing and wanting still more of her.

He collapsed against her, tucking his face into the curve of her neck, nibbling at her skin.

"Dear Lord, what's to become of us?" Her ragged sob reached him over the pounding of their hearts.

Rolling to his side, he hugged her close. Though he had no answer for the fear she voiced, he somehow needed to reassure her. "Shh, sweet one. It'll be all right, I promise you." The salty taste of her tears left a bitter ache in his heart.

A tentative knock at the door jerked Logan upright. When he didn't answer right away, the knocking became insistent.

"Mister Logan, you in there?"

Logan recognized Ezra's voice and scrambled to pull on still-damp trousers. Ezra never came into the main house, much less to interrupt Logan in the middle of the night. He fumbled for his watch. Dawn was two hours away. Dread washed over him.

"What is it, Ezra?" he questioned, throwing the door open.

He quickly glanced back at the bed, hoping Michaela was covered, but at the moment not concerned about the propriety of his being in her bedroom.

Ezra stood twisting his hat in his hands and shuffling from one foot to the other. "They done it again, Mister Logan. Bad this time."

"Done what—did what?" Logan stomped into his boots as he spoke.

"It's bad." The old black man hung his head in sorrow. "We had a guard posted, like you said, but Henry found Arthur with a knot on his noggin' when he went out to take his place. Arthur come 'round, but don't recall nothing and nobody, it being dark and all."

"Ezra, get to the point. *What* happened?" Logan cared about Arthur, but since it appeared the man was all right, he needed to know what new disaster had struck.

"The indigo, Mister Logan. It all been smashed to pieces." Ezra almost cried as he spoke the words.

"Oh, God," Logan moaned, racing down the hall and forgetting all else in his hurry.

***

Mica squirmed restlessly on the bed as Logan spoke with Ezra. Unable to get dressed with the door wide open and the foreman in view, she waited in agitation until Logan raced away.

Now, as she tore through her clothes to locate a skirt and top, she prayed the damage wasn't as bad as Ezra had indicated. Poor Logan! All his hard work all the loving care he took with his plantation—only to have someone destroy it.

The entire household was astir by the time Mica flew down the stairs. Mattie, in nightcap and robe, lit lanterns as her husband, Simon, struggled to hitch up his suspenders. Lana and Annie stood nervously twisting their hands.

"Hurry, Simon," Mica called over her shoulder, grabbing a lantern as she raced out the door. The instant she stepped onto the drive, she began to curse. She'd forgotten to put on shoes. After hopping her way across the crushed shell, she ran through the grass at the side of the drive.

When she rounded the bend, it became immediately apparent exactly where disaster had struck. The drying shed glowed with the light of a dozen lanterns, and dark shadows were racing back and forth past the windows. From this distance, she couldn't see Logan, but knew he'd be right in the middle of everything.

Mica gasped upon entering the shed. Tray after tray of dye cakes were upended, the indigo smashed on the floor or lying crumbled on broken racks. The air, thick with a blue haze, choked her when she tried to breathe.

Logan's workers were silent as they worked to set the shed to rights. Even as they worked, Mica saw their gazes shift continuously to the man who stood in the middle of it all.

Dear Lord, it's so unfair, she silently cried as she watched Logan survey the damage. He'd been so proud of his accomplishments earlier that night, and now his shoulders slumped in defeat. Tears filled her eyes as he bent to pick up one of the larger pieces lying at his feet, only to crumble it in his fist.

A small cry escaped her when his gaze caught hers across the room. His eyes, usually so full of laughter and life, now appeared sunken and hollow with despair. He looked at her, yet Mica doubted he saw her at all.

She reached a hand out in supplication, but he ignored the gesture. His face, contorted with tightly controlled rage, was unfamiliar to her. Mica, fearing for him if he released his anger on some unsuspecting person, walked slowly towards him. The others backed away when they caught sight of Logan, but Mica didn't fear for herself. If she had learned anything at all in her time at Indigo Bay, it was that Logan was a gentle man, not prone to violence. Even to the extent to which this catastrophe had pushed him, she knew he wouldn't harm her.

"Damn them to everlasting hell!"

Mica jumped at his bellowed expletive, but she stood her ground even as he hurled a clump of indigo against a far wall. The solid thunk seemed enough to break him from his stupor, and he began storming up and down each aisle.

"Logan, what are you looking for?" She had to get him to

talk. If he didn't, he would surely explode even more.

"Evidence! Proof! Anything to tell me who wanted so desperately to destroy *me* that he would destroy the entire island!"

He picked up a cake of dye, but apparently found some flaw for he carelessly tossed it back into the pile on the tray. Mica followed him as he wandered aimlessly back and forth.

"You can't find anything in the dark," Mica protested, even as she scoured the edge of a tray for fingerprints. She realized that would do Logan little good since fingerprint identification had yet to be invented. "There isn't enough light to see anything."

She touched his shoulder, her voice gentle. "Come back to the house, Logan. It may not look so terrible in the morning."

He turned on her, eyes flashing fire as he shrugged off her touch. "That's easy enough for you to say. You can go back to your nice, safe life and forget about us. I have to find a way to put food on the table and clothes on the backs of these people. *I* have *responsibilities.*"

Devastated, Mica's mouth dropped open as Logan ranted at her, then spun on his heel and stormed outside. She watched his rigid back until he became swallowed by the night. *He* had responsibilities—like she didn't know what the word meant! Mica started to yell out to him, but she held her silence as she once again surveyed the insurmountable damage.

Logan had every right to be angry—furious, in fact. She had been an available target for that anger, and she really couldn't blame him for lashing out. If a disaster of such proportions had happened to her, she probably wouldn't have been as nice about it.

As she reflected on what he had said, she thought of a way to help him. She hurried down the aisle to the door, anxious to explain her plan.

Mica found Logan leaning against a tree—their tree—his head bent, his shoulders slumped, and his hands stuffed into his pockets.

Although he didn't look up at her approach, he acknowledged her presence by saying, "I apologize for my behavior just now. I had no right to take my anger out on you."

His voice cracked, and Mica realized how hard it was for him. Not the apology, but the feeling that he somehow had failed to live up to his obligations.

"Oh, Logan, this is not your fault. No one could have predicted something like this might happen. We just have to make it right." She allowed a small amount of enthusiasm to enter her voice as her idea took concrete form in her head. "I've come up with a plan."

At least he raised his head to look at her, and she hurried on, hoping he wouldn't take offense at her offer. "I can help. I have loads of money, and quite a few stocks that can be cashed in and..." His look stopped her in mid-sentence.

"*Loads* of money? And how will that help me? We've already discovered that some things don't travel through time very well." He held his hands up in a gesture that encompassed himself. It was the first time he had actually admitted what had happened to them.

Before Mica could respond, he added, "Have the notes of currency not changed over time? If so, they won't come back to my time. And even if they did, the dates on your money alone would make them nonnegotiable."

Mica sighed. He was right. Even if she could bring truckloads of money back, his bank would consider it some kind of hoax.

Logan pushed away from the tree, stuffing his hands once more into his pockets. He turned away from her, staring back at the drying shed, where lights still flickered as workers tried to clean up the mess.

She tucked her arm through his, resting her head on his shoulder. This time, he didn't shrug her away, and Mica was glad she could offer him this comfort, at least.

"This plantation is my life. It's not just pride in producing a product for which the world clamors. It's knowing I can take care of the people who depend on me."

"Didn't you say there would be another harvest?" Mica tried to find something positive to say, though the outlook appeared extremely bleak.

"A harvest which won't occur until mid-September, and dye not ready for market until after the first of the year." He snorted. "And that does not take into account the field which burned. Those plants won't produce this year." He shook his head. "Unless I can find backers to finance me through another season, I will lose the island. Ezra, Arthur and their families will become slaves elsewhere—their freedom papers don't mean much on the mainland."

"There must be a way."

"Michaela, there's no market for indigo cakes crushed to powder."

"Powder?" Mica thought of all the instant food like powdered milk, jello, pudding, and other dissolvable materials like laundry detergent. "Why not sell it that way?" Her question was met with raised eyebrows and an incredulous stare.

"Are you crazy? The Indigo Bay stamp is our reputation—the seal of quality on our product. Do you realize what a laughing stock I would be if I tried such a scheme?" He turned to walk away, but Mica wouldn't let it rest.

"Didn't you say it had to be dissolved with alcohol, anyway?"

"Alkaline."

"Whatever. By having it already crushed, it would dissolve easier and save the textile manufacturers' time."

"You're forgetting our trademark. How would anyone know it was *our* indigo, or dye at all? And how would it be sold—in an open barrel to blow away with the slightest wind?"

Mica could tell by the tone of his voice how desperately he wanted to believe in her plan. She thought of the cardboard boxes so many items came in, but doubted they had been invented.

"Tins?"

"There's no time to find anything of the quantity we would need. Besides, the stamp—"

"I know, I know—the Good Housekeeping Seal of Approval." Did he have to refute every idea she had?

"Good Housekeeping what?"

She ignored his question. "I've got it! You stated once that your island also produced cloth, dyed with your indigo, right?"

"Yes, but—"

"Why couldn't we make cloth bags to be filled with indigo powder? It would be weighed and sold just as it always is, only already crushed and ready to use." Before he could argue with her again, she continued. "Is there any reason you couldn't take the same Indigo Bay imprint used on the cakes and stamp it on the cloth with the dye itself? Sort of a stencil?"

"There's less than a week to market."

"Logan, come on. Are you going to give up when people depend on you? When your reputation is at stake?"

He grinned wryly at the words she threw back in his face. "It would be an incredible amount of work—round the clock with everyone helping."

"If all the people on Indigo Bay have a stake in what becomes of the island, don't you think they will *want* to help?"

He grabbed her in a rough embrace, kissed her soundly, then let loose and shouted across the yard, "Ezra, gather everybody to the drying shed right away. And I mean everyone! We have work to do."

To Mica he added, "Go to the house and tell Mattie and Simon what's to be done. Gather all the sewing materials you can, and bring everyone back with you except Annie and Lana. Annie's to start cooking—lots of food—with Lana to help her. We'll be too busy to stop for any length of time, but the workers will need to be fed."

He turned towards the shed, then stopped. "Once you've set the house staff to their tasks, send Simon out to the stables. We're going to need the stable master's and groom's help, too."

As the sun rose to light the area around the drying and weaving sheds, lanterns were extinguished one by one, but no one stopped long enough to enjoy the sunrise. Logan had divided the workers into groups, each with a different task. The men carefully scooped the indigo from the trays and collected as much as they could from the floor. They crushed then sifted it through screens to eliminate any particles of wood left from the destruction and to insure uniformity. Using large barrels and tubs—anything they could find—they stored the hundreds of pounds of crushed indigo, until the sacks were ready for packaging.

In the weaving shed, the process took longer, and Mica wondered if they would have everything ready when needed. Taking cloth which had been ready to dye, Logan showed the women how to lay it out, estimating the size they would need to hold quantities of indigo. The imprint stamps, normally in the house for safekeeping, had been brought down, and using dye set aside for the cloth, Logan dipped the stamp, then applied it to the sparkling white cloth.

"It works," he stated, almost as though he hadn't expected it to. Mica was glad to hear his voice hold some of his old enthusiasm once again.

"Of course," she replied. "Now go see to the men. We'll manage here."

Without waiting to see if he followed her advice, she divided the women into groups—some to cut and stamp the material, the rest to begin the arduous task of hand sewing the sides, leaving the top open until the indigo had been poured in. Knowing the impossibility of sewing shut the hundreds of bags once they had been filled, she found a coil of thin rope and instructed some of the younger boys to begin cutting it into one-foot lengths.

Logan stood at the door, unable for the moment to continue back to the drying shed. He watched Michaela absently tuck a strand of hair behind her ear as she bent to speak softly to one of the older women.

She had done it again—turned his world from topsy-turvy back to some semblance of normality. While he had serious doubts that the indigo would sell in its present state, he couldn't help being infected by her enthusiasm. As she had pointed out, he had to try. At this point he had nothing to lose.

A chuckle escaped when he looked down to find she stood barefoot, her skirts not quite reaching her ankles. A most unconventional woman, his Michaela Marie, willing to sacrifice anything to insure he succeeded. A sigh escaped as he turned away. He could do no less and had best get after it.

Everyone on the plantation—from the youngest child to the old folks who usually sat in the shade all day—worked tirelessly. Logan would periodically send a group back to their cabins to sleep, and he caught a catnap under the tree now and then. But for the most part he never ventured far from either building. There had been no sign of further trouble, but as insurance, he had sealed off the island, posting a guard at the only road to the mainland.

Logan wanted no intrusions or interruptions. Nor did he want word of their endeavors leaking out before market day. He would have the element of surprise if he could present a new product on that day, without a lot of hearsay and suspicion circulating among the buyers prior to the auction.

The only one to give him any trouble was Michaela, who refused to go to the house to rest. If she wasn't instructing a new group of women, she had several bags in her lap and was bent over the cloth with a needle and thread. He glanced over to the tree to find her there again, sitting cross-legged, the indigo bags scattered around her. He started to turn back to his work, but something stopped him.

He watched for several minutes before he realized what had caught his attention, and then he laughed outright. Several men stopped what they were doing to stare at him, but he didn't care. Love swelled in his heart as he strolled towards the tree, still chuckling.

Squatting down in front of Michaela, he gently removed the needle and bag she clutched in her hands, then tugged on her shoulders until she tilted sideways to lay upon the ground.

"Not now Logan, I have work to do," she murmured, not aware she had fallen asleep sitting up.

"Shh, rest now, sweet one. There will still be plenty to do when you wake." She never even opened her eyes, and it took several minutes before the mist cleared Logan's own eyes enough to see her.

***

Mica woke to a gentle shake of her shoulder. It took her

eyes some time to focus in the absence of light. When she realized where she was, she jerked upright, searching her lap for the bags she had brought outside to stitch.

"They're already done, sweetheart. Don't fret." Logan plunked down beside her, stretching his long legs as he leaned against the tree. "We're finished. Now, we'll see what kind of lawyer I am. I must convince a jury of my peers and indigo buyers that I'm not ready for the loony bin."

He closed his eyes, tilting his head back against the rough bark of the tree, and Mica studied his profile. Even in the dusk before nightfall, she could see the tired lines around his eyes, the creases at the corners of his mouth. She leaned into him, gently kissing the edge of his lips, then up along his cheek to his eyes, hoping to smooth the worry lines.

"Ah, Michaela, ever the soothsayer." As he spoke, he circled her waist with his strong arms and pulled her onto his lap. His hungry kiss ignited fires in her, and for a moment she forgot where they were. Only when she heard laughter a short distance away did she recall their circumstances.

Flushing deeply, she pulled away. "Logan, what will people think?"

He laughed as he jumped up, pulling her to her feet. "They'll think the master of Indigo Bay is in love with the beautiful woman who has crazy ideas." He tugged her along the path, past the tired workers. As they walked, everyone waved or applauded, and Mica's cheeks flamed hotter.

"You didn't tell them it was *my* idea, did you?"

"Of course. Do you want them to think *I'm* crazy?"

She swung at him, and he laughed, racing off down the path towards the ocean. When he disappeared around a bend, Mica hesitated. The sun had set, casting the path in shadows, and she tentatively stepped away from the shrubs onto the sand.

"Logan?" She called into the darkness.

"Right here."

He grabbed her from behind, and she squealed, her heart pounding from the fright. Just as quickly, it gave way to a different beat as Logan nibbled on her neck, munching his way to her ear.

"You did a fine job these past days. You worked harder than anyone, refusing to give up—refusing to let *me* give up, and I shall be eternally grateful."

His tongue tickled her ear, but when Mica tried to turn around, his embrace tightened, holding her back flat against him.

"Say you'll stay here with me always, Michaela, to share my life and have my children." His voice pleaded with her as he spoke the unspeakable.

Instead of answering him, Mica hedged. "I'm twenty-nine. That's too old to have children."

"You're *how* old?" Logan released her, his voice incredulous.

"You knew that. Don't make it sound like I'm ... I'm..." Mica was at a loss for words.

"On the shelf? An old maid? A spinster?" Logan readily supplied a choice of adjectives, laughter apparent in his voice as he slowly stepped away from her.

"Yes...no," she sputtered, reaching out to smack him, even though she knew he was only teasing her.

Spinning around, he raced down the beach, and Mica chased after him. Their laughter carried across the waves, and when Logan slowed so she could catch him, she wrestled him to the ground, determined to show him she was not a spinster yet.

They tore at each other's clothes in their haste to be shed of them. Splashing into the gentle waves that washed upon the shore, Logan loved her so tenderly she wanted to cry. She knew she had to tell him her time here was over. Though her heart broke, she owed it to her father to return as she had promised. After all, she was a responsible adult.

As though Logan sensed her heartache, he didn't speak as they dressed. When she tried to talk, he admonished her to silence once again by saying, "Don't, Michaela. Not just yet. I have something to show you."

Hand in hand, he led her up the path to the house, but then veered toward the garden. Just as they rounded the corner a full moon appeared, casting a mellow light across the flowerbeds.

"They delivered this just today, and I meant to surprise you. But in the midst of the rest of the turmoil, the workmen grew careless and knocked it over, breaking his hand. As soon as things calm down, I'll have it replaced."

His voice was anxious, and at first Mica didn't understand why. Then he turned her around, and her gaze fell on the statue, newly erected in the center of the garden.

Cupid! Tears sprang instantly to her eyes. She was the woman for whom Cupid had been commissioned.

"I was so angry," Logan growled. "I wanted it to be perfect, as you are. And it shall be, as soon—"

"No. I love it just as it is."

"But he has no bow and arrows—no hand, either, for that matter."

Mica couldn't express her emotions at that moment. Could it be there was a way to make dreams come true? She dared not breathe a word, for fear the fairytale of her childhood would turn into a nightmare.

Logan circled her shoulders, pulling her close to his chest. "It matters not that Cupid lost his love arrows. My heart has already been captured by the most wonderful woman in the world, and my love will be hers throughout all time."

Over the past month, Logan had taught Mica to live each day to the fullest, never looking back at what could not be changed. Their love had grown beyond anything she could have imagined. She only wished she had more time.

Mica turned in his arms. "Oh, Logan, please, tell me what to do." She searched his face, trying to find an answer to their dilemma in the depth of his gaze. Once decisive and so sure of herself, Mica felt she would never be the same again.

"I can't make that decision for you." He kissed the top of her head, and she hugged him closer. "I can only tell you what is in my heart."

He placed her palm against his chest, the strong beat of his heart pulsing through her fingers. Her eyes brimmed with tears, but he sadly shook his head.

"I love you, Michaela Marie, with my very heart and soul. You have become my world, around which my happiness and hope revolve. I will love you until the moon and stars are forever gone—until I'm old and stooped and they carry me to my grave. All the riches in the world can't compare to the wealth of love I have to give you. But more than that, I cannot do."

Logan didn't allow Mica further tears. He took her upstairs to his bed, where his caresses and kisses and tender loving carried her slowly on an exquisite journey through passion that made time stand still.

***

Now, hours later, Mica stood at the window, gazing out at the statue of Cupid, shimmering silver in the moonlight. No matter what she wanted—no matter how desperately—she knew time had run out.

"Logan?" She turned back to where he lay sprawled on her bed, hair tousled, the sheet barely covering his hips. He reached a hand out to her, but she shook her head, fearing her courage would fail if she touched him. His hand dropped back to the bed, and he waited in silence.

She wasn't sure where to begin. "I came to Sea Crest for a vacation when my divorce was final. I chose to leave Richard, but even so, I was shattered. I lost court cases I shouldn't have. I forgot important appointments. I was a mess." She shrugged as though to make light of the situation, but she now realized she had been on the verge of a breakdown.

"I guess it was fortuitous that Aunt Theo left me Sea Crest, because coming to the inn no doubt saved my sanity."

"You're far from ready for an asylum." He scooted up against the headboard as he spoke, his gaze intent on her face as he listened to her story.

"You didn't know me before."

"That's all in the past, Michaela. It doesn't matter now that you're here with me."

"But that's the problem. I have to go, don't you see? It's my *life.*"

In a deceptively soft voice, he countered her statement by

saying, "What about *our* life, Michaela? What about me?"

"What do you expect me to do?" She placed her hands over her face and sobbed into them, trembling already from his loss. She had no answers, unless she could convince him to come with her.

She looked up as he swung his legs over the side of the bed. "You could come with me," she pleaded, desperate. "Logan, there's going to be a terrible war here. Thousands of lives—"

At her mention of the future, he sprang from the bed and came to her. Gently, he placed his fingers against her lips, his other hand circling her arm. "I don't want you to predict the future. If you're not here to share it with me, it won't matter."

"Come with me," she begged.

He caressed her cheek, his eyes full of sorrow. "I don't belong in your world, Michaela Marie. You saw what happened to me when I went there with you. I can't share your life and all its wonders."

"There must be a way."

This time he roughly pulled her into his embrace. His hot lips found hers before she could protest, his tongue delving deep to wash away her pleas.

"Does that feel like a specter's caress?" he whispered raggedly when he pulled away from the kiss. His hands slid over her back to her buttocks, pulling her hard against his arousal. "Is this a phantom's passion? In your world, that's all I am—a ghost."

"It's just not fair."

Logan tugged her hand to take her back to bed. "Not much in life is fair. But we have time yet, and we'll find a way."

Mica's heart broke as she resisted.

"No, you don't understand. My father gave me a month to get my life straightened out. *One month.* Then I had to go back to work." Tears obscured her vision, but she had already memorized his face for when she would no longer be in his arms.

"My month is up—tomorrow."

Twelve

Despondent, Mica pulled her knees close to her chest and, with a sigh, rested her chin upon them. She had curled up in the window seat of Katie's living room to stare unseeing out the window. Rain whipped through the trees and pounded the already saturated earth. The dismal weather perfectly reflected her mood.

"They say another tropical storm is brewing, but indications are it won't touch land," Katie commented from the sofa.

"Mmmm."

"Mica, listen to me." Her friend's voice held the exasperated tone she'd used in their youth when Mica would rather study than party. She knew what Katie would say even before she spoke. "You've got to pull yourself together. If it didn't work out with Logan, it didn't work out. You've moped around for over a week, and it's just not going to change anything."

Another tumultuous sigh escaped as Mica tried to pull herself from the emotional stupor that engulfed her on a daily basis. She cried readily—had even broken down in court yesterday, and the judge had been put out. She couldn't eat. She didn't sleep.

Her father was ready to send her to a psychiatrist, but her mother had convinced him it would be bad for the family name. Even her best friend was apparently at her wit's end.

"Oh, Katie, you don't understand. I just left—sneaked off in the middle of the night—without a word. I couldn't help him, and I couldn't face him."

Mica recalled Logan's face in slumber, the worry lines

from days past smoothing out. How she loved him! Even as she had tiptoed down the hall, her heart kept calling her back to his side.

She had never quite figured out what Aunt Theo had meant when she asked Mica to help him. She had tried to help, convincing Logan the crushed indigo would sell. Now, she feared she had messed things up royally by falling in love with him.

As if reading her mind, Katie asked, “If you’re that much in love with the guy, why couldn’t you work things out? Does it really matter if your father doesn’t approve of him?”

When Mica had shown up on Katie’s doorstep in tears, she had only said that she had left him because of her father and responsibilities. After all, how could she explain falling in love with a man who had lived more than a century before? Katie hadn’t asked any questions. She just fed Mica hot tea as if that would fix all her problems.

Mica chewed nervously on a fingernail. Even after a week back in Charleston, she still feared crossing the timeline had jumbled things beyond her understanding. By venturing into the past, she felt she had irrevocably changed hers or Logan’s destiny.

“Mica, you’re doing it again.”

“What?”

“Twisting that key and ribbon you’ve been wearing around your neck.”

She glanced down, not aware of the habit she had acquired since returning to Charleston. She had convinced herself that she’d brought the key from Sea Crest to keep the nosy Barkers or the crazy professor from finding out about the passage. However, in the dark of night as she sobbed into her pillow, she clutched the key to her heart, hoping it would bring her closer to Logan.

“While that necklace might be considered quaint, in an antique sort of way, it hardly matches your outfit.”

Today Mica had come to Katie’s straight from court. Her tailored brown suit and ruffled blouse were the latest fashion. She wiggled her stocking-clad feet, more comfortable now than in her heels, but she'd rather be barefoot in the sand at Indigo Bay.

God, there she went again. Everything in her present world still reminded her of 1850. She twirled the key around her finger.

Katie stood beside the window seat. "Let me see that."

Mica relinquished her grasp on the key, but refused to remove the ribbon from around her neck.

"You know," Katie continued, "if you had the key gold plated and put it on a gold chain, it wouldn't look quite so...scruffy."

"I don't think so," Mica said, retrieving the key. "Besides, it has sentimental value, not monetary."

Katie shrugged. "Well, it couldn't hurt, sentimental or not. After all, gold never loses its value."

"Gold?" Mica swung around, her heels thumping against the base of the window seat. Why hadn't she thought of that? She was a corporate lawyer versed in international trade and had a portfolio worth thousands. Yet she hadn't even thought of the one method of exchange used internationally—and throughout the *past.*

She jumped off her perch and headed for the door. "Where's Matthew?"

"Well, it's an hour prior to dinner on Monday. That means he's in the study reading the *New York Times.*"

Mica didn't wait for her friend to accompany her to the study. They didn't stand on formality at each other's homes. Racing from the room, she pounded on the study door then burst in before Matthew had acknowledged her knock.

"Matthew, you've got to help."

Katie's husband looked up from the paper he perused, then leisurely set it aside. He didn't seem the least concerned that Mica stood shouting at him across the width of his desk. When Katie rushed into the room behind her, he did tilt his head sideways to give her a wink.

A month ago, Mica would have made some facetious remark about their behavior, because they were still very much in love. Her views on that subject, however, had changed radically over the course of just a few weeks.

She paced back and forth, clasping her hands first in front of her, then behind her back. She tried to put into words the outrageous plan she had concocted to help Logan. Thrilled to finally have a course of action, she didn't want Matthew and Katie to think she had slipped off the deep end. Spinning around, she took a breath to calm herself.

"I want you to liquidate my stocks and bonds—all of them." That was easy enough.

Apparently Matthew didn't think so. He glanced from one woman to the other, a frown crinkling his forehead. Katie just shrugged her shoulders.

"You want your entire portfolio turned into cash?"

"Not cash. Gold."

Matthew came around the corner of his desk, hands in the air in a placating gesture. "Now wait a minute." To Katie he said, "I thought you said she was getting better?"

Mica had to laugh. "Surely you two have better things to do than discuss my mental health."

She began pacing again, energy flowing and revitalizing her. She wanted to do this. She needed to help Logan so desperately it scared her. The feeling of being on a crusade gave her a rush of adrenaline like she used to feel when she first became an attorney. Before the disillusionment and frustration and disappointment.

She had acquired a fair-sized portfolio. Converting it to gold would ensure Logan had the money he needed to see him through any hard times. Then it wouldn't matter if this year's crop sold well at market or not.

"Why on Earth would you want gold?" Matthew questioned, bringing her back to their discussion.

"I just need it, that's all. Since when did you become so inquisitive?" Mica countered.

"Since you asked for over one hundred thousand dollars' worth of stocks be converted to gold, that's when." Matthew threw up his hands in exasperation.

"Can it be done?"

"Of course it can be done. Any restrictions on buying gold

were lifted in 1972. That's not the point."

"Then what is the point?"

"You'll gain no interest by converting everything, and you'll run the risk of government questioning."

"Why would the government have any say in what I do with my money?"

"If you try taking that much cash into Castle & Noble Investment House to get gold, believe me, the government will want to know why."

"That's ridiculous. It's not like I'm laundering money." Mica's short temper began to stir.

"But the government doesn't know that. When that much gold is purchased, they won't look at your impeccable credentials as an attorney. The law requires paperwork on any cash transactions to gold over ten thousand dollars."

"How long would I have to wait after I complete the papers?"

"Oh, you wouldn't have to wait at all. The Investment House would give you the gold on the spot, but you'd have official-looking people at your door within twenty-four hours."

"I don't care. Just do it," Mica stated, crossing her arms over her chest in a gesture of finality.

"Mica, look. Katie says you've been under a lot of stress lately. Perhaps you should think about this."

"I am *not* stressed out," Mica shouted at him, then slapped a hand against her mouth. She couldn't believe she had screeched like that.

"Katie, talk to her." Matthew turned away to pour a drink from the sideboard. He could be a sweetheart, and Katie loved him dearly, but Mica couldn't stomach his chauvinistic attitude. He, and many men she knew, thought a woman was *stressed out* if she had a single idea of her own and it didn't agree with theirs.

Katie turned to her, rolling her eyes upward, and Mica put up her hand.

"Okay. You might as well know the real reason behind this *madness.* Although Matthew has politely refrained from saying so, I know that's what he's thinking." She sighed. She would tell them about Logan, and if Matthew didn't haul her away to the loony bin, he'd get her the gold.

For the next hour, Mica recapped her month with Logan. She tried to explain the time warp, how desperately Logan needed the money to help his people, and her love for a man who didn't exist in their century.

"Oh, Mica, how very, very romantic. I never would have thought it." Katie was the first to find her voice when Mica stopped talking.

"Bullshit," Matthew exploded. "That's the most absurd, ridiculous...Mica, if you're doing drugs, as your friends, it's our duty to see you get help."

"That's enough, Matthew," Mica snapped. "I didn't tell you to gain your approval, or your belief. I told you because..." She looked from husband to wife. Katie's eyes were brimming, and Mica truly didn't know whether she believed her or not.

"Katie?"

Katie walked over and clasped Mica's hands, squeezing them almost to the point of pain. She turned to her husband, and in a voice filled with awe and perhaps fright, said, "She's not on drugs, Matthew. Her Logan was in the room the entire time I visited with her. I kept thinking I heard voices down the hall, but it must have been him." She turned teary eyes to Mica. "And...I felt his presence."

Mica gasped. "Why didn't you say something?"

Katie gave a nervous laugh. "For exactly the same reason you didn't. Matthew would have put me away." She glanced fondly at her husband. "In country club style, of course, but still 'off to the funny farm.'"

"I don't believe this." Matthew couldn't, or wouldn't, take their word for what had happened.

Mica knelt down beside the sofa on which he had dropped. Clasping his hands, she spoke earnestly. "Listen, I'll compromise with you. Get me the gold, and by—" she paused, not sure she could make the time table she wanted. "—by next Monday, if I haven't accomplished what I need to, I'll put it all back into your trusting hands."

"What about the Internal Revenue?"

"To hell with the government. It's my money. Besides, if I can get it to Logan, there won't be any trace of it for them to worry about."

"That's just the problem, Mica. How will you explain where it went?" She knew he felt justified in asking her questions, even if he wouldn't be directly involved.

"Let me worry about that. After all, if need be, I know a good lawyer." She gave him a smile. Probably the first real smile she had managed since leaving Indigo Bay.

Matthew capitulated. "All right, give me until Friday."

"Wednesday." Now that she had a plan, she didn't want to wait any longer than necessary.

"That's only two days. I'm not sure it can be done."

"You said my stocks could be cashed on the spot."

"But the market might not be good."

Mica threw up her hands. "Matthew, it doesn't matter. I want my money, however much there is of it. Let's compromise. I'll give you until Thursday."

Mica and Katie left Matthew to his brooding. Katie tried to persuade her to stay, but she declined.

"I'm in court again tomorrow. As much as I hate this particular case, I still should go home and review my briefs."

Katie gave her a hug. "At least you're not a criminal lawyer. I'd hate the thought of you associating with hardened felons and murderers."

"Well, as far as I'm concerned, sometimes the best dressed businessmen are just as bad." Mica replied, then changed the subject as they reached the front door. "Katie, did you really see, I mean feel, Logan, or were you just saying that to help me out with Matthew?"

Katie smiled as she answered. "I thought I was imagining things, but yes, I definitely felt him."

"But you couldn't see him?"

"No, but I'm sure he's just as wonderful and handsome as you say. Besides, he's got to be something special to bring such a smile to your face."

Mica hugged her. "He is."

"Well, I hope so. After all, you wouldn't give Richard

another penny, and here you are giving away a fortune!"

Mica laughed with Katie as she kissed her good-bye, but on the drive back to her apartment she thought about what her friend had said.

Why had she decided to give Logan all her money when that had been a major rift in her relationship with Richard? Soft brown eyes came to mind, the corners crinkled in laughter. Other images intruded—Logan fighting the nasty Mr. Jacobs when he beat up a child, Logan working harder than anyone to put out fires and repackage the indigo. The list could go on and on.

Mica knew he didn't do it for himself, although he was proud of his accomplishments. He did what he needed to protect what had been left in his care—the island, the people—her.

She cried herself to sleep that night, but for the first time since her return, it was a cleansing cry, not one of self-pity. She felt good about what she had to do, and she didn't care if she had to work another fifty years to regain her stock options. She had no use for the money, anyway, so she might as well ensure Logan's success.

The next two days proved extremely stressful. Not only did Mica worry about Matthew's progress, but her current case left her wondering why she had become an attorney.

Seaboard Enterprises had always been a reputable client until now. They were one of the largest corporations in Charleston, and she had conducted mergers and international trade agreements on their behalf. Then sexual harassment charges were filed against the company and Samuel Clancy, an employee. Her father hadn't allowed her to transfer this case to a subordinate.

Samuel Clancy was guilty—had as much as confessed—but she couldn't betray a client's confidence. She came home from court feeling soiled and used, and she stood in the shower long minutes to wash away the emotional dirt.

By Wednesday evening she had reached the end of her endurance. She shut off the phone the minute she walked into the apartment. She didn't even want to hear the answering machine. After her shower, she pulled on soft, silk pajamas and uncorked a bottle of wine. Curling up in a chair by the window, she tried to clear her mind as rain battered the windows.

More rain. The coast should be out of the hurricane season by now, but the weather bureau still predicted the current tropical storm would intensify by the weekend. It was probably a good thing she intended to visit Sea Crest, just to make sure things were secure. Although she didn't have any plans to sell the place or to live there, she still had the responsibility for its upkeep.

The bottle clinked against her crystal glass as she refilled it. A glass of wine normally calmed her nerves and helped her relax, but for whatever reason, it didn't work tonight. A disquieting shroud engulfed her, and it had nothing to do with her current case. Something gnawed at her from the inside—something intangible but still making its presence felt.

"In-two-three-four-five," Mica breathed deeply. "Out-two-three-four-five." Her counselor had taught her the breathing exercise. Usually it worked. Tonight it didn't.

Nothing worked. Half a bottle of wine later, she crawled into bed, determined to sleep. When she closed her eyes, Logan's countenance came immediately to view, and Mica contented herself with thoughts of him. She had visualized several scenarios for giving him the gold, but each ended with her leaving him. Each time with more heartache than the last.

She finally decided she must go to the other side during the day, when he would be gone. She would leave him a note, of course, but she didn't think she could bear to see him. She buried her face in her pillow, hoping to dream of him, as she did every night, knowing her dreams were all she had.

***

"Thursday, the thirteenth day of September, two thousand one. The Court of the State of South Carolina is hereby in session. Case number 560-483, Melissa Reynolds vs. Samuel Clancy and Seaboard Enterprises," the bailiff intoned in a dry, hollow voice.

The judge's gavel pounded in the silence as though it

hammered directly on Mica's brain. She stood beside her clients.

"Has the jury reached a verdict?"

"Yes, Your Honor, we have. The jury finds in the case of the defendant, Samuel Clancy, not guilty on all charges. In the case of the co-defendant, Seaboard Enterprises, not guilty on all charges."

"The Court of the State of South Carolina thanks the jury for their verdict and their time, and they are now dismissed. This court stands adjourned." The gavel pounded again.

Mica snapped her briefcase shut with a sigh. She had nothing to say to her client, who stood there with a huge macho smile, as though he expected her to be happy with the verdict. How could she be, when she knew beyond any reasonable doubt he was guilty as charged?

Hell, the bastard had propositioned her more times than she could count, and in his firm's corporate boardroom, no less, when she had to see him on business. In her mind, his employers, Seaboard Enterprises, were just as guilty for backing his claim of innocence.

She recalled her visit with the plaintiff, Melissa Reynolds, in the process of trying to negotiate a settlement. She wasn't a headliner. She hadn't been out to create a scandal or to climb the corporate ladder. She had only wanted her executive position and the right to work in a harassment-free atmosphere. Now, she had neither, because the company would find some way to eliminate her position and thereby dispose of the unobliging Ms. Reynolds.

Mica should be happy that she had accomplished her job. She had removed the blemish from Seaboard's corporate image, and the exorbitant fee she would charge them for doing so would be paid without a quiver of conscience on their part. Mica tucked a stray lock of hair behind her ear and turned to leave the courtroom.

"Let me buy you a drink, Michaela." The touch on her arm drew goose bumps.

"Mr. Clancy, my name is Ms. Chadwick. And no, I do *not* care to drink with you." *Or ever see your lecherous face again,* she longed to add, yet knew she couldn't. "You'll receive a statement from our firm."

Her cool remarks dismissed him as surely as her rigid back. She turned to her secretary, Suzy, who had just hurried into the courtroom, and she welcomed the interruption.

"Ms. Taylor called twice, but since her case is in settlement, I told her you would be in contact and she needn't call back."

Mica quickened her pace. She didn't care about Helen Taylor. She didn't even care about winning again. She had an inexplicable urge to get as far away from Charleston as possible. Right now. Her breathing quickened. Her determination to leave was so intense she didn't catch the deliberate pause in her secretary's recitation until they stepped into the elevator.

"Well, what is it you don't want to tell me?" One glance at Suzy's face, and Mica knew the answer even before the other woman spoke.

"Richard called."

"Damn!" The elevator doors opened on a rush of humanity, precluding further discussion until they walked into the underground parking lot. Mica wasn't about to ask for particulars, but Suzy proceeded to tell her anyway.

"He wanted an appointment. When I told him I didn't schedule your personal matters, he said this was business."

"I told him two weeks ago I wouldn't bail him out again. I'm already paying him plenty." The mention of her ex-husband still fueled Mica's anger. So much so, she jammed the wrong key into the car's lock. The high-pitched screech of the alarm obscured the remainder of the not-so-polite adjectives she used to describe him.

She took a deep breath, held it for the count of five, then slowly exhaled. Her hands shook too hard to remove the key. Without a word, Suzy took over, inserting the correct key to open the door, and then punching the alarm button. The instant quiet soothed Mica's nerves. She dropped her chin to her chest and closed her eyes for an instant.

"Cancel or reschedule tomorrow's appointments." She tossed her briefcase onto the back seat of the Cougar as she gave instructions to her ever-faithful secretary. "I'm driving to Sea Crest, but under no circumstances are you to tell anyone where I am." She didn't have to say who *anyone* meant. She slid behind the wheel, but didn't start the engine. Suzy was probably the only person who had any idea what Mica had gone through the past six months.

"Thanks, Suzy. You'll never know..."

"Yeah, I do." Suzy grinned and gave her arm a pat.

***

By the time Mica crossed town, Matthew had left for the day, making her wait until the following morning to receive a cashier's check for her stocks. Disregarding his arguments that she wait until he completed the sale of her blue chip stocks, she took what he had managed to convert and raced back across town to Castle & Noble Investment House. Matthew had called ahead, and they were expecting her.

Panic had seized her yesterday outside the courthouse, and she felt compelled to hurry up the coast as fast as possible. The restlessness she had felt the night before descended on her with a vengeance. She couldn't explain it, but she didn't doubt it had something to do with Logan.

They asked no questions at Castle & Noble, for which she was grateful. She signed the necessary papers as they counted out her gold in American Eagles. Even dated, the gold coins would travel through time and Mica figured she could worry about melting it down later. Given the current price of three-hundred-ninety dollars per troy ounce, she left with a briefcase containing only seventeen pounds of twenty-four carat gold.

She didn't know how much purchasing power the gold would have in 1850, but she figured it would be a lot more than today, considering the inflation they experienced. It really didn't matter. The gold would help see Logan and his people through this year's rough times, at least.

Mica turned north onto Highway 17. There was no reason to stop at her apartment. She had clothes at Sea Crest, and didn't plan on staying long, anyway. What would happen after that she had no idea. She didn't want to visualize her life at some later date, so she concentrated only on getting to Sea Crest before the storm hit.

"Damn!" Mica slammed on the brakes as taillights in front of her blinked red. Traffic slowed to a stop, but with the rain beating against her windshield, even the wipers couldn't help her see the cause.

She jumped when a large hand knocked at her window. Rolling it down just enough to see out, she spied a yellow-slickered highway patrolman, water running off the brim of his hat.

"Sorry, ma'am, but we're closing Highway 17 due to the storm. You'll have to return to Charleston."

"But Officer, this highway is always open for evacuation. Besides, I have a home at Cameron, and I need to see that everything is boarded up." A heaviness squeezed her heart, and she felt an even greater sense of urgency.

"We have reports of gusty winds near the coast, and motorists are advised not to travel. We're just trying to protect you, ma'am." Mica could tell by his tone that the officer was in no mood to argue, but neither was she.

She rolled up her window, made a U-turn as other cars were doing, and drove south. At the first intersection, she turned west. Having grown up in the area, she knew every back road and circular route, some of which weren't even on a map. In a matter of minutes, she was again headed north through a residential area.

She encountered very little traffic and no police. Apparently the highway patrol had focused their efforts on the main highways, which didn't surprise her. In all the years she had lived through hurricanes, evacuation always occurred on the four-lane roads, not the county byways.

She drove at a reasonable speed, not stopping at any of the little towns that crowded the highway. Visibility dropped to zero at times, compelling her to slow down to avoid going off onto the shoulder. When her hands cramped from gripping the steering wheel, she forced herself to relax, reaching down to flick the knob on her radio.

A soothing melody coursed through her—a melody that

reminded her of the time she and Logan had loved the night away in the music room. She could almost see him as he caressed the piano keys, his music wrapping her in warmth and love.

Thomas Logan Rutledge. She recalled the many times he had praised her for helping him, and his unfailing faith in her ability and willingness to share in his life. She finally understood the turmoil of the last few weeks, especially after her day in court where she would rather have been on the losing side.

While her clients paid their bills, they didn't go out of their way to express their appreciation. Even her father took her for granted in terms of her efforts. He just *expected* her to win cases and negotiate international trade agreements because that was what she had been trained to do.

Useless. That was exactly the word to describe her current life. Entrenched in the family law firm that specialized in corporate law and worked with only the largest corporations in Charleston, she didn't feel she made any contribution to society. Especially when a scum like Samuel Clancy still had his job.

Aggravation mounted as she mentally catalogued her dull, responsible life. She couldn't say she had *never* felt needed, but lately that feeling had been replaced by dissatisfaction, not to mention boredom and restlessness. Yet she felt caught in a perpetual cycle from which she had no hope of extricating herself.

The rain lessened, and Mica sped up, anxious to arrive at Sea Crest. She tried not to think about encountering Logan. Instead, she concentrated on the necessary precautions needed to take at the bed & breakfast, just in case this storm escalated in strength and moved up the coast.

Static erupted on the radio, and she punched the button for another station. The song was cut short by the DJ's voice.

"It's Friday, September fourteenth, and this is the latest bulletin from the National Hurricane Center. Hurricane Charley is expected to hit the South Carolina coast near Charleston late tonight or early tomorrow morning. Residents are advised to take necessary precautions and seek shelter inland."

Mica stomped on the accelerator. She had to get to Logan before the hurricane hit. If she didn't…

She didn't let herself finish the thought, because she knew that if she didn't get there in time, she might never see Logan again.

Thirteen

Mica arrived at Sea Crest to find Anna firmly in control. Workmen had boarded up the windows and were just closing and latching the front shutters. Mica dropped her briefcase in the apartment, then went to check the food and water storage. Hopefully, Charley would veer out to sea and their supplies would not be necessary.

"Did you reschedule the guests for flights home?" she asked Anna as they hurried through the house to the kitchen in search of flashlights.

"Most of our reservations were up yesterday, and since flights have been canceled, our newest guests won't arrive until after the storm has passed. That just leaves two rooms occupied."

"Two rooms—I thought you said everyone was out?" Mica didn't want to be responsible for others during a storm.

"The Barkers refused to leave, even though their time is up. Said they couldn't get a flight out because of the storm, so they would just have to ride it out here."

"Oh, great. I suppose they're hoping the storm blows the place down so it'll be easier to search for their treasure."

Anna laughed with her, though Mica was hardly kidding. "Who else?" she asked.

"The professor's reservations aren't up for another week, so he said he'd be glad to stay and keep me and the Barkers company."

Mica thought she detected a blush on Anna's cheeks and wondered if she had an infatuation for the gray-haired professor.

"Well, I suppose there's nothing we can do about it now.

Until a couple of hours ago, I really thought this storm would leave us alone. As long as our guests stay out of the way and observe the rules, we should be all right. After all, Sea Crest has weathered storms before. You have reviewed the rules with them, haven't you?"

"Yes, of course." Anna ticked them off on her fingers, "Stay on the main floor away from the windows, leave the TV and radio turned to the weather channel, and ration food and water."

"Good. I'll leave you to see to our guests. I need to make sure all is secure in my apartment." Using that excuse, Mica hurried down the hall. She must get the gold upstairs before the weather worsened.

She dumped her aunt's jewelry from a small wooden chest onto the bed. Flipping open the latches on her briefcase, she began unrolling the gold American Eagles and dumping them into the box. Regardless of whether paper would *time travel,* she didn't want Logan to see the telltale signs of modern investment brokers.

Mica clicked the latch shut on the small box. She left her apartment through the French doors, rounded the house through the gardens and re-entered in the kitchen. Since the guests had all been instructed to remain on the main floor, she hoped they wouldn't detect her movement towards the stairs. The rain had slowed to a drizzle, but the wind had picked up. She crossed her fingers, hoping the outside noise would cover her footsteps.

As quietly as possible, she slipped around the corner and sped up the stairs two at a time. She didn't hesitate, but fit the key in the lock and turned it, then she stepped through and closed the door behind her. The unmistakable scent of beeswax candles greeted her, and she wondered how she had ever thought Indigo Bay was a simple extension of the existing bed and breakfast.

The gold clinked as she shifted the box to her other arm. The individual coins were small, but they were heavy when you put a bunch of them together. Determined to leave her present for Logan and be gone as fast as possible, she tiptoed down the hall. She had almost reached the study when she detected angry voices from beyond the partly open door.

"I want what's due me! My father and I were stuck on this stinking piece of dirt while you partied away your time up North, attending balls and seducing all the women you could find. How do you think I felt when I learned the will was entailed and all my hard work was for nothing?"

Neil's voice rose in anger, and Mica feared he might try to harm Logan. She crept closer, trying to see around the corner of the door without being spotted.

"You could hardly categorize as work what you and your father did to this island," Logan snorted. "If you had been in control much longer, there would be nothing left."

There was a pause, and Mica longed to see Logan's face. Before she could move, he continued the discussion.

"I told you no more, Neil. If you can't make a contribution to this island and its inhabitants, I refuse to give you any more money to squander at the gambling tables."

Logan's voice held more exasperation than anger, and Mica's heart when out to him. Neil could be her ex-husband's twin.

"If you think I'm going to work side-by-side with darkies, think again. There are other ways to insure I get what I deserve."

Mica felt guilty listening to their private conversation and she decided to leave the box in Logan's bedroom. He must have seen her shadow on the wall, however, for he called to her as she turned.

"Michaela Marie, what are you doing here? It isn't midnight and the witching hour yet," he said, sarcasm lacing his voice.

His face came into view when she stepped inside the doorway and stopped. His brown eyes flashed with fury and he looked as though he would throttle her.

"Did you come back, like Neil, in hopes I have to sign over the island because my crops failed and I'm unable to pay my debts?" He stood magnificently proud and stubborn. His hair was tousled, as though he'd been out in the wind. His white linen shirt clung to the contours of his work-hardened chest.

She couldn't blame him for being angry with her. She had made a habit of disappearing. Still, he didn't have to be quite so rude, not after everything they had shared.

With deliberate strides, she walked to his desk. The gold jingled as she thunked the wooden chest onto the desk and slid it across the smooth surface close to where his hands rested. "I came back to help, like I said I would."

"You said many things, and some were far from believable. I don't know whether to trust your word—on any of it." His gaze locked with hers, and she recognized his hurt because of her deception. His eyes, always portraying hope and laughter, were now were full of betrayal and cynicism.

She had told him she loved him, but she couldn't stay. She had tried to warn him, but that didn't make her sneaking out on him right, and she knew it.

She gestured towards the box. "This will help, in case—"

"I don't need your help." He bit out the words, making no move to open the box. He straightened to his full height, his whole body offended by her gesture. His gaze flickered from her to Neil. "Regardless of what you both might think, I can take care of my own."

He turned back to her. "I don't need your charity. The auction was held over a week ago. Though skeptical, most of the buyers trust the Indigo Bay name enough they still bought our dye. The price was only slightly lower than last year."

"Oh, Logan, I'm happy for you, I really am." Tears misted her vision. His posture rejected both her money and her, and she knew his stubborn pride would prevent him from accepting her gift.

Neil moved closer to the desk, his green eyes flashing with defiance. "This is all very touching, but it doesn't solve my problem." He reached for the box. "If your pride won't allow you to accept this lovely lady's money, I most certainly have no such scruples."

With a flick of his wrist, he flipped open the box. "Holy jumping mother of Moses! It's full of gold!" He grabbed for the glittering coins, only to have his wrist clinched by Logan.

"Get out, Neil." Logan spoke harshly, but his penetrating gaze never left Mica's face. She paled, unable to understand the emotions that washed across his features. "Leave the island today, and don't return until you're willing to work."

He released his grip on Neil's wrist, thrusting him away as he had the broken pieces of indigo.

Neil bristled, his gaze still on the gold. "There must be thousands there. You don't need it. You have your precious island," he sneered, his voice full of hate.

Logan slammed the lid shut. "Out!"

Neil backed slowly towards the door. "You can't have it all, Brother. Never fear, I will be back." He roughly shoved Mica aside, storming down the hallway.

Deadly silence spoke louder than words as Logan stared across the width of the room. When Mica could stand it no longer, she reached out a hand, pleading with her gaze that he understand her motives—both in leaving and giving him the gold.

"Logan?"

"I don't need your gold, Michaela. I need you." Angry strides brought him right in front of her, and she stepped back. "I need you here beside me, day in and day out, to share my life and happiness. Can you do that? Or will I wake up one morning and find you gone again?"

She gasped when he grabbed her upper arms and dragged her into an embrace. Before she could answer his questions, he kissed her. But instead of passion, his kiss was full of anger and hunger and desperation. She clung to him, answering his need with her own.

When he finally released her, she wept against his shoulder. This had been her reason for not wanting to see him.

"I have to go," she whispered brokenly.

His hands dropped to his sides, his breath soft and warm against her temple. "I love you, Michaela Marie. Does that count for naught?"

"I'm not what you *need,"* she said, sobbing even as she backed towards the door.

"But you're all I'll ever *want.*" He turned his back on her, and Mica knew he was giving her a choice. He wouldn't stop her this time, and he wouldn't beg her to stay.

With a sob, she turned and fled.

***

Mica stood at the edge of the beach. She should be inside, but everything had been done that could be done. The shutters were up, food stored, lamps and flashlights available should Hurricane Charley not go out to sea as predicted.

The wind had picked up considerably, tossing rain and sea mist against her. She didn't notice, because the moisture mixed with the tears that slid silently down her face.

She turned and glanced down the beach. Apparently other people on the island also thought Charley would veer away. Quite a few lights flickered from the many homes on the waterfront—homes she no longer thought of as part of Logan's Indigo Bay.

Pieces of litter blew against her legs. She yelled out angrily, "Why are you trying to destroy Logan's island?" The wind provided no answer to her fury.

She hugged herself against the bits of blowing sand, her tears obscuring the rolling clouds and black horizon. How could her life have changed so radically in such a short time? Could she honestly go back to Charleston and resume her life? She laughed, a mirthless echo against the strengthening wind.

Her life seemed only to have begun with Logan. He had shown her the marvels of unspoiled beauty, hard work and love. He had opened her eyes to the wonders shared by two people working towards a common goal.

If she returned to Charleston, Logan would be lost to her forever. He said he wanted *her*—her love, her undivided attention—not her money or any other material thing she had to offer. It had been heartbreaking to leave him, his stiff back turned to her, not in rejection, but in affirmation of her right to choose. She loved him all the more for allowing her that right, though she wished it could be otherwise. Could she go to him now, only for the weekend, and not want to stay wrapped in his arms forever?

She clutched the key she wore—the talisman to her dreams. "What should I do? How am I to live without him?" Her cries of anguish faded into the coming night, and her tears mingled with the salt spray from the breakers.

The wind answered this time, for above the thunder of ocean and storm, she heard the sweet melody of a waltz. Compelling and exotic, it beckoned her. She began to run, realizing at last that she really had no choice. The decision had been made more than a century before. With each step, her heart pounded, anxious to claim that which she had almost denied forever.

Abruptly, every light along the shore went out, forcing Mica to slow her pace. Knowing from past experience that the storm would keep the electricity out for the duration, she hesitated. Should she check on her guests before abandoning her aunt's home forever?

"I'm not really leaving," she whispered as she trotted up the path. "I'll always take good care of your island, Aunt Theo." She sent a silent thank you to her beloved aunt, for without her gift of Sea Crest, Mica might never have found Logan.

She had the distinct feeling Aunt Theo and Logan's Aunt Margaret had planned this from the very beginning. Mica only wished they had made it easier, but then she might not have appreciated what she had found in Logan.

She entered the kitchen, feeling her way along the south wall to avoid stubbing a toe on the appliances. A flickering light in the vicinity of the living room caught her eye, and she carefully made her way in that direction.

Two indefinable shapes huddled on the sofa in the dark. The flashlight blinked on and off in the corner, but the small circle of light did little to illuminate the room.

"Anna?" Mica took a cautious step forward.

One of the dark silhouettes answered. "Yes, it's me. The batteries must not be very good."

Mica moved towards the couch as her manager continued nervously, "Never did care for storms. Most of the time, I go up to Orlando and stay with my sister. Even if a hurricane comes inland, it usually loses its punch before it hits Molly's."

Anna's wistful voice reminded Mica that soon the older woman would be in full charge of Sea Crest. Mica now wondered if she could handle it.

"Mrs. Harris, there's something you should know."

"Now, dear, don't worry about me. I just get a little melancholy when a storm hits. You see, I lost my husband in a storm at sea. He was a fisherman." She spoke to no one in particular, but Mica understood her need for conversation to chase away her fears.

She had moved close enough to recognize Mr. Barker sitting next to Anna, his bald head glowing in the meager light. That could only mean the domineering Mrs. Barker had control of the only other light.

Mica turned toward that corner of the sitting room. Nadine Barker had begun pulling books from the shelves. The flashlight, tucked under one arm, cast distorted shadows on the wall.

"Mrs. Barker, I'd prefer you stay away from the windows. Come over here with the rest of us. Besides, you have no right to dig through the personal library."

"I'm not going to sit in the middle of the room like a ninny, just because of a little storm. Besides, we're so close to discovery. Harold, come here and hold this damned light." She tapped the flashlight against her palm as it went out again. As though God took exception to Mrs. Barker's criticism of His handiwork, a roll of thunder, followed by a loud crash, echoed from above.

Anna twisted her hands in agitation. "I do hope that wasn't Professor Bigley. He refused to come downstairs, you know."

"No, I didn't know." Mica sighed but headed for the stairs. Why was it that when she had finally reached a satisfactory conclusion to her personal dilemma, everything began working against her? She certainly couldn't chance going through the door with the professor upstairs.

"Professor Bigley, where are you?" She kept one hand on the banister as she crept up the stairs and turned down the hall. She had just reached his door when it slammed open. The professor and his squealing ghost machine tumbled out into the hall.

"Sorry. Had to go back for more film. I accidentally knocked over the water pitcher and bowl." He didn't slow down, but tossed his explanation over a shoulder as he hurried towards the far end of the corridor. Right towards the door to Indigo Bay!

Mica's breath caught. Surely he couldn't know. She tried to calm herself as she raced to catch up with him.

"Please, Professor, you must come downstairs. If the wind gets much worse, I can't be responsible for your safety. The trees, telephone poles..." Her voice trailed off, but her mouth remained open.

The professor's contraption glowed with lights. Every bulb on the machine was blinking in a series of reds, greens or blues. Fortunately, he had turned the volume down, but Mica couldn't stop staring in amazement. The closer he moved to the door, the faster the lights blinked.

"There's a great disturbance on the other side of that door. The same sort I noticed weeks ago, only much stronger."

"It's probably just the weather," Mica spoke to divert the professor's attention. She recalled the episode when Logan had accidentally crossed over. She didn't doubt the professor's machine could really detect spectral phenomena. Now she must get him downstairs so she could investigate. Was Logan standing on the other side of the door yearning for her? Waiting for her?

"No, no, it's not the storm, nor the electrical currents generated by the lightning. Something horrendous is happening beyond that door, and we must help!" He set the box down and wrapped both hands around the doorknob, twisting and jerking in an attempt to open it. "Where's the key? There used to be a key in this lock."

Mica quickly slipped the key down the front of her shirt. Nobody, not even the professor, could be allowed access to Indigo Bay. She would protect it and its inhabitants with her life. But if what the professor said was true, Logan was in trouble.

Anna's cry of alarm sounded from downstairs. Mica froze,

uncertain which direction to go. The manager's next words made her decision for her.

"Fire!" Anna's cry became one of panic and Mica had no choice. She was happy to note, however, that the professor raced her to the stairs.

They came upon Harold and Anna slapping ineffectively at a small flame on the edge of a throw rug. Mica grabbed the fire extinguisher behind the desk and quickly doused the area. It hadn't been a large blaze, but Mica rounded on Harold, whose red face tattled on him.

"What the hell were you thinking?" she shouted right in his face.

"I'm terribly sorry. *Naddie* didn't have enough light to see the books, so I thought to light one of those small lamps to help her out." He shrank from Mica's vicious glare.

"Of all the idiotic ideas. I told you not to disturb my property." She took a step forward, not sure that, at the moment, she didn't intend to do him bodily harm.

Nadine came to her husband's defense as the professor led a distraught Anna over to the couch. "My goodness, Ms. Chadwick, it's not like it was a raging inferno. Just a little disturbance, that's all."

Raging inferno? Disturbance? That's what had been written in the—

"Where's that journal?" Mica questioned the woman, her voice brooking no argument.

Nadine gave her one, anyway. "Now see here, you have no right to our book."

"Where *is* it?" She spit the words, grabbing the woman by the arm and shaking her with all her might.

"Here, here!" Harold thrust the book into her hands, forcing her to let go of his wife, whom he cuddled as she feigned injury.

Mica ignored them as she frantically flipped through the pages, searching for the passage she had read before. "Where is it?" she mumbled, scanning the erratic handwriting.

"Not only does he have the land, but now the gold as well...a raging inferno consumes all he holds dear. Then I

shall have my revenge!"

Dear God, *she* had given Neil yet another reason to covet what belonged to Logan. No wonder it hadn't made sense before. She had read the journal entry before she had taken the gold to Logan.

In court they would call it circumstantial evidence—a journal with no dates or names, and nonsensical comments about spectral disturbances from a professor who believed in ghosts. Mica didn't care, because this time she relied on her heart. Racing up the stairs and stumbling in the dark, she staggered down the hall. Fumbling for the key, her hands shook so badly she had difficulty fitting it properly.

"Please, please, don't let it be too late," she begged. "Not now. Not after I've finally learned to love."

The door gave beneath her shoulder, and she fell through the entrance, thick smoke immediately causing her to choke. She slammed the door and dropped to her knees, though the air wasn't much easier to breathe. She held her shirttails up to cover her mouth and nose.

"Logan," she yelled as loudly as she dared, knowing that to breathe too deeply would only make it more difficult. Crawling on hands and knees, she checked every room as she came to it.

The room in which she slept showed signs of a search. Bed linens were strewn across the floor, and the draperies hung at crooked angles against the windows. Apparently Neil thought she lived permanently at Indigo Bay and he had searched her room for the gold.

The smoke and heat intensified as Mica crept down the hall. Though she shouted Logan's name until her voice grew hoarse, she could hear no response. Perhaps he had gotten out, but Mica's heart told her otherwise.

The study was shut tight, but smoke rolled from beneath the door. She heard a timber crack and then thunder to the floor somewhere within.

"Logan," she shouted again as she reached for the door handle. "Ouch! Damn it!" She jerked her hand back, blisters already forming where the hot metal had bitten into her palm.

She couldn't even conjure up enough spit to moisten it.

Rising to her knees, she wrapped the tails of her shirt around her hand before attempting to touch the knob again. As she felt the latch give, she dropped back to the floor and rolled up against the wall. She had heard too many horror stories about flash fires erupting when new oxygen became accessible.

A blast of bone-melting heat escaped when the door opened further, and Mica was thankful for the wall's thin protection. When the smoke cleared a little, she cautiously peered around the doorjamb. Flames cracked and sizzled, licking up the walls to consume the wallpaper and timbers beneath.

The fire appeared contained along the outside wall of the study, and Mica searched the floor and closer areas for signs of life. This room, too, showed signs of invasion—Logan's precious law books laid helter-skelter on the floor, and papers from his desk were scattered to become more fuel for the fire.

"Logan, I know you're here somewhere. I can feel it." She crawled into the room, her gaze moving constantly in search of him. Then she heard a moan.

"Logan!" This time she shouted, scrambling to her feet as she came around the back of the desk.

***

Logan tried to make sense of his world. His lungs burned, the back of his skull felt like someone had cracked it wide open, and a sharp pain invaded his right shoulder to travel down his arm. Smoke and tears blurred his vision.

He thought perhaps Neil had gotten the best of him after all, for kneeling beside him was the most beautiful angel he would ever see. Her wet tears dropped to his face to become balm for his soul.

"Michaela...Marie," he croaked. "Ever the salvation of this wretched soul, aren't you?" He reached with his uninjured arm to circle her neck and draw her closer. "Have you come to gloat over what my stubborn pride has cost me?"

"You are stubborn," she said, sobbing as she hugged him. "But if there's anything to gloat over, it'll have to be done later."

She was tugging at his arm, trying to get him to his feet. At her words, he became aware of the heat. He swiveled his head to survey the damage, intense pain ricocheting inside his skull.

"Damnation!" Leaning heavily on her for support, Logan managed to shift from his knees to his feet. When Michaela grabbed his right wrist and tried to wrap his arm around her shoulder in support, he cried out in agony.

"I'm sorry, but we've got to get out of here! I can't call 911 to come to our rescue."

As they shuffled over to the door, Logan didn't have time to wonder about her choice of words. It took all his strength and willpower just to move his feet one in front of the other.

They entered the hallway, and he slumped against the wall, unable to take another step. Black crept into the edges of his vision, and he feared he would pass out.

"We must stop—just for a moment," he wheezed, for the smoke still captured in his lungs made it difficult to say the simplest words.

"We can't," she replied. Her hands felt cool against his cheeks as she cradled his head. Still, the black crept closer, sucking the strength from his legs. He began to slide down the wall.

"Look at me!" He couldn't recall ever hearing such determination in her voice before. "I love you, Thomas Logan Rutledge, and I didn't come back to you just to have you die on me."

Her words gave him strength, for he truly thought when she left this afternoon he would never see her again. She had become his world, more precious than the land he held so dear, and more valuable than any gold she might give him.

Too late, he had gone in search of her. He would have pleaded, begged on bended knee, for her to come back. Unable to find her, he had gone to the music room, pleading his case with his music. He had prayed she would hear, as she had before, and return to his side.

Now, his angel had no mercy as she tugged him away

from the wall by his shirtfront, and together they stumbled down the hallway.

Fortunately, Simon met them at the top of the stairs, and between Michaela and him, Logan managed to get to the bottom.

"Mister Logan, I got everyone out, but I thought you had gone into town." Simon informed him.

Logan had intended a visit with friends before Neil's arrival, and he had earlier told Simon not to wait dinner.

"It's ... all right." His voice cracked, and he coughed.

Once outside in the fresh air, Logan's senses became more tuned to his surroundings. He found his people already forming a bucket brigade, but he seriously doubted anything could be saved. Fortunately, a rain had begun to fall, and it would help put out the flames. He had no strength to help. He could only stand and watch the fire consume his home, and he hugged Michaela tightly to his side.

"Thank the heavens you weren't there when Neil returned," he told her, his voice harsh with emotion. He kissed her forehead. Her solid presence felt so right.

"It was all my fault."

Her whisper held anguish, and he hugged her tighter to let her know he was all right.

"No, you're not to blame. I should have listened to you when you tried to warn me about Neil." He sighed. "He wasn't satisfied with a share, nor was he willing to work for it. He wanted it all and tried to kill me to get it." Logan swiveled his head, trying to release the tension and dull ache that still clung to his brain.

A groomsman interrupted with a discreet cough. Logan glanced over Michaela's head to where the man stood, bathed in wavering light from the fire.

"Excuse me for bothering you, Mister Logan, and I'm sorry to be the bearer of bad news, but I thought you'd want to know." He nervously twisted and untwisted his felt hat.

"What is it?" Logan couldn't think of any news worse than watching his home burn to the ground.

"It's your brother, sir." He coughed again, his gaze shifting from the ground to the house and back, looking anywhere but directly into Logan's eyes.

"Get on with it, man."

"Well, sir, he come tearing out to the stables, insisting on a horse. Knowing how you feel about your animals, I argued with him, but he struck me and grabbed the first one he could saddle. The horse must have smelled the smoke and panicked, for she reared and threw Mister Neil." Another deliberate pause, and Logan raised a brow in question.

"He's dead, sir. Broke his fool neck, begging your pardon."

With no outward display of emotion, Logan thanked his groomsman and turned away, curling his good arm around Michaela's shoulders to pull her close against his chest.

"I'm sorry, Logan. He committed a terrible crime against you, but I still wouldn't have wished him dead."

He kissed the top of her head. "Sweet, sweet Michaela. How did you ever manage to be a lawyer when you have such a soft heart?"

She turned in his arms and reached up to kiss him, her lips cool and moist. Logan clung to her, wanting to absorb her into himself, to forever have her close. He had thought all he would ever have were memories of her, but perhaps now his prayers had been answered.

He whispered against her cheek, "I have nothing to offer you now, except a pocketful of dreams." Even before she answered, Logan knew what her response would be. He wasn't disappointed.

"It doesn't matter. I'll trade my responsible and dull life for your pocketful of dreams any day."

Logan's chest was real and solid against Mica's back. His uninjured arm hugged her tightly to him. They stood together, watching as the rain smothered the remaining fire, the smoke thick in the damp air.

"Do we rebuild?" he asked her referring to the future. A future they had irreversibly changed. But perhaps they hadn't changed it, after all, because her Cupid statue remained as evidence of their destiny.

"I suppose we must. After all, what will the Barkers have

to look forward to if there is no Sea Crest and no treasure?" Mica spun around, panic in her voice. "Oh, heavens, Logan, the gold!" She didn't care about the gold for herself, but for what it could have done for Logan's island.

He chuckled hoarsely. "Regardless of the fool I acted at the time, I am grateful for your financial backing." He kissed the tip of her nose. "The gold is what brought Neil back. We argued, and in the midst of our fight, he clubbed me over the head.

"He must have started the blaze in a fit of fury when he couldn't find the gold. You see, I had already removed it from the house and buried it beneath your Cupid. It seemed only sentimental at the time, but it proved fortuitous."

"Then Neil was searching in vain, yet he almost killed you."

"Hush, sweet. It's all right." The crash of timbers turned their attention back to the remains of Indigo Bay. Silhouetted against the first rays of dawn, the gutted building was a grisly reminder of all Mica had nearly lost.

The passage door, oddly enough, was the only piece of wood not burned beyond recognition, and it swayed on the charred remains of its frame.

A chill swept through Mica to settle in the key she now clutched. The door groaned as if to beckon her, and the key grew colder in her hand. The ribbon from which it hung seemed to tighten against her neck, constricting her throat and cutting off her air.

"Logan?" She whispered his name fearfully, though she knew he had not ventured from her side.

His arm tightened in reassurance. She didn't hesitate this time, but quickly removed the key from around her neck and tossed it into the middle of the smoldering rubble. The instant it landed, the door creaked and swayed, then appeared to melt down the charred framework to the ground. Presently, only the rain and wind could be heard over the loud beat of her heart.

"You're stuck here now." His voice warmed her heart. She leaned her head back against his shoulder, knowing that she'd made the right choice. This was the life she wanted—the life that would give her the happiness she'd never have found in her own time.

"No, I'm not stuck here. I belong here now."

Epilogue

Charleston — Present Day

Hurricane Charley Blamed for Attorney's Disappearance. The headline of the *New York Times* jumped out at Matthew French. He rapidly scanned the article, his analytical brain unable to comprehend the implications.

> Charleston, South Carolina, is still reeling from the devastation left by Hurricane Charley,the most powerful hurricane to hit the US in two decades. Sixty miles north, in the small town of Cameron, police are blaming the storm for the disappearance of Charleston attorney Michaela Marie Chadwick. Reports indicate Ms. Chadwick was last seen near Sea Crest, her family's resort home on Cameron Island. An official investigation is in progress.

Matthew dropped the paper back on his desk and left to find Katie. He had the feeling, though, that she probably already knew.